ENEMIES of OZ
of GREATEST IMPORTANCE!
This book stolen from

The "Dan in Oz" Trilogy

1. The Unknown Witches of Oz

2. Jellia, Maid of Oz

3. That Ozzy Feeling

THE UNKNOWN WITCHES OF OZ

Locasta and the Three Adepts

David Hardenbrook

illustrated by

Kerry Rouleau

2001

Galde Press, Inc.

Lakeville, Minnesota, U.S.A.

The Unknown Witches of Oz

Printed in the United States of America

First Edition
First Printing, 2001

Cover painting and interior illustrations by Kerry Rouleau
Map by David Hardenbrook

Library of Congress Cataloging-in-Publication Data
Hardenbrook, David, 1967–
The unknown witches of Oz : Locasta and the three adepts / David Hardenbrook.—1st ed.
p. cm.
ISBN 1–880090–23–6 (trade pbk.)
1. Oz (imaginary place)—Fiction. 2. Witchcraft—Fiction. 3. Boys—Fiction. I. Title.

PS3558.A6188 U5 2000
813'.6—dc21

00–021023

Galde Press, Inc.
PO Box 460
Lakeville, Minnesota 55044–0460

Contents

To Mama-Bach with love

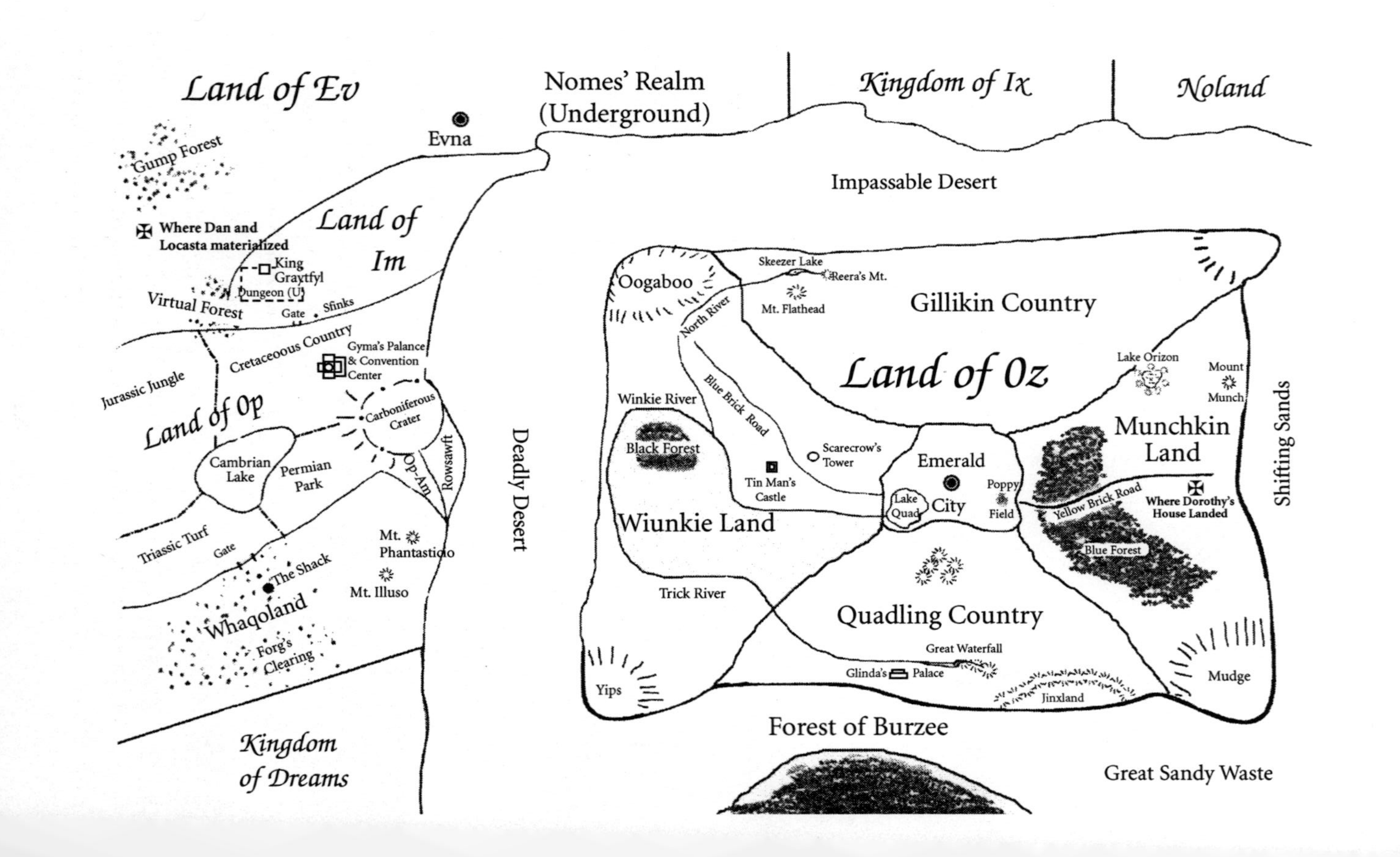

Land of Ev
Nomes' Realm
(Underground)
Kingdom of Ix
Noland
Evna
Gump Forest
Impassable Desert
Where Dan and
Locasta materialized
Land of
Im
King
Graytfyl
Dungeon (U)
Virtual Forest
Gate
Sfinks
Cretaceoous Country
Gyma's Palance
& Convention
Center
Jurassic Jungle
Land of Op
Carboniferous
Crater
Cambrian
Lake
Permian
Park
Op-Am
Rowsawft
Deadly Desert
Triassic Turf
Gate
The Shack
Mt.
Phantastico
Mt. Illuso
Whaqoland
Forg's
Clearing
Kingdom
of Dreams
Oogaboo
Skeezer Lake
Reera's Mt.
Mt. Flathead
Gillikin Country
North River
Land of Oz
Lake Orizon
Mount
Munch
Shifting Sands
Winkie River
Blue Brick Road
Black Forest
Scarecrow's
Tower
Emerald
City
Munchkin
Land
Tin Man's
Castle
Lake
Quad
Poppy
Field
Yellow Brick Road
Where Dorothy's
House Landed
Wiunkie Land
Blue Forest
Trick River
Quadling Country
Great Waterfall
Glinda's
Palace
Yips
Jinxland
Mudge
Forest of Burzee
Great Sandy Waste

The Story So Far

Prologue

IN a parallel universe very similar to ours lies a galaxy very like our own Milky Way. High above the plane of this galaxy, visible in the distance as a glorious and majestic spiral of stars, drifts a star virtually identical to our sun circled by a family of planets virtually identical to the planets of our system.

Aside from having two extra moons and a polychromatic ring system, the planet that corresponds to Earth follows the history of our Earth very closely. But in the South Pacific of this parallel Earth lies an archipelago of small island continents—Dodgesonia, Geiselgea, Wedland, Krofftgea, and, at the very center, Baumgea.

Baumgea is a beautiful and pristine land populated by a diversity of peoples and cultures. There are the Evixians of the northern part of the continent, the midget-sized Munchkins, the tall and brawny Winkies, the graceful and serene Quadlings, the Polynesian-like Gillikins, the lovely nymphs and elf-like knooks and ryls of the great southern Forest of Burzee, and the fat and antisocial Nomes who long ago took to living underground.

Some of the people who live on the continent find that their seemingly supernatural connection to polydimensional space allows them to harness the energies of the universe and use them to create miracles for the benefit of the world. These special people with scientific prowess centuries ahead of the rest of the world call themselves "fairies," "wizards," or "sorceresses," and they refer to their high technology as "magic."

Some centuries ago, a powerful fairy named Lurline ruled over a large band of fairies in the Forest of Burzee. These fairies were of two races: the Wood Nymphs, who considered themselves above and beyond mortal men, and the Veela, who looked and acted very human, except that they utilized powerful magic and sustained good relations with mortals, frequently serving as their guardians, companions, and lovers. One day Lurline called a council of her Veela and Wood Nymphs and announced that she had discovered a new country, cut off from the rest of the world by a hellish desert, at the very heart of the continent—a land of vast beauty that surpassed even the rest of the Nonestic Archipelago. Lurline proposed making this land a place where people could live in eternal peace and harmony and put the mortal world to shame.

The fairies all agreed this was a good plan. "What name shall be bestowed upon this new and greatest of all fairylands?" asked Zurline, the Queen of the Wood Nymphs.

"I wish to call it *Oz*," Lurline replied.

"What a dull name," Zurline remarked.

"I think it an excellent name," asserted Ak, the powerful Master Woodsman. "*Oz* is Old Baumgeanese for 'Great and Good.'"

The other fairies nodded in assent, so Oz it was.

This proved to be a big mistake. Before long, a rift developed between the Wood Nymphs and the Veela. The Veela—who had long associated with humans, and indeed reproduced as they did—wanted mortals to be allowed to live in Oz and enjoy its peace and tranquility. But the Wood Nymphs—who had all been created *ex nihilo* due to quantum fluctuations following the formation of the Baumgean continent eons ago—prided themselves with their independence from "those vile mortals," and insisted that Oz must be forever protected from the corrupting influence of mortals.

The arguments raged between them for centuries, and in the meantime Oz was invaded by four wicked witches from the superlatively evil Whaqoland on the other side of the Deadly Desert. They partitioned Oz between themselves into four countries——Munchkinland in the east, Winkie country in the west, the Gillikin rain forests in the tropical north, and the Quadling valleys in the south.

Unable to settle their differences, the Veela eventually departed for another forest and the Wood Nymphs washed their hands of them and of Oz. In their new home in the Land of Ev, the Veela observed the goings-on in neighboring Oz. All four of the wicked witches had imposed a brutal feudal system upon the hapless citizens in each of their respective territories, and Oz became a very unpleasant place indeed.

The Veela were anxious to overthrow them and fulfill Lurline's grand design for Oz, but they themselves were not powerful enough to confront such powerful witches. So they sent vanguards to search Baumgea for powerful good witches. Eventually they found two. Against four wicked witches, it seemed a hopeless case, but by this time the Oz witches had turned against each other, and as it was now every witch for herself, at least two of them could be conquered and progress toward a peaceful and happy Oz could commence.

Locasta, a plump and elderly witch, easily conquered old Mombi, the witch of the north, and liberated the Gillikins; and the tall, regal, and devastatingly lovely Glinda successfully drove the witch Taarna the Terrible out of the southern Quadling Country. Glinda became the good witch ruling in the south of Oz, and Locasta was known henceforth as the Good Witch of the North.

The Veela also stumbled upon a strange little man who was hopelessly lost in a hot air balloon. Seeing the letters O.Z. printed on the balloon (which were in fact his initials, Oscar Zoroaster), they assumed he had been sent by Lurline to aid Oz. So they generated a magical wind to blow him into the green area at the heart of Oz, where the people proclaimed him a great wizard. There he caused to be built the sparkling and glorious Emerald City. Although in fact he was only capable of a few conjuring tricks, he possessed a sly shrewdness that enabled him to at least pacify the two remaining unconquered witches—for the time being.

Some years later a girl named Dorothy ran afoul of a vicious tornado on the Kansas prairies. The raging storm swept her up in her house and shot her through a polydimensional hyperspace wormhole into Oz. The house emerged from the wormhole in the skies over Munchkinland and dropped upon the Witch of the East, Old Sand-Eye (who per usual had collapsed into an unexpected doze and never knew what hit her). Dorothy then proceeded to "liquidate" Old Snarl-Spats, the Wicked Witch of the West, and expose the Wonderful Wizard of Oz as a humbug from America.

After Dorothy and the Wizard returned to their homeland, Glinda (now so great in her magic that she was really a sorceress, not a mere witch) initiated a search for the long-lost Princess Ozma.

Princess Ozma was the sweet and lovely teenaged daughter of Lurline and King Pastoria (an early, benevolent mortal ruler in the Emerald City).

The Unknown Witches of Oz

Lurline had decreed that one day, when the enchantment of Oz was complete, Ozma would ascend the throne and benevolently rule and care for the good people of Oz for all eternity. But suddenly and mysteriously, the lovely young ruler-to-be utterly vanished.

Now that the wicked witches were finally all destroyed and Lurline's enchantment of Oz near completion, Glinda was determined to find Ozma and place her on the throne. Glinda engaged in much research—interviewing of citizens, and even a little spying and Oz-o-phone-tapping—and she deduced that old Mombi, the witch that Locasta had defeated, was responsible for Ozma's disappearance.

Glinda called up Locasta on the Oz-o-phone and asked her to assist her in capturing Mombi, who, though no longer ruler of the Gillikins, was still scurrying around and causing mischief.

"I will! I will!" Locasta cried, and putting down the phone she dashed out of her little cottage in the midst of the balmy, tropical Gillikin marshes. She stopped abruptly as she found herself standing face-to-face with old Mombi herself!

"Where's the fire?!" Mombi snarled, and to Locasta's horror, a wall of orange-hot flames rose up from behind Mombi like a tidal wave of starstuff and crashed down mercilessly on the Good Witch of the North...

1

The Nome and the Genie

LOCASTA had utterly vanished. But more pressing issues diverted Glinda's attention from the loss of her friend and colleague. She succeeded in capturing Mombi and forcing her to reveal that she had transformed Ozma into an eight-year-old boy. At bucket-of-water-point, Mombi disenchanted Ozma so that she was a lovely maiden once more, and then Glinda stripped Mombi of her powers, ending the Era of Wicked Witches in Oz once and for all.

Ozma's coronation ceremony was the greatest event in Oz history thus far, and was attended by numerous human Ozites as well as many of Oz's exotic citizens—the Scarecrow, the Tin Man, the Cowardly Lion, the Winged Monkeys, Jack Pumpkinhead, the Wogglebug, and many others. To Glinda's relief, even the Good Witch of the North showed up, although Glinda was puzzled as to why her old friend was so uncharacteristically low-keyed and taciturn, and especially taken aback by the little witch's announcement that she had changed her name to "Tattypoo."

In any case, Ozma assumed the throne, becoming Supreme Ruler of Oz, and Lurline's enchantment was at last complete. Present-day Oz is an exceedingly beautiful fairy country populated by diverse people and other beings. As part of Lurline's enchantment, no one in Oz ages (unless they want to), dies, gets sick, goes hungry, or is poverty-stricken. A new era of love, joy, peace, plenty, and guilt-free relationships began and will never end.

The four old quadrants of Oz remain, now each with a kind and benevolent sovereign, but all in Oz pledge ultimate allegiance to Princess Ozma in the Emerald City, the only world leader with an unwavering one-hundred-percent job approval rating!

Oz is inhabited by many queer and magical personalities, from the Scarecrow, the Tin Man, and Scraps the Patchwork Girl to the Cowardly Lion, the Glass Cat, and the cubical Woozy. However, according to a law passed by Ozma for the safety of her citizens, magical arts and sorcery may be practiced in Oz only by herself, Glinda (the most powerful sorceress in Baumgea), the Wizard of Oz (who has returned to Oz and learned from Glinda how to perform true magic), and a few other masters and mistresses of various types of prestidigitation.

Nearly everyone in Oz is good, generous, and kind-hearted, but even in this idyllic land there are a few who are of a foul, vile, and mean-spirited nature. Just before the nineteenth anniversary of the beginning of Ozma's Glorious Reign, one of the formerly most mean-spirited and vile personages in all Baumgea was enjoying a recently found peaceful and quiet existence.

He was Ruggedo the Nome, who lived in a little cottage just outside the Emerald City. Ruggedo once had been the King of all the Nomes, who were elf-like beings who lived in underground caverns beneath Ev, another fairy country in Baumgea. He had been a cruel, evil, and downright foul-tempered king feared by all his subjects.

When Ruggedo had been king, he had owned a Magic Belt that gave him enormous powers, but Dorothy, who also returned to Oz and became a close friend of Ozma, stole the Belt from him in order to free the Royal family of Ev whom he was holding prisoner. The Belt now belonged to Ozma, and the Nome King vowed to conquer Oz, enslave its people, and regain his lost treasure.

Chapter One

So he and his army of Nomes and other frightful beings dug a tunnel underneath the untraversable Deadly Desert to make a sneak attack on the Emerald City. But Ozma saw the approaching threat to her kingdom in her Magic Picture, and by magic she filled the tunnel with dust that made Ruggedo and his army thirsty, so when they burst forth from the ground in the Emerald City, they immediately drank from a nearby fountain containing the so-called "Water of Oblivion," which made anyone who drank of it forget everything they ever knew.

After the Nome King Ruggedo and his army drank the water, they became as harmless and innocent as babies, and Ozma then magically transported them all back to their homelands.

But back in his underground kingdom, Ruggedo soon reacquired his evil ways. He made another attempt to conquer Oz, but this one, like the first, failed miserably and ended with his inadvertent consumption of the Water of Oblivion.

To prevent Ruggedo from once again reverting to his former wickedness, Ozma gave him a home in Oz where he would live in peaceful harmony with the rest of the denizens of the "Merry Old Land of Oz."

Ruggedo had indeed lived a very peaceful existence since then, and had no recollections of his past evil deeds. This day, as he sat relaxed in a rocking chair in his cottage, placidly puffing his pipe (as he did every day at three), he thought about how kind Ozma had been to him in the last few years since he had lived in Oz. He decided to give Ozma a present to show his gratitude. He had a faint recollection of a beautiful ornament that he had found—somewhere—and that he had carried with him until he had established his cottage in Oz.

He remembered he had placed it in his attic for safekeeping, so he hurried upstairs. With a spring in his step and a song in his heart, he rummaged through his collection of old shoes, washboards, nutcrackers, back issues of the *Ozmapolitan,* ball bearings, paper clips, light bulbs, bloomers, fan belts, playing cards, Staunton chess pieces, and half-consumed salami sandwiches.

After two hours of carefree but unsuccessful rummaging, Ruggedo decided to try looking for something that he did not wish to find (an egg, which he detested, because eggs are poisonous to his race), and in two minutes he finally found what he was looking for!

It was a small, cylinder-shaped object lined with rubies and with a golden cap on top. He of course didn't remember it, but he had first found it when he and his army were tunneling under the Deadly Desert in his first unsuccessful attempt to conquer Oz. He had carried it with him during his wanderings, but had never been able to figure out what it was or what it was for. Anyone from turn-of-the-twenty-first-century America would have recognized it instantly as an aerosol spray can (albeit a very flashy one), but as a resident of Fairyland in the early 1920s, Ruggedo did not recognize it as such.

He did think it would be a very wonderful present for his beloved queen, so he picked it up and headed downstairs to find some gift-wrapping paper.

As he bounded down the stairs, he dropped the can, and it bounced to the bottom of the stairway and rolled on the floor. Ruggedo got a big kick out of this, so he picked up the can, raced up the stairs, and bounced it downstairs again.

He did this several dozen times, and as the can bounced and rolled, he laughed contentedly like an innocent child.

When he got tired of the rolling, he picked up the can and pulled off the cap. He stared in awe and wonder at the push button, and then he pressed it. A fine mist and a delightful SSSSSSSSS sound emerged from the can. The ex-King of the Nomes laughed like a little boy and released the button, and instantly the mist and the sound ceased.

Ruggedo really liked this game, so he pressed the button again. But this time, when he released his finger, the mist and the SSSSS-ing continued. In a few seconds, the sound became deep like a bursting dam, and the mist turned into a reddish smoke!

His delight turning to fear, Ruggedo repeatedly pressed the button in a desperate attempt to stop the smoke, which only continued to billow from the can and was now filling the room. In a panic, Ruggedo ran outdoors, but the smoke followed him like a menacing storm cloud!

Chapter One

As he stood in fear at the rising smoke, he suddenly heard a deep and menacing voice from nowhere laughing fiendishly and exclaiming, "Free! Free! I'm free!"

Now the huge mass of smoke organized itself into a human-looking form, and then the smoke cleared to reveal a giant, horrifying-looking woman!

She had eyes like balls of flame, a nose like a scimitar, and a lopsided grin that showed her armory of sharp teeth. Her emerald-green hair was done up in a Mideastern pony tail, and her muscular arms ended in frightfully clawed hands. She was dressed in a Mideastern-style outfit that looked about two sizes too small, and each of her wrists was adorned with a shining gold bracelet.

"I'm free at last! Free to wreak revenge and wreckage on the wretched powers of good!" the woman cried, gleefully rolling every *r*. Then suddenly her gold bracelets glowed ominously.

"Curses!" the woman hissed. "I am an All-Powerful Genie, and yet I am the subservient slave of a spray can!"

"I…I…I…D…D…D…W…W…W…W…W…" Ruggedo stammered.

"You have a way with words," the woman remarked sarcastically. "Ever considered a career in politics?"

Some words finally escaped the terrified Ruggedo's mouth: "W—Who are you?"

"I am Taarna, the Terrible, formerly the Wicked Witch of the South and Daughter of Old Sand-Eye, the Wicked Witch of the East; but now I am the Genie of the Spray Can, and I thank you, master, for releasing me from my imprisonment."

"G—G—Genie?" Ruggedo said, still very much afraid.

"Yes," Taarna said. "I have infinite cosmic powers, but I am forced to obey the wishes of my master and to dwell in the cramped confines of that sickening spray can! Years ago, Nan-Kerr the Cloud Queen imprisoned me in that can using the Fairy Queen Lurline's Great Magic Orb, which ended my wicked deeds, and made Fairyland safe for goody-goodies like Ozma and Glinda! And now I shall have revenge on them all!"

Taarna's bracelets glowed again, this time even brighter.

"You see?" said Taarna dismally. "As a Genie, I am forbidden to do anything for myself—I have to obey my master!"

"Who is your master?" Ruggedo asked.

"You are, since you released me," Taarna replied.

"Me?"

"Yes! You have three wishes. Any three wishes you care to make, I will grant."

"Three wishes," mulled Ruggedo. "You know, I'm so happy I don't know what I would wish for!"

Chapter One

"Really?" said Taarna, amazed. No Genie had ever had a master who was entirely happy before.

"Oh, yes," said Ruggedo, emphatically. "Everyone in the Land of Oz is happy and contented."

"So they would lead you to believe," Taarna snarled, "Honestly, fella, you may be my master, but you talk as though your head were empty!"

Suddenly, Taarna took a closer look at Ruggedo. There was something about him that looked familiar.

"Say, didn't you used to be King of the Nomes?" she asked.

"I don't know; when I came to Oz, I drank from the Fountain of Oblivion and lost all memories of my past life!"

"The Fountain of Oblivion! So that's their game is it?" Taarna said to herself, then out loud to Ruggedo, "Lost your memory you say? That's awful! But I'm sure you're the Nome King. We Genies aren't stupid (to say the least)!"

"Well, it's of no matter," said Ruggedo. "No past life I may have had could ever compare with the happiness and contentment I enjoy now."

"What are you, weird?" Taarna said. "You sit around here all day smoking your pipe? When you could be a totalitarian ruler tyrannically controlling millions of people?"

"I don't want to control anyone!" Ruggedo said indignantly. "I'm happy, and I don't care what may have happened in my past."

"But don't you care that a part—perhaps a major part of your mind has been totally erased?" Taarna pressed, thinking that if only she could get Ruggedo to be evil again, he would help her get revenge on her enemies.

"I'm quite content, honestly," said Ruggedo, playfully twirling his snow-white hair with one finger.

"But how do you know that Ozma, or Glinda, or that wretched Wizard haven't taken away important things?" said Taarna, whose patience was wearing thin. "Things you should know?"

"But when I'm so happy, there couldn't be anything else I should know," said Ruggedo.

"You are a fool!" roared Taarna, losing all patience. "The people of Oz stole away all your knowledge, and knowledge is the most precious possession of any living being!"

"I don't like it when you talk at me that way!" said Ruggedo. "It scares me!"

"Forgive me, master," said Taarna, in a calmer voice. "I just don't like the idea of one man erasing another's mind! I mean, for all you know, you had discovered some terrific new magic that would have revolutionized Fairyland!"

"What new magic?" Ruggedo asked.

"Oh, I don't know—Maybe a spell that makes a fly find its way through a half-open window. Not even I can get a fly to do that!"

"I'm going to have to think about this," said Ruggedo.

"What's to think about, since your brain is empty anyway?" Taarna snapped.

"Well, maybe you're right," Ruggedo said, suddenly thinking that it might be a fun game. "What do I have to do to get my memory back?"

"Just wish me to restore your memory," said Taarna. "That will be your first wish, and you will then have two remaining."

"Okay—Genie, I wish for my memory to be restored!"

Taarna smiled fiendishly. "Your wish is my command!"

Ruggedo remembered his childhood in the City of Despair, Nomeland. He remembered how his father had sent him to Nome Boarding School where they knocked all the wimpy, lovey-dovey ideas out of him and taught him to be evil and cruel, like all other "real Nomes."

He remembered how he had defeated his brother for control of the throne of Nomeland and became the new tyrant of the Nomes.

He remembered how he had acquired the Magic Belt that gave him phenomenal powers, and how he had enslaved the royal family of Ev and transformed them into ornaments to decorate his palace.

Chapter One

Then he remembered how Ozma and the people of Oz had come and saved the royal family and robbed him of his precious Magic Belt.

And he remembered how the Oz people had come back and kicked him off his throne.

And he remembered how he had tried to get revenge and had been defeated by the Ozites, and how they had finally stolen his memory by making him drink from the Fountain of Oblivion.

"Those scoundrels!" Ruggedo screamed so loud that even Taarna jumped. "That rotten Ozma and those other meddling fools! Give me a sword. I'll cut them to ribbons. I'll be king of Oz, and I'll make all the Oz people weep with regret!"

"That's better!" Taarna said, smiling grimly. "Now we can get on to important business!"

"But wait! What if the Oz people try to dunk me in that horrid Fountain of Oblivion again?" said Ruggedo.

"Don't worry, master," Taarna assured him. "When I restored your memory, I also rendered you immune to the Water of Oblivion. Next time they try that on you, you'll retain your memory. You can just pretend to lose it, so that silly Ozma will think you're harmless and will let you go. Then you can make a quick escape and hide somewhere to plot your revenge. But I don't think that will be necessary. With me to help you, your next war with Oz will be the one you win."

"What do you mean, with you to help me?" Ruggedo growled.

"I mean that now that we have a common goal, to exact vengeance on the Oz people, you can use your second wish to..."

"Oh, no you don't!" Ruggedo screamed. "You just want to cheat me out of Oz and the Magic Belt. Well, you won't do it."

"But..." Taarna tried to say.

"I'll conquer Oz, and I'll conquer it myself in my own way," Ruggedo cried, and started to march off.

"Where are you going?" Taarna demanded.

"I'm going to find an underground hideout where I can formulate my plans to get back at the Oz people, and I'm going to carve my history in rock so that I will never forget it again."

"You've got me wrong!" cried Taarna. "I want to help you. (Since you're my master, I have no choice.) And, like I said, I made you immune to..."

"A likely story. You just want to trick me. Well, you can forget it!" Ruggedo screamed, and he took the can and threw it, with Taarna's misty form following, into a nearby gravel pit. Having no other choice, Taarna retreated back into the can, and the can hit the bottom of the pit with a thump.

"There!" Ruggedo said with a satisfied giggle. "That's rid me for good of a potential rival." And he marched off to embark on a series of futile attempts to conquer the Land of Oz, culminating in his metamorphosis into a harmless cactus, which Ozma placed on display as a warning to all others who might attempt to cause unhappiness in Oz.

2 The Adepts at Sorcery

IN the northernmost region of Oz stands a majestic, plateau-like mountain called Mount Flathead. On Mount Flathead live three beautiful and clever witches known as the Three Adepts at Sorcery. The Adepts are the granddaughters of Locasta, the Good Witch of the North, and they are among the most powerful sorceresses in the world; indeed, only Glinda exceeds them in power. The first Adept, Zsuzsa, has silvery hair and soft brown eyes. She is very regal and dignified, and her specialty is artistic and musical magic. The second Adept is Sofia, with golden hair and bright blue eyes. She is free-spirited and sprightly, and her forte is sorcery garnered from nature. And last but light years from least is Judit, whose flowing reddish-brown hair and sparkling green eyes are bewitching to all. She speaks with a gentle, soft-spoken voice and moves with demure grace, and she is a skillful and brilliant specialist in mechanical magic, as well as the great and mysterious magic forces of the space-time continuum itself. She even comprehends the "Magic of Everything," that most fundamental and cosmic of all magic.

The Adepts have performed many miracles over the years. It was they who discovered the long-distance hyperspatial transportation magic that opened up the wormhole that first brought Dorothy to Oz (though she mistook it for a cyclone). They also mastered nonorganic animation that allowed a scarecrow to come to life and a woodman named Nick Chopper to exchange his severed flesh for tin.

There was only one problem that evaded the Adepts. Through the early years of Ozma's reign, the Adepts were locked in a spell that a wicked witch named Coo-ee-oh had placed upon them that had turned them into fishes. When at last the spell was broken (about six years before Ruggedo's encounter with Taarna), they had even forgotten their real names—they called themselves Audah, Aujah, and Aurah. Only months later did they remember who they truly were. And they also realized that during their absence their Grandmama Locasta had vanished. The Adepts searched all through Oz for her to no avail, and in increasing desperation they decided to travel to Virtual Forest in the Land of Ev to consult their mother, who was Queen of the Veela.

After flying over the desert on a magical wind of their own devising, they descended into the forest. But instead of finding the Veela dancing, singing, and otherwise enjoying themselves, they found themselves in a deserted clearing.

"Where is everybody?" Zszusa cried.

She was answered by an unearthly roar. They turned and saw a grizzly bear, black as soot and as big as a small house, advancing on them. It was a Major Ursa, a big grizzly bear and leader of the animals who guarded the Baumgean forests from mortals and other unwanted trespassers.

"Who goes there?!" growled the bear, as the saliva dripped from his steel-trap-like jaws.

"We're the Adepts at Sorcery," Judit explained with brave calmness. "We have come to see our mum."

"On important business," Sofia added hastily.

Chapter Two

"Authorized by our queen, Princess Ozma, daughter of Queen Lurline!" Zsuzsa appended.

"Ozma has no jurisdiction here!" the bear explained aggressively. "And my spies inform me that you Three Adepts are the illegitimate products of Locasta the Witch's illegal carnal relationship with a mortal man!"

"What are you driveling about?" Zsuzsa demanded.

Major Ursa produced a document from somewhere under his black fur and read: "By order of her majesty, Queen Zurline the ($e^{\pi i} + 1$)th, the Three Adepts at Sorcery—having illegitimately been called into existence through heinous violations of the Law of the Forest committed by Locasta the Witch of the North by procreating—are hereby sentenced to death in inconceivable agony."

"What kind of twaddle are you spewing?" Zsuzsa demanded.

"We are not 'illegitimate'! Our mum is Queen of the Veela. Where is she?"

Major Ursa snarled malevolently. "A more sordid tale I never did hear! Veela are traitorous renegades from Zurline's band of chaste and obedient Wood Nymphs, and the idea of an Ozian magic worker having carnal relations! Blatant violation of the Law of the Forest!"

"All the Law of the Forest says," Judit asserted, "is to exhibit responsible forethought before making a rash commitment, and it advises devoted fairies of Baumgea to consider romantic entanglements extremely carefully and cautiously in order to assess the feasibility of balancing their loving relationship with commitment to their duties as an immortal and defender of fairylands. But it does not unequivocally forbid magic-workers from having carnal relations with mortals!"

"If it does, boy are we in trouble!" Zsuzsa muttered.

"Silence!" the Bear screamed. "You and your recreant Veela relatives have been condemned by the Fairy Tribunal of Burzee; and I must now execute my duty to tear you limb from limb!"

"That kind of threat doesn't scare us," said Judit boldly.

"Yes, it does!" Zsuzsa and Sofia asserted in a panicky chorus.

"Come on, sisters!" Judit said angrily, and she turned on her heels and walked straight into a twenty-foot deep gravel pit.

"Har! Har! Har!" laughed the Bear vindictively, so hard that it blew gentle Zsuzsa and sweet Sofia into the pit as well.

"Where the hippikaloric are we?" Zsuzsa muttered, as she and her sisters scrambled to their feet and daintily brushed the dirt from their Grecian gowns.

"I don't know," Sofia replied. "But I'd sure like to know why the sky is flickering like a strobe light."

"I see what you mean," observed Judit. "It looks like day and night are passing at lightning speed."

"You know what I think?" Sofia cried in alarm. "I think day and night are passing at lightning speed!"

"You're right, sister!" Zsuzsa gasped. "Look! If you watch the flickering carefully, when it's light you can see the sun shifting with the solstices, and when it's dark you can see all three moons zip by in their orbits!"

Chapter Two

"Of course!" said Judit. "This pit is a time-dilation envelope—an isolated pocket of space-time where the arrow of time progresses at an abnormal rate!"

"Yes of course," Zsuzsa said, assuming an all-knowing air. "That's *just* what I was thinking…'An isolated pocket of space-time,' I said to myself, 'where the arrow of time progresses at an abnormal rate.' You're an uncanny mind reader, Judit!"

"Well, it occurs to me," Sofia interjected, "that in that case we are getting projected forward in time at a catastrophic rate, so *let's get out of here!*"

Judit and Zsuzsa took her point, and they tried to glide out on their magical wind, but an invisible barrier that marked the boundary of the time-dilation envelope at the top of the pit impeded their escape. Unfortunately, the time-slowing effects meant that they emerged from their captivity a full *eighty-eight* years later in real time! The Adepts flew out of the forest at once and returned to Oz. They went first to Mount Flathead, where they ruled, and to their relief found that their friend the Skeezer mortal Ervic had taken it upon himself to rule in their stead. He likewise was relieved to find them alive and well. After a brief but affectionate reunion, Ervic agreed to keep things on Mount Flathead running smoothly a little longer while they went to the court of Princess Ozma to ask for her advice.

The Adepts found Ozma sitting regally in her royal dais, surrounded by her odd court of humans, animals, grotesques, and so on, and they were astonished at how much she had changed. No longer physically a little girl, like a feminine version of the boy Tip she had once been, Ozma had matured into a young woman of about seventeen, even though people generally never age in Oz. She was very beautiful with her flowing dark hair with two big red poppies, her blue eyes, soft red lips, blushing cheeks, and her long, strapless, fitted red gown.

"It's times like this I'm glad I'm a girl!" Sofia whispered to her sisters, as she imagined a young man bowling over at the mere sight of the lovely Queen.

"Well, my dear Adepts, what brings you to the Emerald City?" Ozma asked sweetly.

"Your majesty," Judit informed the fairy queen of Oz, "we have come from Virtual Forest in Ev, where we were assaulted by a particularly unpleasant bear from Burzee and imprisoned in a time-dilation envelope that shot us forward in time by almost a century."

"Oh, how terrible!" Ozma cried. "That would explain why I haven't heard from you for so long. Are you all right?"

"Oh, yes; from our point of view only a few minutes ticked by, but in the outside world eighty-eight years passed! After we escaped from that highly unusual space-time anomaly, we came here."

"But what were you doing in Ev?" the Wonderful Wizard of Oz inquired.

"We were searching for our Grandmama, who is lost," Sofia said. "But it appears that our mum, the Queen of the Veela, has disappeared too, along with all their subjects."

"No...Remember what mum said to us, sisters," said Zsuzsa, "when her husband ran off and she decided to leave us in Grandmama's care? She said she was sure that Zurline would seek revenge on the Veela who had rebelled against her, and that the best place for them was in Virtual Forest, which is full of all sorts of weird, magical anomalies that would stymie an orthodox fairy like Zurline. So I'm sure mum and the other Veela merely hid themselves deep within those anomalies to hide from Zurline and her goons."

"I didn't realize that you were part Veela," the Wizard said.

"Oh, yes—We learned technology-based Krumbic magic from our dad before he took a powder," said Zsuzsa with a note of bitterness. "And we learned about magic garnered from nature—"

"—And provocative dancing," Sofia added mischievously.

"—from our Veela mum.

"Yes, you're right," Judit agreed. "Veela are very cunning about attracting nice people and evading the hostile folks. It's our dear Grandmama that we should worry about."

"Who *is* your Grandmama?" Princess Dorothy asked. (Dorothy had also grown into an attractive teenager).

"Locasta," Sofia replied.

Everyone looked blank.

"Otherwise known as the Good Witch of the North," Zsuzsa added.

Chapter Two

"But I thought Queen Orin of the Ozure Isles was the Good Witch of the North," the Wizard said. "And that old Mombi was jealous of Orin and so changed her into an ugly old witch named Tattypoo, and Orin lived thereafter as the Good Witch of the North until she was disenchanted."

"That's only half of the story," Zsuzsa observed.

"I assure you that we met with Tattypoo several times, and she was definitely *not* our Grandmama," Judit said regretfully.

"Old our Grandmama may be, but certainly not ugly!" Zsuzsa remarked.

"And when we met with Tattypoo, she didn't know who we were," Sofia lamented.

"And Grandmama is the foremost authority on the Magic of Everything, the ultimate, fundamental physics of sorcery, but Tattypoo had never heard of it," explained Judit. "She was definitely not Grandmama, and we think our real Grandmama is still lost somewhere, perhaps in Baumgea, perhaps on another continent, perhaps even on another planet altogether!"

"I thought as much," Glinda said with a sigh. "When Tattypoo was disenchanted, I knew as well that she was not my old friend from fairy school, but I know not how to find her."

"Don't you have any spell that could help locate her?" Ozma asked. "What about your Great Book of Records?"

"What's that?" Sofia asked.

"My Great Book of Records is an incredible magical set of volumes that record all important world events at the very instant that they occur. It's an invaluable aid to find out what's going on in the world, especially in Oz, so that Ozma can know what people in her realm need her help. But as far as finding Locasta, it has drawn a blank.

"I have plenty of other spells for finding lost persons as well," continued Glinda, "but they have not helped either. The problem is trying to find someone that there's *two* of. My spells seem to get confused and pinpoint Orin as the disenchanted Good Witch. Tattypoo was so similar to Locasta in every detail that for years even my powerful cosmic sorcery thought she was Locasta."

"Well, it seems to me," Zsuzsa cried, "that if Mombi transformed Orin, then it must have been because she inflicted some hideous enchantment on our dear Grandmama as well, but wanted to make everyone think Grandmama was all right and still ruling the Gillikins as always."

"Yes, but *how?*" said Sofia. "What did she transform Grandmama into, and what kind of spell did she use?"

"And where is Grandmama now?" Judit added.

"We should do as detectives do," Glinda remarked, "and look for a *modus operandi*."

"A what-dus what-a-di?" cried Zsuzsa.

"*Modus operandi*—That's Latin for 'manner of behavior,'" Glinda explained, "a characteristic pattern that someone follows over and over. And I see a definite *modus operandi* with the way Mombi performs enchantments."

"Which is—?" said Judit.

"Why don't you try to find it for yourselves?" said Glinda with a playful smile.

"Who do you think we are, Holmes, Poirot, and Columbo?" cried Zsuzsa.

"Well, wait a minute; let's think about it a minute," said Sofia. "Besides Orin, Mombi also enchanted Ozma into Tip."

"And didn't she at one point enchant *herself*?" said Judit.

"Yes, she disguised herself as the palace housekeeper Jellia Jamb," Ozma confirmed, "and poor Jellia assumed the appearance of Mombi."

"What a rat!" observed Zsuzsa. "Making it so everyone would be out to get Jellia instead of her!"

"What a minute!" cried Judit with a burst of insight. "You mean to say that that little switcheroo was not just to confuse herself and Jellia with everyone, but that it's the way Mombi *repeatedly* performs transformations?"

"It makes sense," Zsuzsa said contemptuously. "It is by far the easiest method to perform a transformation, and probably the only method comprehensible to a hack witch like Mombi was."

"Yes, when Mombi enchanted Ozma, she switched Ozma's form with that of the boy Tippetarius," Glinda said.

Sofia jumped in: "And so when she changed Queen Orin into a—a—"

Chapter Two

"Carbon copy," Judit said, offering what she considered to be the technical term.

"—of Grandmama," Sofia continued, "Grandmama likewise assumed Orin's physical appearance!"

"That is correct," said Glinda. "I have tried on many occasions to find out about Locasta in my Great Book of Records, but it has no reference to Locasta after the year that Dorothy first visited Oz. Clearly Locasta assumed a different form at that point—almost certainly Orin's—and Orin assumed Locasta's form."

"All of which probably muddled the Book of Records into not reporting events about either of them," said Zsuzsa.

"Yes, the Book is very powerful,"said Glinda wistfully, "but it is not perfect. Sometimes it gets confused and makes omissions or reports slightly erroneous facts. I'll never forget the day when I read in the Book that *The Mifkets of Snark Island are feeding weary and hungry sailors with the local Boojums.* When I saw that, I used my sorcery to direct a lost ship in distress toward the island. It was only when Ozma observed the ship arriving at the island in the Magic Picture that we realized the terrible truth—that the Book had made a tiny error, and what it should have said was, *The Mifkets of Snark Island are feeding weary and hungry sailors* to *the local Boojums.*

"Luckily, the sailors on the ship knew about the Boojums and other perilous beasts of Snark Island, and retreated as soon as they realized where they were, so no harm was done. But still, I felt badly about the whole affair, and resolved that from then on I would always verify what the Book said in Ozma's Magic Picture."

"What about Ozma's Magic Picture?" Sofia asked. "Won't it tell us where Grandmama is? It's supposed to show you anything in the world you want to see just by commanding it, right?"

"Yes, and I've tried the Magic Picture, but when I ask to see Locasta, all I get is static," said Glinda.

"It's obviously muddled about Grandmama too," Sofia said.

"Is that Mombi's doing, too, do you suppose?" Zsuzsa asked.

"Obviously. But I can't help wondering if there are *other* things going on behind the scenes," Judit said grimly. "That Bear in the forest said something very odd. He said that we were the products of our Grandmama's having violated the Law of the Forest, and that we therefore did not deserve to live. He claimed that he was acting on the orders of Zurline."

"He was speaking rubbish!" the Wizard remarked.

"Yes, but it just seems an odd excuse to think up on the spur of the moment," Judit remarked. "Or even on the spur of the eon. I think that Zurline was after our Grandmama, claiming that she was in violation of the Law of the Forest by having grandchildren—not by cloning, quantum fluctuations, or the Stork Adoption Agency as fairies frequently do, but in what mortals would call 'the traditional fashion.' "

"Yes, I fear that you are right," Glinda admitted. "Mombi admitted that many of her powers were given to her by the wizard Nikidik, who was once a servant to Zurline. The Law of the Forest is a very touchy subject, and it has been used as an excuse by evil beings like Mombi to persecute the innocent."

"This is a problematic situation that has been looming over me for a long time," Ozma said gravely. "The supreme fairies have always regarded me as a radical and a rabble-rouser, all because I wished to rule Oz as I saw fit. But they believe my interpretations of the Law of the Forest are way too liberal and accommodating to my mortal subjects. Some very powerful fairies have leveled various threats at me over the years—threats to impeach me if I continued to espouse my 'dangerous' ideas, such as that all beings are created equal (even cowardly lions and winged monkeys), and that Oz should offer Universal Magic Care Coverage. They're also not big on my habit of allowing worthy mortals like Dorothy and the Wizard to come and live in Oz. They claim that 'worthy mortal' is a contradiction in terms."

"Surely Lurline doesn't feel that way," Judit said. "She's supremest of the supreme, and you are her daughter."

"Yes," said Ozma sadly, "but Lurline founded Oz in order to create a fairyland that would put the world of mortals to shame. My guess is that in her heart of hearts, she's as contemptuous of mortals as anyone."

"Well, don't guess; ask her!" Zsuzsa suggested.

"But Lurline has been gone for centuries," Ozma explained. "No one knows where she's travelled to. And her subordinates are always on my back, trying to keep me in line—*their* line. And more than anything, they resent my decision to allow myself to mature from a little girl into a grown woman. They see that as opening the door to abandoning my innocence."

"Which is absurd!" Glinda interjected. "Your majesty is still as good, sweet, kind, and gentle as you ever were. You just have a better perspective on adulthood now."

"Do suitors ever come seeking your hand?" asked Sofia.

"All the time," Ozma replied. "But I've never found one who was good, kind, sensitive, loving, and caring enough to suit me. And I never shall marry until I do. In the meantime, I'm not going to let fundamentalist fairies and their draconian interpretations of the Law intimidate me!"

"Very wise," said Zsuzsa. "But can we get back to the subject our Grandmama now?"

"A word in your majesty's ear?" Glinda requested. Ozma nodded and Glinda whispered something into the royal inner ear. Ozma whispered back. Glinda smiled and nodded.

"I have a plan," announced Ozma out loud. "In order to develop a more mature attitude to care for my subjects, I have allowed myself to grow and mature physically into a young woman, and consequently I'm finding it an increasing strain to repress my romantic and other— um, *adolescent* longings. I openly admit that I want to love a young man and marry him and make him the happiest man in the world! Many fairies insist that any human relationship will invariably undermine a fairy's devotion to duty, but I *know* I could strike a balance between royal duties and personal happiness. I must! Fairies and people don't realize it, but even a great queen like me desires companionship. So I want there to be a man in my life, not only for myself, but also so that I can have more empathy for my married subjects, so that I can more effectively help them with their problems. So do you think you could locate a worthy young man—someone sweet, gentle, sensitive and kind—whom I could care for, as well as find your Grandmama?"

"I think we could do that," Sofia replied.

"Yes, indeed!" her sisters agreed. All three of them were much touched by knowing Ozma's feelings.

"I wonder how," murmured Zsuzsa dismally.

"I just had a thought!" Judit suddenly exclaimed. "Have we considered using the same wormhole technology that first brought Dorothy to Oz?"

"Sister, you know that that technology is in a very rudimentary state," Zsuzsa pointed out.

"Well, we have to try," Judit insisted. "After all, even Chopin had to start by learning to find middle *C*."

"Yes, I quite agree!" said Sofia, dancing gaily about. "We can do it! We will find a way, because we are motivated both to find our beloved Grandmama and to find a man for our gracious Queen Ozma to love!"

"But what about the supreme fairies?" Dorothy asked.

"I'm tired of letting them intimidate me!" Ozma proclaimed. "And I certainly will not tolerate their bullying my good subjects the way they have the Adepts! *I* am queen of Oz, not they, and I intend from here on out to *act* like the queen! Romantic, carnal love is *not* an evil thing! It is a *good* thing, no matter what the Burzeean Fairies think, when the love is real and true!"

"Then—I can go out on dates?" said Dorothy in delight.

"Yes, my dear. *All* Oz people can. And now, I consider it a priority to bring Locasta back to Oz. Her banishment on the grounds of falling in love and producing three wonderful granddaughters was unjust. And from now on, I shall be as assertive and effectual a queen as I can possibly be—and if the Fairies of Burzee don't like it, too bad!"

Everyone applauded Ozma's decree. The Adepts thanked their queen and gratefully decided to return to their home on Mount Flathead to commence their search.

"I have just one question," said Sofia as they flew home on their magical wind. "Who was the man that Grandmama was involved with? Who is our grandpa?"

"One search at a time, sister," Judit said gently.

3

The Wogglebug College

SEVERAL days later, the Adepts paid a visit to Glinda. They expressed frustration, for all their attempts so far to find Locasta had been in vain. Glinda granted them full access to the numerous think volumes in her Great Library of Knowledge, but unfortunately they were of no help either.

"Does Oz have any other reference books besides the ones in your possession that might give us some kind of clue to what was going on between Mombi and Grandmama just before she vanished?" Judit asked Glinda.

"Well, there are quite a few good books in Professor Wogglebug's possession, including the Royal Book of Oz," said Glinda.

"What is the Royal Book of Oz?" Sofia asked.

"It is a book that describes the ancestry, lineage, pedigree, and noble parentage of the people of Oz," Glinda explained.

"Gee, no one ever asked us about our noble lineage," said Sofia.

"Yes, I guess the Wogglebug forgot to ask you," Glinda said apologetically.

"Or maybe he assumed we just rose up from the waves!" snarled Zsuzsa.

"Sister, please!" Sofia remonstrated.

"We must have been in that time-dilation envelope when the Wogglebug wrote the book," Judit deduced.

"Well then, he should have saved us, shouldn't he?" said Zsuzsa, seemingly determined to look on the negative side.

"Well, can you show us this book?" Judit said, ignoring her. "After all, even if it says nothing about us, it might say something about Grandmama, and her lineage and pedigree is ours as well!"

"Better still, let's stroll on over to the college and meet with the prof in person!" Sofia cried, and she did an excited somersault, now more hopeful of finding Locasta.

"It would be a long stroll!" laughed Glinda. "But we'll take my flying chariot; it will get us there in no time!"

"Good! Then we can see the college. We've never been there before," Judit said, also in higher spirits now.

"And the college museum as well," Glinda said. "It is filled with all sorts of artifacts from Ozian history. We can even show you Ruggedo."

"Who?" Zsuzsa asked.

"The Old Nome King," Sofia said. "The one who was always trying to conquer Oz."

"Why should we want to see him?" Zsuzsa said contemptuously.

"Well, as you know, after a couple of attempts to conquer Oz, Ruggedo drank of the Fountain of Oblivion and lost his memory," explained Glinda. "And with no memory of his past evilness, he was a good and benevolent friend of Oz for several years. But then for some reason—it is still a bit of a mystery—he regained his memory and became evil again and tried several more times to invade and destroy us, until at last we defeated him for good, and we now keep him housed in the Wogglebug College Museum in a highly interesting form where he can never do any harm again."

"Famous last words!" Zsuzsa muttered to herself as they departed for the College.

Chapter Three

In her great chariot pulled by a team of swans, Glinda, along with the Three Adepts at Sorcery, glided above Oz's beautiful, green countryside until they came to a great, stately building with tall marble pillars.

"This is it—Wogglebug College," Glinda said.

The chariot came to a stop just in front of the college's main entrance, where they were met by Professor H.M. Wogglebug, T.E., himself!

"Greetings, my friends!" the Professor said jovially. "It is a pleasure to see you all."

"Hello, Professor," Glinda said and, indicating the Adepts, added, "This is Judit, Zsuzsa, and Sofia—the Adepts of Sorcery and rulers of Flathead Mountain."

"I'm delighted," he said. "What may I do for you?"

"Well," Sofia said, "we came to visit your school and library…"

"…to research our ancestry…," Judit continued.

"…in the hope of find a clue as to the whereabouts of our lost Grandmama," Zsuzsa concluded.

"I also wanted to show the Adepts some of the things in the College museum," said Glinda.

"Wonderful!" the Wogglebug said jovially. "If you'll follow me…" He led the party up the great steps and into the main hall of the college, where they were joined by the famous Scarecrow of Oz, Jellia Jamb the royal maid, and Princess Ozma herself.

"We're visiting the college as guest lecturers," Ozma explained.

"What are you lecturing on?" asked Sofia.

"I'm speaking on Ozzy politics and modern fairy diplomacy," said Ozma.

"I'm lecturing on formal logic, with special emphasis on the 'straw man' fallacy," said the Scarecrow.

"And I'm discussing the use of song and wit to lighten domestic labor," said Jellia Jamb.

"Well, if you will all follow me, I will show the Adepts the college," said the Wogglebug.

"I follow nothing but my heart," said Jellia with a smile, as they started down the main corridor.

"This college is the chief center of all knowledge in Oz, except for Glinda's library and Book of Records, and our boys all receive a capital education here," the Wogglebug said proudly.

"Boys?" Zsuzsa said in a dangerous voice.

"Girls, too!" reassured the Scarecrow.

"Yes, our—uh, student body," said the Wogglebug, "get a healthy dosage of education with every meal."

"What do you mean?" Judit asked. "You make it sound as though they took a pill or something."

"They do!" The Wogglebug said. "English pills, literature pills, mathematics pills, history pills, science pills, civics pills—"

"You see," Glinda explained, "in conventional schools, students have to sit in classes for hours a day absorbing knowledge—"

"A horrendous waste of both the students' and the teacher's time!" the Wogglebug said indignantly. "I mean, what is the purpose of education anyway?"

"To fill young minds with the riches of knowledge," Judit said.

"No!" the Wogglebug said, incensed. "The purpose of education is to teach young people to think for themselves so that they can get on with their lives! And how can they learn that when all their precious time is taken up with things like decoding the inner meaning in Shakespeare or memorizing the presidents in chronological order?"

"But those things taught in conventional schools are important, aren't they?" Sofia said.

"Yes, but with the magic pills of my school, they can absorb all the academics with one swallow, and then they're free to pursue things like athletics, free inquiry and exploration, and creative artistic endeavors, where the young minds learn the really important tasks like how to solve problems, how to help others, and generally how to be good, decent people!"

Chapter Three

He then led them into the "Laboratory of Learning," where all the pills were kept. The room was filled with rows and rows of bottles—each filled with pills for a different subject. There were writing pills, grammar pills, classical history pills, medieval history pills, modern history pills, English lit pills, drama pills, algebra pills, calculus pills, analytic geometry pills, chemistry pills, physics pills, astronomy pills, music appreciation pills, and many more.

"Do you have a how-to-find-the-whereabouts-of-one's-grandmama pill?" Zsuzsa asked.

Unfortunately, the college did not, so they moved on. After touring the athletic wing of the college, where hundreds of boys and girls were having the time of their lives playing all manner of games, they walked over to the college museum, where they saw many paintings, sculptures, and historical fairy documents.

"Now let's head over to the Botanical Gardens," the Wogglebug said.

"Oh, wonderful!" Judit said. "We're great nature lovers!"

"Judit especially," said Zsuzsa. "Last week she not only stopped the war between the two ant hills outside our palace but even got them to sign a test ban treaty."

"And when we get to the Botanical Gardens, we must be sure to show you Ruggedo!" Glinda said.

"Yeah, right," Zsuzsa said in a less-than-enthused tone.

The College Botanical Gardens were filled with many different plants from all parts of Oz. There were red roses, white roses, blue roses, daisies, daffodils, six-leaf clovers, watermelons, chocolate-milk-melons, domestic grasses, crab grasses, 092-magnetic grasses, pine trees, maple trees, fur trees, feather trees, Ozfruit trees, and many others.

"Well, this is all very beautiful," Sofia said after they had seen the whole of the gardens, "but can we go to the library now? We're hoping that the Royal Book of Oz may give us a clue of what might have become of our Grandmama."

"Who is your Grandmama?" the Wogglebug asked.

"Locasta, the Good Witch of the North," Sofia said.

"Hmmm," Professor Wogglebug mulled. "I may have written something in the Royal Book about her...If you follow me, we'll go to the library at once."

The Wogglebug, jovially swinging his cane, strode through a door and everyone followed him back into the college. Judit stopped at the door, however, as her lovely green eyes fell on a old, wilting cactus in one corner of the room. The cactus was clearly languishing from neglect and lack of watering.

"Cactuses are known for their ability to retain water, but not forever!" Judit observed to herself. "Poor thing, I'll give it a dose of Magic Revitalizing Water."

Magic Revitalizing Water is an invention of the Adepts (a base mixture of heavy deuterium water and water from the Truth Pond) that not only restores health to ailing plants and animals alike, but also restores enchanted things to their proper forms. Judit produced a bottle of the magical water from her robes and tenderly poured a generous amount onto the sickly cactus.

After a pause, the cactus began to shake and quiver. Then Judit stared at the cactus in astonishment as the cactus stared back at her! The cactus now actually had eyes...and a second later it had ears...then a nose...a mouth...a white beard...a pair of angry, white eyebrows...

"I almost forgot!" the Wogglebug laughed as he led the others back into the garden. "I didn't show you the cactus that is the enchanted form of—"

He and the others stopped in horror as they arrived just in time to see the cactus suddenly explode into the fearful form of...

"Ruggedo!" they all said in a horrified chorus.

"That's right! It is I, Ruggedo!" the old Nome sneered at them with glee. "I am free at last, thanks to the foolish and indulgent munificence of this asinine Adept!"

"Did you understand a word he just said?" Jellia whispered to Ozma.

"I believe he just called my sister stupid!" Sofia said with fury.

"And what'cha gonna do about it?" Ruggedo sneered. "I am now at liberty, and I promise you that I shall conquer Oz and mash the lot of you like little bugs!"

Chapter Three

"I resent that remark most emphatically!" the Wogglebug said indignantly.

"You'd better not try anything, or you'll regret it," the Scarecrow warned.

"Oh, I'm sooooo scared!" Ruggedo jeered. Glinda tried to raise her hands to put a spell upon him, but he was too fast, and he quickly bounded across the garden and leaped a six-foot wall, saying. "So long, Ozites! See you when you're my slaves!" And he laughed as he vanished.

The others raced out to door to try to catch him, but when they were outside, he was gone.

"Nice going, Judit!" Zsuzsa said acidly.

"I'm so sorry," poor Judit said, nearly in tears. "I thought it was an ordinary cactus; no one ever said it was the Nome King!"

"It's not your fault, dear," said Sofia in her sweet, compassionate voice. "I didn't know either. The last I heard, Ruggedo had been enchanted into some form where he could cause no trouble."

"Oh, he was," Jellia replied. "But you know Ruggedo, the Comeback Kid of Oz's adversaries—He escaped, and Ozma decided to put him back as a cactus. Clearly the most stable and foolproof form for him to be in...or so we thought."

"So what happens now? I suppose our search for Grandmama is on the back burner now," Judit said.

"Yes, my dear Adepts," Glinda said. "With Ruggedo on the loose, the situation is very grave and urgent indeed. There's just no telling what he might do. We'll have to devote our resources now to stopping him from doing the Oz people any harm. So I'm afraid you'll have to continue the search for your Grandmama without me for the time being."

"I see," Zsuzsa said dryly.

"We understand, of course," Sofia said sadly.

"I don't!" Zsuzsa said crossly.

"We do, I promise," Judit said. "Is there anything we can do to stop Ruggedo?"

"I suggest that you go back to Flathead Mountain, just in case Ruggedo is headed that way and your people there need protection," said Glinda.

"We will!" Sofia said.

"But what about Grandmama—?" Zsuzsa protested. "What if someone tries to do her harm? We've got to find her!"

"I have an idea," said Ozma. "The Adepts can go back to Flathead Mountain and protect their people, and search for Locasta from there as best they can; Glinda, you go back to the Emerald City and organize a search party for Ruggedo so he can be stopped; and Jellia and I will explore the Baumgean countryside for both Locasta and Ruggedo."

"What shall I do?" the Scarecrow asked.

"Would you look after the Emerald City in my absence?" said Ozma.

"Of course!" the Scarecrow replied.

"I think that is a wise plan," said Glinda. "Then we can find both Locasta and Ruggedo and everyone can help."

"Yes," Jellia agreed. "We will find both the Adepts' dear, long-lost Grandmama and that fat, rotten, annoying little Nome!"

Back on Flathead Mountain

THE magical trio returned to their home on Flathead Mountain and worked diligently, researching all aspects of magic, spells, and incantations, including the fundamental Magic of Everything. To maximize the depth of their concentration, each isolated herself in her own room and, with an intensity worthy of chess grandmasters, they tried to work out the necessary formulae that would search the space-time continuum until their Grandmama was found.

After weeks of hard work, Judit announced that she had something important to show them—a way to go about finding their grandmama.

"Even though Zurline thinks we're 'illegitimate!'" Zsuzsa said derisively.

"I don't understand what's happened to Zurline—Glinda says she used to be gentle, tolerant and kind...Now she's become the vengeful and arrogant Queen Zurline the $(e^{\pi i} + 1)$th," Judit said.

"What kind of ordinal title is that anyway?" Zsuzsa wondered. "I know about Ptolemy the First and George the Third and Henry the Eighth, but what does Queen Zurline the '$(e^{\pi i} + 1)$th' denote?"

"It's a mathematical expression with all constants: Euler's number raised to the power of pi times the square root of minus one, all added to one. Well, you're the math whiz around here, Judit," Sofia observed.

Taking the gentle hint, Judit got out her memo book and performed the sum: $(e^{\pi i} + 1) = 0$.

"Ah, I see now—Queen Zurline the Zeroith. It all makes sense now," said Zsuzsa bitterly.

"Should we go tell her to stop meddling in the affairs of Oz?" Judit inquired.

"First we have to find Grandmama, and then find a sweet, kind, gentle young man for Ozma to marry," Sofia asserted.

"And if Zurline has any objections, we'll remind her that the vision is now complete," Judit said. "We have a perfect fairyland ruled by the kindest fairy queen in history. Oz has come of age, and we no longer need Zurline or anyone to tell us what to do."

"And if Zurline still objects, we'll tell her to go boil her head!"

"Zsuzsa!"

"I'm sorry, Sofia," Zsuzsa apologized, "but I find it difficult to have any other attitude toward someone who banished our Grandmama and tried to have us assassinated."

"If in fact she did—Ozma insists that she couldn't have," Sofia gently reminded her.

"I think we should pinpoint Grandmama, then direct her via her magic slate to the home of the lucky young man whom we choose to bring to Oz, then we can bring them here together," said Judit.

"That is altogether a very resourceful plan, sister, but how do you propose to do all that?" Zsuzsa remarked.

"I'll show you," Judit said.

Gripped by curiosity, her two sisters followed Judit over to the other side of the mountain where a glass dome enclosed a fantastic-looking machine. It was as big as a small house and had numerous gears, springs, flywheels, and other gadgets protruding from it. There was also a piano and a waterwheel with a pump attached to the machine by pipes, and connected by a thick wire at the very base of this incredible contraption was a small typewriter.

"This is my latest invention—my Total Cosmic Interconnectedness Entity Tracking Mechanism," Judit announced.

"English translation, please." said Zsuzsa.

"It's a Grandmama-finding machine," said Judit.

"This ridiculous contraption is going to find Grandmama? And I have a bridge over Winkie River I'd like to sell!" Zsuzsa said.

"Come on, dear; let her explain it to us at least," Sofia said.

"Oh, very well," sighed Zsuzsa.

Judit proceeded to explain: "Now, it is well know amongst us Krumbic sorceresses that all things in the universe are interconnected, right?"

"Right!" said Sofia.

"Therefore, it stands to reason that all the myriad life forms here in Oz are connected by magical forces to all life in the Great Outside World..."

"Agreed," said Zsuzsa.

"So by tracing the magical link between us and Grandmama, we should be able to pinpoint her!"

"I'd better watch myself," Zsuzsa said. "You're starting to make sense."

"So I went back to Wogglebug College the other day and borrowed all the books he had on 'Nature, Twentieth Century Technology, and Their Relationship with Sorcery,'" continued Judit. "Researching them has given me insight on how to build this machine, which is capable of tracing the magical forces linking all of nature's living things. It will tell us how and where to find Grandmama!"

"Bravo!" Sofia cried.

"It's somewhat of the same principle that makes the Book of Records and Magic Picture work," said Judit. "With it, we'll pinpoint Grandmama and find an ideal man for Ozma. All we need is for all three of us to use our Krumbic Sorcery to make the machine run. Now since I'm the machine's inventor, I'll sit at the helm and run the life-nourishing waterfall pump. As our musical genius, you, Zsuzsa, shall play the piano—"

"What good will that do?" Zsuzsa asked.

"Please, dear; it's all part of the Krumbic machinery," Sofia said.

"How about one of those wonderful songs that Jellia sings?" Judit suggested.

"That sounds good!" Zsuzsa said. "But which one? 'Winkie River Flow'? 'Book of Records'? 'Munchkin Country Blue'?"

"How about that beautiful, ethereal one that she been singing recently?" Sofia suggested.

"'Only If You're Ozzy'? Yes, that one is perfect!" Judit said. "And you, Sofia, since you're a queen of the dance—shall stand upon the metal pedestal at the top of the machine and pirouette like mad!"

"How fun!" Sofia cried with delight.

"Um, how long are we supposed to do all this?" Zsuzsa asked.

"However long it takes," replied Judit.

Chapter Four

"Why do I have this mystical fairy premonition that this is going to be a total flop?" Zsuzsa asked.

"Oh, please, let's just try!" Sofia implored. "For Grandmama!"

"Okay, you talked me into it," Zsuzsa said, and she levitated to the piano.

"That's the spirit!" Judit said. She glided over to the crank that ran the pump and the waterwheel. "Okay girls...stand by...contact...SWITCH ON!"

As she said this, she grabbed the crank and turned it with all her strength (which was surprisingly substantial), and when she got the water flowing at a good rate over the wheel and into a vat below that pumped the water to a nearby encirclement of tall bamboo, she let go of the crank, which continued to turn of its own magical accord, and she started going through a series of incantations.

Meanwhile, Zsuzsa played "Only If You're Ozzy" as loud as she could, and Sofia pirouetted on one tiptoe as fast as she could. Every gear and piston in the machine was moving full speed now, and soon steam was billowing from the pipes.

Suddenly, the typewriter at the bottom of the machine started working, just for a second. Judit raced over to read what it had written. All that was written on the paper was: *dmaryk@tursiops.com.*

"What in the Nonestic Archipelago does that mean?" said the still-playing Zsuzsa and still-pirouetting Sofia when Judit read it to them.

"Oh, well I, uh—I think it's perfectly obvious...yes, very, very obvious," Judit said.

"You don't have the foggiest idea, do you?" Zsuzsa said.

"I do!" Sofia said. "*Tursiops truncatus* is the famous bottlenose dolphin, so the machine is obviously telling us to...um...consult the famous dolphin of Deemaryk!"

"Well, what does the 'com' mean?"

"The comical dolphin at Deemaryk? The comet dolphin at Deemaryk? The commiserating dolphin at—"

"And where, pray, is Deemaryk located?" Zsuzsa inquired.

"Uh—well, it doesn't know—but don't worry, the machine will find it!" Judit assured her. "All we do now is, while the machine is still going, stand in single file, and we will go through an incantation to contact the Comet Dolphin at Deemaryk!"

"What if we get a busy signal?" Zsuzsa asked.

"Oh, please! It's worth a try!" Sofia said, floating down from the machine.

"Hey, I don't mean to sound skeptical," Zsuzsa said, also gliding down. "I just don't think there is any such place as 'Deemaryk'—It could just as easily be some guy's name!"

"Well, let's try, anyway," Judit said.

So they stood in a row, and facing the steaming machine, they swayed and waved their arms in mystical patterns and chanted: "O great forces of the universe...We are trying to reach the Celebrated Comet Dolphin of Deemaryk (or Celebrated Dolphin at Comet named Deemaryk)...Please contact us, O great Dolphin of psychic wisdom...only you can help us find our Grandmama, Locasta the Good Witch of the North...Speak to us! Speak to us, O great Dolphin! Speak!"

Suddenly the typewriter typed another message, this time a much longer one. With joy, they bounded over to read the salutation from the great mystic dolphin they had contacted, and were perplexed beyond belief and puzzled out of their wits when they read the message:

> *** TURSIOPS SERVER VERSION 3.2 ***
> **** RUNNING UNDER LINUX ****
>
> Welcome! You are now signed on to Smith & Tinker's Tursiops computer network server!
>
> Your assigned internet address is:
> adepts@mtflathead.gillikin.oz

Dan and Locasta

THE elderly woman at the reference desk in the public library in Los Angeles, California, was busy chatting on the phone with her friend and so took no notice of the sixteen-year-old boy who eagerly made his way to the public computer terminals. He had short, light brownish hair and a fair-skinned face with blue eyes and freckles, a tall, slender build, and a western shirt that made him look like someone who longed for adventure.

But adventure had so far eluded him. He had been an orphan for several long and painful years, during which time he periodically was moved from one foster home to another, each no better than the last; for each of the dreary, scummy slum apartments that he was required to call home was ruled by abusive, tyrannical guardians who regarded him as little more than the basis for a larger welfare check. And the other kids he encountered cruelly teased and shunned him for his fondness of things like astronomy, natural history, and mathematics and his unwillingness to take part in stickball, rap music, stealing hubcaps, and their other pastimes. Only recently had he found some relief to his lonely existence when he discovered the wonderful computers in the library with their Internet access, which allowed him to communicate with kind and friendly people all over the world.

He sat down at one of the computer terminals and started to type out his latest electronic mail message to the three strange girls he recently met through an Internet chat room. They seemed to be really nice girls; in fact they were by far the most terrific girls he had ever met, either in person or through the computer network. But what made it strange was that these girls insisted that they neither owned a computer, knew how to use a computer, or had ever even seen a computer!

He had asked them how, then, they could communicate with him as though they were on the Internet, and they would say that it was one of those "miracles of the universe," and refused to elaborate. They also said that they first made contact with him and the computer network as part of some sort of search mission, but they said that they couldn't say more until the time was right.

As these three were the first really wonderful girls he had ever encountered, and since he had waited for so long to meet such kind and compassionate people as these, he quickly came to regard them as his dearest friends. He disregarded their oddities and continued to converse with them via computer mail about everything from nature to music to the interconnectedness of all things. The three girls were obviously all very wise and kind and sweet, and he was feeling much better than he had for a very long time.

Just as he began to type the first message of the fourth month of his dialogue with these incredible girls, he became aware of someone peering over his shoulder. He slowly turned around, expecting to see the librarian waiting to eject him, or his guardian come to drag him home and thrash him again.

But instead his eyes met those of a plump, rosy-faced little old lady in purple robes and a tall, pointed purple hat. She carried under one chubby arm a small blackboard slate and held in the other hand a long, gilded staff with an *N* at one end.

Chapter Five

"Pardon me," she said, her eyes twinkling, "but can you tell me what country I'm in?"

"The United States of America," he replied awkwardly.

The lady shook her head. "Oh, dear, dear! I must be very far from home." She wrote "United States of America" on the little blackboard slate.

"Yes," she mused, with a tone that sounded more amused than distressed. "Any country with a name that long must very far from home indeed. I'm clearly very, very lost."

"Gee, I'm awfully sorry... My name is Dan Maryk."

"Dan. What a delightful name!" the old woman said with a chuckle as she exuberantly shook his hand.

"Shhh!" hissed the librarian. "You have to be quiet in the library!" And she went back to chit-chatting with her friend, her voice at a sufficient decibel level that she could be heard in the rest rooms.

"I don't think I caught your name?" whispered Dan.

"Did I throw it at you?"

"What is your name?" he asked patiently.

"Locasta."

"Locasta? That's a very pretty name...just like you, if I may say so!"

Locasta's wrinkled face beamed at the complement.

"Locasta...Is that Greek?" he asked.

"I don't think so," Locasta mused. "In fact, I think Glinda once told me it was Merrylandian."

"Glinda? Like Glinda in *The Wizard of Oz?*"

"Oh, that movie," Locasta said with a tone of derision as she casually balanced the slate on her nose. "Yes, sort of like that. But that movie is just wrought with historical inaccuracies!"

"May I ask why you're balancing that slate on your nose?"

"I do this at noon every day," she said brightly. "It's good for my magical vibrations. Yes, that movie had quite an unacceptable number of factual errors—merging me and my dear friend Glinda into one character, for a start."

"What do you mean, your 'dear friend'?" Dan said.

"Oh, I know Glinda very well; we went to fairy school together," Locasta explained. "But she's not at all like she's portrayed in that film...She's really a very wise and astute sorceress."

"Do you mean to say that you are the Good Witch of the North, and that you know Glinda?" Dan said, incredulous.

"Yes indeed!" cried Locasta with enthusiasm.

"Shhh!" Dan cautioned.

"Oh, it's all right. I just cast a small spell that has rendered us invisible and inaudible. No one can see or hear us!"

Dan was still skeptical, but Locasta proved it by clapping her hands in front of the face of the librarian, who took no notice and continued her gossip with her friend. Then Dan did something he had always wanted to do, for the librarian was a mean old crone who liked to kick him out of the library if he stayed over half an hour, which she thought was long enough for riffraff like him to haunt a respectable *bibliothèque.*

"You fat, ugly, mean, rotten, stupid, slobbering old COW!" he cried next to the librarian's ear. As before, she took no notice.

"Remarkable!" said Dan, who now believed in the power of his new friend. "So you say you know Glinda? Then do you live in the Land of Oz?"

"Sadly, no. I have been exiled from Oz for some years now."

"Why did they exile you?"

"For many years, I ruled over the Gillikins in the Northern part of Oz," she explained. "But then one day old Mombi, the wicked witch I had conquered years earlier, decided to get revenge on me. She kidnapped me and used some terrible sort of powerful magic I have no inkling of to send me to a remote and uncivilized corner of Australia!

"I wandered aimlessly and desperately around that bleak and alien wilderness for a few days, and then I suddenly blacked out! When I came to, I was in a hospital in Sydney. I had lost my memory and I had assumed the form of a beautiful young woman! The only thing that I had to identify myself to the medicos was a name bracelet they found on me engraved "Princess Orin Oopyttat." From that they concluded that I was in fact the Princess of Liechtenstein, so they released me and sent me to the Liechtenstein embassy. When I arrived, the ambassadors knew right away that I wasn't their princess, but a princess nonetheless, so to avoid scandal (what scandal I can't imagine) they set up a lavish flat for me in the heart of Sydney, where I lived a life of luxury (and utter boredom) for the better part of twenty years!"

"Twenty years!" cried Dan in sympathetic alarm.

"I think the only reason I stayed so long," Locasta continued, "was that I was still amnesia-stricken and I just didn't feel secure going out of the house without my memory. But then one day, at a party thrown by some ambassador or another, I was introduced to the famous silent-screen star Arnie Hunk, who was on vacation in Australia and had heard about the famous Unknown Princess. He seemed to think that I might be able to act in his films. Sure enough, Arnie pulled some strings with Monumental

Pictures, and I immediately became a great leading lady with many starring roles. I was very happy as a silent screen star for about eight years, until one morning I awoke to find that I had reverted overnight to this, my natural form, and my memory had returned. I realized that I was really the Good Witch of the North from Oz! Arnie Hunk was livid; the invention of talkies was calamity enough for him and the studio, but to have their leading lady suddenly go geriatric on them—that was too much! So they nullified my contract and sent me away, which was all the same to me, because now that I remembered who I was, I wanted to get back to my real home—Oz!

"So ever since then, I've been wandering the world, trying in vain to find my way back to Oz. The most inconvenient part of it all has been that very little of my magic will work here, except for a few conjuring tricks, my magic slate, my invisibility spell, and my nonaging immortality that all natural-born citizens of Oz possess."

"What does your magic slate do?" Dan asked. "Besides stand on you nose, I mean."

Suddenly the piece of chalk attached to the slate by a string lifted itself up and by itself wrote: "There are more things in heaven and earth!"

Dan was too stunned to speak, so he didn't. Locasta took the slate from her nose and examined it lovingly.

"My magic slate tells me important things when I need to know them," she explained. "It told me that if I came here, you would help me find my way home."

"How?" asked Dan.

"I don't know, but the message said that my granddaughters, the Three Adepts at Sorcery, had found a way to get me back home—"

"Did you say Three Adepts?" Dan cried. "You mean that the three magical Adepts of Oz are the three girls I've been corresponding with...and are your granddaughters?"

"Yes," the Good Witch replied with a smile.

"I don't believe it!" cried Dan. "I've established contact with Oz!"

"Or more accurately, my granddaughters have established contact with you," said Locasta.

Chapter Five

"Yes!" Dan said. "You see, I've been corresponding with them by e-mail on this computer—"

"What's a computer?" Locasta asked.

"Well, it's a machine used for doing calculations and communicating with people long-distance, among other things," Dan explained. "But I guess you don't have computers in Oz, which makes me wonder how your granddaughters can communicate with me."

"Being the Adepts at Sorcery that they are, my granddaughters are very powerful," Locasta said. "They no doubt found a way to link up the ebbs and flows of the Magic of Oz to the computer network."

"But how did they ever come to communicate with me? I'm nobody!" cried Dan.

"I'm sure you're not nobody, my boy," said Locasta. "Nobody is nobody! But maybe my granddaughters made contact with you because you are unconsciously in touch with fairy forces. Many people are, you know, and sadly go through life without ever knowing it. Poor souls! Anyway, since you have communicated with my granddaughters, they obviously have in mind transporting us both to Oz."

"You mean...," Dan breathed with excitement, "I'll never have to go back to those awful slums—ever again?"

"Never again!"

"Ouch!"

"What are you doing, my boy?"

"Just trying to pinch myself awake," Dan explained.

"You're not dreaming," Locasta assured him. "The message on my slate said that my granddaughters were making preparations now, and that they would transport us in a few days."

"A few days!" Dan cried. Once he absorbed the idea of never having to set eyes on his cruel guardians again, he was very anxious to be off at once.

"Don't worry!" said Locasta. "We shall just stay here, and being invisible, no one will know. Which is a good thing, since I had better bone up on the events that have transpired in Oz in these ninety-odd years since I left, or else when we go there I might feel as disoriented as Rip Van Winkle upon awakening. So, do you know if this library has any Oz books? I'd ask the librarian, but every library I've gone into and asked for books about Oz, they hand me a book about either Australia, a maximum-security prison, or something called Buffy the Vampire Slayer."

Dan laughed. "Actually this library is quite an enlightened one as far as Oz goes. They have all of the Oz books that were by written by L. Frank Baum, and many more besides. I've loved the Oz books since I was a little boy, but I never realized before that they were historical books. Just think, Oz is real!" And Dan trembled with excitement at the idea, and that he would soon be there.

So Locasta spent the next few days at the "X 398" shelf reading all the Oz books there, while Dan surfed the web and sent e-mail to the Adepts to tell them their grandmama was with him.

Going through the several shelves of Oz books with remarkable speed, Locasta read all about how Ozma became queen; how Dorothy and the Wizard returned to Oz to stay; how her granddaughters had been cruelly enchanted by the witch Coo-ee-oh and then restored by Red Reera the Yookoohoo; how Scraps the Patchwork Girl came to be; how Betsy Bobbin, Trot, and Cap'n Bill came to Oz; and many, many other things.

Locasta put down *The Giant Horse of Oz* one night long after the library had closed and the two of them were alone. "It's all very clear to me now," she said. "Right after old Mombi dispelled me from Oz, she captured the fairy Queen Orin of the Ozure Isles and transformed her into me, so no one would know I was gone, and me into her, which is why I became a young woman. Then when the spell was broken twenty-eight years later, our bodies switched back, and we both resumed our correct forms. But nearly everyone in Oz thinks that Orin was the one and only Good Witch of the North and don't know about me, which I'm sure is what Mombi wanted. So now I'm doubly anxious to get back home and assert my true identity, and be reunited with my beloved granddaughters."

"Well, they e-mailed me this evening—" Dan began.

"'E-mailed' you?"

"Uh, that means they sent me a message through the computer," Dan explained. "They e-mailed me and said that they would transport both of us to Baumgea today!"

Chapter Five

"How does that make you feel, my boy?" asked Locasta.

"Wonderful!" Dan proclaimed. "Uh—what's Baumgea?'

"The continent where Oz and other fairy countries lie," Locasta said. "There are several continents in the Nonestic Archipelago: Baumgea; Dodgsonia, where Wonderland and the Looking-Glass land are; Wedland, home to the Seven Jeweled Hills, the Seven Woods and Willows, and the Seven Deserts; Krofftgea, continent of Lidsville, the Land of the Lost, Living Island and Tranquillity Forest; and others. The rest of the world beyond the Nonestic Ocean, the self-described 'World of Reality,' is referred to as the 'Collective Hunch' by Nonesticans."

"Well I've lived in the 'Collective Hunch' all my life," said Dan, "and I long to escape it and its wars, crime, selfishness, and cruelty. You mean we're actually going to Oz?" Dan was still unable to believe that his dreams were about to come true. "And meet your granddaughters, and Dorothy, and Glinda, and the Scarecrow, and the Patchwork Girl, and—Ozma?"

"You said Ozma's name with considerable emphasis," Locasta observed.

"Well, I admit that I've had a crush on Ozma ever since I read the Oz books as a kid. But I don't know if I could ever meet her person," Dan lamented.

"Why not?" Locasta inquired. "I'm sure she would adore a sweet and loving man like you. Everyone in Oz would."

"You really think so?"

"Of course, my boy!" Locasta said jovially. "They will be so grateful to you for helping me."

"How have I helped you?" asked Dan.

"Just by showing kindness and compassion," said Locasta. "I've been stuck in the Collective Hunch for enough years now to see that people like you are very rare and precious."

"But I've always been crazy about Ozma," he stammered bashfully. "She's so sweet and beautiful...and if I meet her, I'd like...well, that is to say...I'd sort of...like to...uh...ask her out?"

"I see," Locasta replied thoughtfully.

"But I know I'd be too shy to ask her," Dan said hopelessly.

"Faint heart never won fair maiden, my boy," said Locasta with a knowing smile.

"But what can I do?" cried Dan. "Every time I open my mouth and try to talk to a girl, I get tongue-tied. I guess I can't help feeling that the lovely and much-beloved Queen of Oz could never be interested in a common computer nerd from America like me."

"You are not common and you are not a nerd!" said Locasta forcefully. After a pause, she added, "What is a nerd, anyway?"

"Someone who's hateful or repulsive," said Dan.

"Well, that certainly does not describe you," said Locasta, "and if it's a phrase that is supposed to imply that all computer people are hateful and repulsive, I'm glad I live in a fairyland that doesn't use such inane phraseology. As far as talking to Ozma—share some stories about yourself and talk to her about the things you love best. Your interest in computers should give you quite a bit to talk about."

"What if I bore her to tears?"

"Then she is not the right one for you," his white-haired friend answered softly. "Ozma may love you in return or she may not. But you will not know until you try. And remember that it's not the end of the world if she doesn't."

Dan nodded and said, "So when will we be on our way?"

"Just as soon as my granddaughters get their magical machines to work right...and they will! But I guess the computers here in your country have no magic." Locasta then listened with fascination as Dan showed her how the computer worked and some of the things on the World Wide Web.

"How often do you have to wind it?" she asked at last.

"You don't have to wind it; it works by electricity," said Dan with a laugh.

"Thrilling! Absolutely thrilling!" Locasta said in astonishment. Turning back to the screen, on which was displayed the web page of a well-known computer animator, she asked, "What part of the world are we looking at now?"

"It's not any real place," Dan explained. "This is virtual reality—a realistic-looking landscape mathematically generated by the computer."

"Of course!" Locasta cried. "It's Virtual Forest! The great woodland in the southern part of the Fairyland of Ev!"

Chapter Five

"Of course not," laughed Dan. "It's not real; it's just a picture."

Then Dan looked closely at the screen.

"It certainly looks real, though, doesn't it?" he observed. "Remarkable how much realism these 3D animation programs are capable of now… But it all looks so real! The trees, the grass, the sky, the river—it all looks as though it were really in front of us, and that I could reach out and touch it. In fact, I actually feel a country breeze blowing around me. It feels almost as though we were actually there ourselves…"

And to Dan's astonishment, the picture leapt up off of the computer screen and grew to the size of a doorway. Locasta smiled in delight and grandmotherly pride. "They did it! My granddaughters have opened up a…a…"

"Wormhole?" asked Dan.

"I'm afraid I don't know the technical term, but it is definitely a magic portal to Oz or a neighboring land. Come, my boy!"

His heart throbbing with excitement, Dan picked up his satchel in which he had stuffed his few but much-prized belongings and followed Locasta into Fairyland.

6

The Experiment Succeeds

"IT'S worked! It's worked!" Judit cried. "I just talked with Ozma on the fairy-phone, and her Magic Picture tells her that Grandmama is in the Land of Ev! She's back in Baumgea!"

"Hooray!" Sofia cheered, and danced a jig.

"It would have been nice if that fool machine of yours could have gotten her into Oz," Zsuzsa said.

"It doesn't matter! She's back! And you did it!" Sofia cried, hugging Judit.

"Thank you, sweetie," Judit said, "but I just built the machine; I couldn't have done it without you both."

"Is that sweet young man from the Collective Hunch with her?" Zsuzsa asked.

"Danny? He sure is, and after these months of corresponding with him by way of Judit's machine and this magical thing called the Internet, I can't wait to meet him in person," said Sofia.

Chapter One

"Well, at least we can stop the machine now," Zsuzsa observed. "It's so noisy it's been keeping me awake nights."

"Yes, of course," Judit said. "I'll do it at once, and then we'll get our winds going and fly over to our beloved Grandmama."

"At last! Oh, I can't wait!" Sofia cried, and pirouetted with joy.

Judit was about to throw the switch to stop the magical machine when Zsuzsa shouted. "Wait a minute! The typewriter is writing something!"

Judit raced over to the typewriter, and watched in amazement as it typed out these words:

I bring uplifting news my friends.
Oz's perils are near an end.
To invade and plunder Oz your foes
Will decide to have one final go.
For a while you may be where
You all feel you're in despair.
But their "perfect" plan will reach a hitch—
A very special teacher and a long-time-lost Good Witch!
Then demise befalls each fiend and crone
And Oz is ever after left alone.
And then eternal peace and cheer
Will reign in Oz, now free from fear.
The truth of my words you'll be convinced
The day the gremlin becomes a prince!

"What in Baumgea does that mean?" Zsuzsa said.

"It's a prophecy of some sort," Sofia said.

"Oh dear! You mean Oz is in danger?" Judit said in agitation.

"For the last time apparently," Sofia said, looking on the bright side.

"I think it's inane nonsense!" Zsuzsa said.

"No, it's not!" Sofia said. "It mentions a long-lost Good Witch—that must mean Grandmama."

"Yes, but who's the very special teacher, what are these fiends and crones, and what gremlin? There are no gremlins in Baumgea that I know of."

"Well, I don't know, but if that's what they say—" Sofia said.

"That's what who says? Some crackpot tea-leaf reader in Hollywood?" Zsuzsa said. "I'm not sure how much I like Oz being linked to the rest of the world by this Internet thing!"

"You may be right, Zsuzsa," Judit said. "Now that Grandmama and Danny are safely here maybe I'd better dismantle the machine...We don't want to attract lunatics from the Outside World, after all."

"All the same, I think we should tell Ozma about this," Sofia said.

"Oh yes, I can just hear ourselves," Zsuzsa said. "'Your majesty, there's this quack in the Collective Hunch who's predicting an invasion of Oz...True, his only credentials are card tricks at the city carnival, but we knew what you really needed now was for us to fill your mind with needless and pointless worries when we really ought to be reuniting with our Grandmama.'"

"Yes, you're right," Judit said as she switched off the machine. "Grandmama is a much more tangible concern that we should be dealing with."

"And besides, if any invaders dared march into Oz, I guess Glinda and the Wizard would soon use their great sorcery to defeat them," Sofia said.

"Quite right!" Zsuzsa said. "So lets go get Grandmama!"

"Yes, lets!" Sofia said.

"Just think," Judit said. "Grandmama safe and sound in Baumgea again, and we're about to see her again. Nothing can happen to her now!"

Ozma and the Virtual Sprites

"THE Adepts just called on my portable Oz-o-phone," Ozma told Jellia as they trekked across the Ozian countryside in Ozma's Red Wagon in search of Ruggedo. "They found Locasta and Danny in my Magic Picture—they've just arrived in Baumgea, and they're waiting for us and the Adepts in Ev near Virtual Forest."

"Who's Danny?" asked Jellia.

"The young man in America who found Locasta," Ozma said. "The Adepts have been communicating with him for some time, and he sounds like a real sweet guy. I can't wait to meet him!"

"They've been communicating with him?" said Jellia.

"With something called the 'Internet,' which I gather is some magical contraption the Adepts have invented," Ozma explained. "Anyway the Adepts have been corresponding very happily with him—"

"While we've trudging across mountains, valleys, and forests searching for that rotten Ruggedo," said Jellia. "Look, Ozma, I hate to sound disagreeable, but don't you think if Ruggedo really had some evil plot up his sleeve he would have made his move by now?"

"Perhaps you're right," Ozma said thoughtfully. "All the same, I want to know where he is, and deny him any possibility of doing my people harm. Actually, I have been thinking about the fruitlessness of our quest so far, and now that we're in Winkie Country approaching the desert, I have an idea: If I used the Magic Belt to transport us to Southern Ev, I could call on my cousin Princess Gyma in the Land of Op. She knows all about finding people and other tricks and could probably help us find Ruggedo much quicker. And if we stop in Ev first, we could meet Locasta and Danny and the Adepts, and all go to Op together."

"That sounds good, but there's something I don't understand," said Jellia. "If you wanted to find Ruggedo, why didn't you just look in the Magic Picture? It shows you everything."

"That's what I did when we stopped back at the Emerald City for supplies," Ozma said. "I knew one glance at it would tell me right away where he was and save us a long, hard journey; but nothing came up—just static. Ruggedo has obviously acquired some powerful magic that is shielding him from the Magic Picture, and Glinda's Book of Records as well, for Glinda reported that it, too, is revealing nothing of his whereabouts."

"He has magic that can resist yours and Glinda's? That's very worrisome," said Jellia.

"Don't worry, my dear; we'll stop him and his magic, whatever form it takes," Ozma proclaimed. "And at least this trip has given me a chance to visit my people outside the Emerald City and make sure they're getting on well."

"So we're going to Ev, then?" said Jellia.

"Yes, I'll transport us there with the Magic Belt," said Ozma, clasping the jeweled belt around her waist.

"The wagon too?"

"I want to conserve as much power in the Magic Belt as I can, in case of emergency," Ozma said. "So I'll leave the Wagon here and make one command to get us over the desert into Ev, and then we'll walk the rest of the way."

Chapter Seven

"Okay, I'm with you," said Jellia.

"I'm not," remarked the wooden Sawhorse who pulled the Wagon. "But I'll wait here for you anyway."

Ozma closed her eyes and whispered a command to the Belt…

"Where are we?" Jellia gasped a second later. They suddenly found themselves in a deep, dark, and forbidding forest.

"We must be in Ev, in Virtual Forest," said Ozma. "The Adepts said that Danny and Locasta were waiting between Virtual Forest and Gump Forest, to the east."

"Then I would strongly suggest we get out of this forest, unless you plan to open a seaside resort," said Jellia, freeing her leg from some brambles.

"I hate to admit it," said Ozma, scanning the nearby trees, "but I'm not sure which way we need to go…Isn't there something about the moss on the trees that tells you the direction?"

"Yeah, the moss always points toward Hollywood," said Jellia.

"Thanks," Ozma replied flatly. "Look, let's go that way—I think the light is brighter there."

Jellia followed faithfully after her mistress. But as they walked, the already meager light only faded further.

"Are you still there, Jellia?" Ozma called out suddenly.

"No," Jellia replied.

"I could've sworn the way out of the wood was this way," said Ozma.

"Is it my imagination, or are we lost?" asked Jellia.

"It's not your imagination, my dear," said Ozma. "But neither do I think we're lost—at least not much longer. Look at this sign."

"What sign? I can't see a thing!" said Jellia.

"Oh, I'm sorry, my dear! I forgot—" Ozma reached into her robes as she spoke and drew out a several small berries. "Here, this gives one the ability to see in the dark."

Jellia munched on one of the berries and, although the night vision she then acquired was not as clear or bright as daylight, it was enough for her read the sign: "For all the information worth having, ask the Virtual Sprites." And an arrow pointed straight ahead.

So they followed the arrow and soon arrived at a clearing where the near-darkness was pierced by numerous little globes of light flitting through the air and winking on and off like fireflies.

"Hello? Are we in the presence of the Virtual Sprites?" Ozma called out.

"Yes…we…are…the…Vir…tu…al…Sprites," they said in quick, scratchy tones, like a bad phone connection.

Chapter Seven

"We need your assistance," said Ozma, trying to follow their movements, which were very confusing. A pair of them would seem to appear from nowhere, swirl about in chaotic loops for about a second, and then the pair would collide and seemingly vanish.

"We...can...not...give...as...sis...tance...We...don't...last...long...e...nough," they said, each sprite uttering one syllable before it hit its partner and vanished.

"Why do you keep appearing and disappearing?" said Ozma, getting quite annoyed.

"We...are...Vir...tu...al...Sprites."

"What does that mean?" pressed Jellia.

"We...used...to...be...real...sprites...but...we...were...en...chant...ed...by...the...witch...es...and...de...mons...of...Whaq...o...land...so...we...would... not...try...to...in...ter...fere...in...their...ev...il...do...ings." The sprites then explained that the demons had imprisoned them in an astral plane cut off from our world, and that they only appeared for a second at a time in our world, along with their mirror images, and after a fleeting instant of freedom they merged with their mirror images and vanished into captivity once more.

"That's horrible!" Ozma cried. "Those witches and demons must have very powerful magic, but they haven't met up with me yet. I'll free you!"

"How?" said the sprites despairingly.

"You say that you appear along with your mirror image when you appear for a second?" Ozma inquired thoughtfully.

"Yes."

"But don't mirror images belong in mirrors, or in something else reflective, like that little pond over there?"

"Of...course...if...we...were...sep...a...rat...ed...from...our...re...flec...tions...for...more...than...a...second...we...would...be...free...and...our...re...flec...tions...would...go...in...the...pond...where...they...be...long.... But...this...en...chant...ment...makes...us...and...our...mir...ror...im...age...at...tract...each...oth...er...like...mag...nets...and...come...back...to...geth...er."

Ozma now knew what to do. She waited for a sprite to materialize near her, and then she reached out and grabbed it and held the little fairy-like creature tight in her fist. Its companion mirror image tried to get back to it and flew frantically around Ozma's closed fist like a moth at a street lamp, but Ozma held on to the sprite as tightly as she could. In a few seconds, the mirror-image screamed as if in agony and tumbled head-over-heels into the pond.

"I'm free!" the sprite cried in ecstasy. It gloated at its reflection in the pond and then did three triple somersaults in the air. "I'm free from those devious demons, and may all of Fairyland be free of them someday!"

"Who? What demons?" asked Jellia.

"The demons and witches of Whaqoland!" the sprite said. "They're horrible! They want to invade, conquer, terrorize, and rule all of Baumgea. All they need is a leader to get them marching."

"This is serious!" Ozma cried. "What if Ruggedo decides to lead these creatures? And what might they do to Locasta and Danny if they find them?"

"Where is this Whaqoland?" asked Jellia.

"Just south of here, and Ev, where your friends are, is to the west. Just go in the opposite direction from how you arrived here, and you'll find your way. But first, won't you release my colleagues?"

"Yes, of course!" Ozma cried. "Come on Jellia, grab all the Virtual Sprites you can!"

So Ozma and Jellia raced about, grabbing Virtual Sprites one-by-one and leaving the mirror images to fall back into the pond. The faster they grabbed, the faster the sprites were freed, until with an explosion of fairy light, the sprites all broke free and, now liberated, flew up through the trees like a flock of pigeons. "Thank you!" they cried.

"Glad to help. Oh, by the way," Ozma called after them, "what became of all the Veela of Virtual Forest?"

"They have encoded themselves into the strange and elaborate network of magical fields in this forest," they cried as they vanished in the distance, "until a young man of worthy cleverness and tenderness can release them. Anyway, they are safe and sound until then. Good-bye to you. And remember—beware the Whaqolanders!"

The Witches of Whaqoland

DAN and Locasta found themselves in a grassy field at the edge of a forest. Opposite the forest was a clear, flowing river. Beyond the river were green, rolling hills, and another forest lay beyond the hills. The sky was clear and blue, and the air was cool and sweet-smelling.

"Where are we?" Dan asked.

"We're in the Land of Ev!" Locasta said, delighted. "I'm not sure how we got here, but here we are. We are at the border of Virtual Forest, and over in the distance we can see Gump Forest."

"Gump Forest?" Dan inquired.

"The home of a species of moose-like creatures whose motto is 'Antlered is as antlered does.'"

"I see," Dan said.

"Now all we have to do is wait for my granddaughters," said Locasta. The message on my slate said that they would come and fetch us within minutes of our arrival."

"I just can't believe it!" Dan said. "In a few minutes we're going to be in the Land of Oz! It's all so—"

But he stopped speaking with a start as he and Locasta were suddenly clutched by long, bony fingers. They twisted their heads around and saw that their arms and legs were being bound in ropes by two of the most hideous old witches imaginable. One was tall and bony and the other was short and globular. Both were unique in their awfulness.

"Now you are our prisoners!" they cackled with glee.

"Who are you?" Dan asked as the hags secured their captors with butterfly knots.

"We are two of the Witches of Whaqoland," the tall one explained. "I'm S-Slinger and she's Reed."

"Pleased to make your acquaintance," said Reed nastily.

"What kind of ridiculous names are those?" Locasta asked boldly.

"Silence, mortals!" S-Slinger snapped. (Of course, she did not know that Locasta was the Good Witch of the North.)

"What are you going to do to us?" Dan stammered.

"We haven't decided yet," leered Reed. "We will decide when we get you to Whaqoland. We might set you to work selling candy bars..."

"Or singing the entire score of *The Sound of Music*," said S-Slinger.

"We might make you write a three-volume essay on the presidential achievements of Millard Fillmore," said Reed.

"Or if we decide you won't make decent slaves," S-Slinger hissed, "we'll put you in the D Square."

"What's the D Square?" asked Dan.

"The most horrible torture a mortal being can endure!" sneered S-Slinger. "But our gracious queen will no doubt devise an appropriately ghoulish fate for you. Now if you'll just come along with us—"

Suddenly the two hags were blinded by a puff of smoke. When it cleared, Dan and Locasta were gone!

Chapter Eight

"How did you do that?" Dan panted. They were fleeing as fast as they could.

"Elementary magic," Locasta replied. "Breaking away from two fantastically horrible witches who plan to enslave you and put you in the D Square is covered in witch kindergarten."

"There they go!" Reed screeched. "You'd better start slinging, Slinger!"

"With pleasure!" S-Slinger said. She hopped aboard her broomstick and darted off after Dan and Locasta like a rocket.

As she gained on them, S-Slinger waved her hand and conjured up a bar of soap and slung it at them, but Dan and Locasta quickly dodged it. S-Slinger then produced a hot bowl of soup and slung that at them, but before it could hit them, Locasta turned it into harmless confetti.

With a shriek of rage, S-Slinger bombarded them with a shower of snowballs, salami sandwiches, six-pointed stars, sand crabs, saxophones, shells, sacks of sunflower seeds, socks, songbooks, soufflés, soybeans, surfboards, sleds called "Rosebud," spoons, saucepans, seismograms, and sailfish wearing sandals. But as quickly as S-Slinger's magic hurtled these objects upon them, Locasta's magic deflected them.

As Reed observed the flight of Dan and Locasta and the failure of S-Slinger's slinging, she decided that drastic measures were called for. She raised her chubby, long-nailed hands over her bloated head and chanted: "O grim elementals that overwhelm,/blow your gusts upon our foe;/they shall despair enslaved in the realm/of our generalissimo!"

In obedience, the grim elementals (which are evil gusts of wind who work for the witches) stirred up a tornado that whisked up Dan and Locasta. It blew them over many miles of countryside and finally dropped them into the swampy depths of the Whaqoland forest. There, Nan-Kerr, Queen of Whaqoland, met in counsel with the wicked witches and frightful demons who were her subjects.

The winds landed them inside the circle of Whaqolanders, right in front of Nan-Kerr herself. Unlike the other witches, Nan-Kerr was a seemingly beautiful young woman with flowing black hair and a youthful, rosy face. She wore silky black robes, and on her head was a sparkling, golden crown. As she looked upon her two prisoners, her face did its best to assume an expression of wicked malevolence, but somehow the effect was not convincing, especially as it almost immediately turned into an expression of total surprise.

"Locasta!" she cried.

"Nan-Kerr!" Locasta cried, in equal surprise.

"You mean you know these creatures?" snarled Old Skin-Droop, the head of the Whaqoland witches.

"I—ah—No! Of course not!" Nan-Kerr stammered, in obvious fear.

"Well, then shall we deal with them?" Skin-Droop hissed.

"Yes, of course," Nan-Kerr muttered.

"Nan-Kerr, what on Earth—" Locasta began.

"Quiet, Locasta," Nan-Kerr hissed at her. "You don't want to get me plopped in the D Square, do you?" Then, out loud, she said, "Summon the chief demon!"

Immediately Forg, the chief of the tribe of Whaqoland demons, stepped forward. He had a squat body and a snake-like tail, and he was dressed in skins like a caveman. He had tiny but fiery eyes, a pug nose, and fanged teeth. From his face grew four horns— two long ones, one slightly shorter and directly above the other, jutting up from his domed forehead, and the two shorter ones sprouting from each side of his sharp jaw. His face was filled with hate for all creation, and he spoke in a roaring voice like a crocodile with ingrown toenails. All the demons of Whaqoland were terrible, but Forg was the most malevolent demon of all.

"How may I assist you, oh princess of profanity?" growled Forg.

"Chief demon," Nan-Kerr said, "I want you to tell me who—"

"Who these turkeys are?" said Forg, taking out a pair of binoculars and scrutinizing Dan and Locasta through them.

"Precisely," said Nan-Kerr, and waited for Forg to finish his scrutiny.

"Probably socialists!" Forg said at last, stashing the binoculars back into his robes.

"What are socialists?" Nan-Kerr asked, puzzled.

"People who don't agree with us!" said Forg.

"Quite right! We must deal with these treacherous fools at once!" Skin-Droop cried.

Chapter Eight

"But who exactly are they? That's the question!" Forg hissed.

"The boy is obviously an intellectual elitist nerd of some sort," said Old Skin-Droop.

"Probably wasted all his time in school learning things!" said a demon named Pe-rude-ian. "Pathetic little twerp!"

"Actually, he's kind of handsome!" Nan-Kerr observed. "How'd you like to date a slightly evil sorceress, good-looking?"

"I—I—I—" Dan said, not sure how to reply when asked out by a witch.

"And the other is—Yes, it's the Good Witch of the North!" Forg announced as he scrutinized Locasta.

"Oh, of course! I didn't even recognize her!" Nan-Kerr lied.

"Nan-Kerr, will you please—" Locasta said.

"I told you to keep quiet," Nan-Kerr hissed, and then stammered out loud: "Um, what do you suggest I do with them, Forg?"

"Find out the great secret from her!" Forg cried.

"What great secret?" said Nan-Kerr.

"You know—The Great Secret!" Forg cried. Then he turned to Locasta and said, "We demand that you tell us the Great Secret!"

"What great secret?" said Locasta, with an innocent twinkle in her eye.

"You know what!" Forg barked. "The M.O.E.!"

"The Music of Elgar?" chirped Locasta.

"You know that's not it, you witch!"

"Of Enya?"

"The Magic of Everything! Tell us about THE MAGIC OF EVERYTHING!"

"Oh sure," Locasta said. "Sometime over coffee and donuts. I'll buy."

"If you don't tell me, the torture you will endure will be unspeakable! Now, tell us!"

"No comment," said Locasta.

"Well, she won't tell," said Nan-Kerr. "What a rotten bit of luck! Well that's the way it goes...so why don't we let them go?"

"Are you nuts!?" Forg snarled. "If she won't tell, we must torture them until she does!"

"How should I torture them?" Nan-Kerr asked nervously.

"Hang 'em from the ceiling!" Skin-Droop advised.

"Turn them into salamanders!" Pe-rude-ian suggested.

"Make them run for Congress!" Forg recommended.

"You don't scare us!" Locasta proclaimed.

"They don't?" Dan whispered.

"So many wonderfully awful things we could do to them," Forg muttered. "Decisions! Decisions!"

As Locasta tried to do some quick thinking, her magic chalk raised itself up and wrote on the slate. "Forg, why don't you sleep on it?"

"Er, uh—That's a good idea!" Nan-Kerr stammered. "There's nothing, um—like a bad night's sleep to clear the evil mind of mercy!"

The witches and demons snarled and hooted in agreement.

"Yes, we'll give them lodgings at the Shack for tonight, and then tomorrow morning..." Forg finished the sentence with a scream of evil, gleeful laughter with which the other witches and demons joined in.

Chapter Eight

The laughing became louder and louder until Dan and Locasta had to cover their ears. Then came a loud BANG! and Dan and Locasta suddenly found themselves alone in a clearing of the forest just in front of a little old shack.

"Where are we?" stammered Dan. "I'm scared!"

"Don't worry, my boy," Locasta said firmly. "I'll get you out of this Lurline-forsaken place as sure as the Emerald City is green!"

"What is this Magic of Everything that they want to know so badly?"

"What...? Oh, that...," Locasta said carelessly. "Just the most powerful bit of magic in all of Fairyland!"

The Magic of Everything

LOCASTA went on: "In the entire Fairy World, there are thousands of intricate spells, runes, and incantations. For centuries, witches, wizards, and sorcerers have searched for the All-Encompassing magical formula—the set of fundamental incantations that govern the workings of all other incantations in the magical universe. The Magic of Everything explains the very intertwining of magic with the fabric of space and time. It tells us the very reason that magic exists."

"Why does magic exist?" Dan asked, not at all understanding how magic could possibly be compatible with the scientific universe he come to know and love during his life.

"In general, it doesn't, as lifelong experience in the Collective Hunch would correctly tell you. If magic could exist as a rule, there would be total anarchy everywhere and the universe would soon fall to pieces. So in general, magic is disallowed by the laws of nature, but there are isolated pockets in the universe where the invisible barrier between the everyday world and the ebbs and flows of the cosmic forces of nature are torn away, and people with a dynamic connection to those intricate cosmic forces are said to have magical powers. And the magnitude of their powers is merely a measure of how greatly they are capable of changing the natural course of the ebbs and flows. Any magic spell that is executed—by me or Glinda or the Wizard of Oz or anyone—calls on and executes lower and lower levels of magic, and ultimately the lowest level, the Magic of Everything, the most fundamental of all incantations, is executed and causes subatomic fluctuations in the cosmic ebbs and flows, and thus makes magical things happen."

"It's like a computer's operating system!" Dan observed, though Locasta admitted that she didn't understand what he was talking about.

"But are there only limited areas in the universe where this manipulation of ebbs and flows is possible—even by those who know how?" asked Dan.

"Yes," said Locasta. "As you know, we live in three-dimensional space—the dimensions of width, length, and height. But there are little pockets of our space that protrude into the fourth dimension of hyperspace—the sea of fluctuations in space and time—and create a so-called gravity-well wormhole that is usually cut off from the outside world, but that is in close contact with the multidimensional ebbs and flows of the universe, thus making magic possible. The local well happens to intersect the earth right in the Nonestic Ocean, where Oz and other fairylands reside."

"Incredible!" Dan said in awe.

"And in spite of all the power of these ultimate cosmic incantations," Locasta said, returning to the Magic of Everything, "they are so elegantly simple that they could be written on a tunic. Yet the incantations themselves contain so much information about other incantations derived from them that mere knowledge of the Magic of Everything can be more precious than having an equivalent level of actual magical powers. Many sorcerers and witches would give half their existing powers to know the incantations that make up the Magic of Everything, so that it is kept a precious secret...In fact, I am the only one that I know of that both knows the Magic of Everything and understands it. That's the hard part—really understanding what those incantations are saying, and making use of them."

"And these spells offer final, complete knowledge of everything?" Dan said.

"Oh, no! There's no such thing as final, complete knowledge," Locasta explained. "No matter how much we learn about the universe, there's always an infinite wealth of new things to discover. The Magic of Everything just explains the workings of other common forms of ultra-powerful magic, including Classical Magical Mechanics, the Special and General Theories of Magical Relativity, Particle Magic, Supersymmetric Magic, Electroweak Magic, and Grand Unified Magic Spells (GUMS)."

"But if some evil being succeeded in comprehending the Magic of Everything, would they then really have the power to control the rest of Fairyland?" asked Dan with a shudder.

"That depends on how knowledgeable that being would be in other types of magic," Locasta explained. "There are many different kinds of magic, and the more different kinds you command, the greater your overall powers can potentially be. You see, every fairy and other magical being in the world exists on a scale that measures the overall magnitude of the sum total of all their magical prowess, and knowledge of the Magic of Everything effectively moves one's Magic Index up a whole level."

"I'd like to see that Magic Index scale," Dan said.

In reply, Locasta's magic chalk came to life again and wrote on the slate:

Magic Index (M.I.) Scale

Index	Examples
9.9	("All-Powerful" Genies)
9	Glinda (Sorceress)
8	The Adepts at Sorcery
7	The Wizard of Oz
6	Ozma (Fairy)
5	Locasta (Witch)
4	Polychrome (Fairy)
3	Mrs. Yoop (Yookoohoo)
2	Mombi (Quasi-Witch)
1	(Immortals Without Magic)

Chapter Nine

"As you see, it's quite an informative scale," Locasta said, "and it is clear from it—"

Locasta was interrupted by a loud creaking. They turned and saw that the door of the shack was swinging open to reveal another old witch. This witch, however, lacked the look of hostile malevolence inherent in her colleagues—indeed, she seemed very cordial as she spoke.

"You are Nan-Kerr's prisoners, I presume?" she said.

"We are," Locasta proclaimed— almost proudly, Dan thought.

"I'm Witch Shacklet, and this is my shack," said the witch. "Please come in."

"Are you going to hurt us?" Dan asked bluntly.

"No, I'm retired, so I'm just an old crab. Won't you come in for a spot of tea, or are you going to stand there all night like a couple of clods?"

Dan looked doubtfully at Locasta as she confidently swept into the little shack, saying, "Thank you. Don't mind if we do."

"Well, are you a guy or a guidepost?" Shacklet said to Dan.

Dan decided that he should not allow his comrade to meet any peril that awaited them alone, so he reluctantly followed her into the witch's hut.

It was small, only one room, dimly lit by a fireplace. In one corner was a long bed of nails (where witches usually sleep), and in another corner was a table piled with magic paraphernalia such as playing cards, rare herbs, astrological charts, and a Parker Brothers Ouija Board.

The room was dominated by a large, round table where about ten witches were sipping tea and munching scones.

"Sisters," Shacklet announced, "these are Nan-Kerr's prisoners. They've come to share our tea."

"Welcome!" said one witch.

"Hi there!" said another.

"Pleased to meet you!" said another.

Locasta thanked them kindly, but Dan was too perplexed by this courtesy to speak.

"Would you like China or India tea?" Shacklet asked as they seated themselves.

"Oh, China please," said Locasta. "India disagrees with my Magical Force Fields."

"You?" Shacklet asked of Dan.

"Ah—I don't suppose there's any chance you have a Cherry Coke?" Dan said.

"None," Shacklet said flatly.

"Dr Pepper?" Dan grasped at straws.

"Have a scone," one of the witches offered.

As Dan and Locasta ate and drank, Shacklet scrutinized her guests.

"So, the witches and demons are to perform their evilness on you, yes?" she said.

"Not if we can help it!" said Locasta confidently.

"How do we know *you're* not going to hurt us?" Dan asked nervously.

"We won't," Shacklet asserted. "Mark you, we're supposed to. We Whaqoland witches were born to be mean, hateful, spiteful, nasty, vicious, cruel, and barbaric. More tea?" she said to Locasta.

"Thank you. Don't mind if I do," she replied.

"Even though the Code of Whaqoland requires all witches to molest every innocent, defenseless creature we meet," Shacklet said, "we in this abode openly defy the law and treat others with kindness and respect."

"We're conscientious objectors," another witch explained.

"Mind you, don't tell a soul about us!" Shacklet said uneasily. "If Forg ever found out about our silent rebellion, he'd set his fellow demons on us, and that would be the end."

"But what made you into rebels?" Dan asked.

"And what is Nan-Kerr doing ruling this horrible country?" Locasta said. "We were chums in fairy school, and she was Queen of the Cloud Fairies, last I heard."

"Have another scone," Shacklet said to Dan and Locasta, "and we will tell you the tale that will answer both of your questions."

The Story of the Witches

"ONCE, very long ago, we Whaqoland witches were all equally mean and vicious and nasty," Shacklet began. "In those days, we were ruled by a witch named Taarna the Terrible. For many years, she ruled over us and the demons of Whaqoland, which in those days was a large and prosperous country, taking up much of the land that is now the Land of Ev, and together we all performed many wonderfully wicked deeds."

The assembled witches chuckled to themselves in happy recollection, to Dan's vague uneasiness.

"Across the Deadly Desert from us was the Land of Oz," Shacklet continued, "which at that time (before Glinda and Locasta showed up) was ruled by a number of equally horrible witches.

"Ruling the Gillikins in the Northern part of Oz was a 'witch' named Mombi, although she wasn't a real witch, but just a dabbler—a phony of the highest caliber."

"She was a jack-of-all-magical-trades and a master of none," another of the witches added with disgust. "Always had to buy her charms and potions and incantations off the shelf, as it were. She couldn't even operate a crystal ball if her life depended on it."

"She always refused to read the manual," Shacklet remarked, and then continued: "Mombi was very jealous of Taarna, not only for her superior powers, but because she ruled over all of Whaqoland—a country that was then substantially larger than Mombi's realm.

"So Mombi said to herself, 'It's not fair for her to have a bigger country than mine. I must conquer all of Oz so that my realm will be bigger than hers.'

"And that's how Mombi got the idea to conquer Oz. But before she could take any action, Locasta and Glinda came and Locasta took control of the Gillikin country away from Mombi. Mombi was so enraged by this defeat that she went into hiding to work out some sort of strategy for getting revenge on Locasta and conquering Oz."

"So that Taarna would no longer have a bigger country than Mombi had?" Dan said.

"Precisely," Shacklet said. "For a long time Mombi got nowhere, on account of her very limited powers, and as the years passed and the good witches and fairies in Oz gradually increased in power—especially Glinda—Mombi became very worried that the powers of good would take total control of Oz and that she and her sister witches would be destroyed altogether.

"Now it so happens that while Mombi was buried in these worries, here in Whaqoland Queen Taarna was developing jealousies of her own—specifically, she was jealous of Nan-Kerr the Cloud Queen, who, unlike Taarna, had a beautiful kingdom in the sky, was herself very beautiful, was wooed by many handsome princes, and was also a much better skater.

"In order to satisfy her jealousy, Taarna devised a magic concoction that would knock Nan-Kerr right out of the sky. She mixed the formula in her cauldron, and when all was ready, she said an incantation that made a bolt of lightning shoot out of the mixture in the cauldron. The magic lightning boomed upward—the opposite of what normal lightning does—soared into the Cloud Kingdom, bashed a big hole in the walls of Nan-Kerr's palace, and struck Nan-Kerr right on the leg.

"With a scream of pain, Nan-Kerr tumbled right out of her palace and fell through the air until she landed in Whaqoland right at Taarna's feet!

"'Why did you do that!?' Nan-Kerr demanded, as she cringed with pain from the blow to her leg.

"'I didn't do it!' Taarna lied, and added with a wicked leer, 'but I'll admit that I'm enjoying every minute of it!'

"'You'll pay for this!' Nan-Kerr cried.

"'No, you will be my slave,' Taarna said with a vindictive laugh, 'and you can never return to your precious kingdom in the sky!'

"In fury, Nan-Kerr tried to enchant Taarna, but the injury to her leg stopped her from rising in order to execute any spell, and Taarna was too powerful for her anyway, so she had no choice but to become a faithful citizen of Whaqoland. But she resolved someday to even the score.

"Sometime thereafter, after she secretly concocted a formula that cured her crippled leg, she found out that Mombi had malicious feelings for Taarna. So Nan-Kerr decided to work against Taarna by helping Mombi. She didn't know at that time that Mombi was evil and plotting to conquer Oz.

"Nan-Kerr traveled to Oz and showered Mombi with a series of magical gifts, including a powder that brings an early monsoon, a crystal that colorizes gray skies, a powerful switcheroo formula for quick-and-clean transformations, and various books on elementary-school witchcraft that Mombi was in dire need of, such as *The Joy of Hex, Voodoo for Dummies, 101 More Enchantments to Try at Home,* and *The Do-It-Yourself Witchcraft Kit.* Mombi gazed upon these treasures longingly, but she was somewhat suspicious, as well she might have been, of Nan-Kerr's true motives.

"'All these wonderful magical items can be yours—and for free,' Nan-Kerr told Mombi persuasively.

"'What's the catch?' Mombi demanded.

"'The catch is that you must help me overthrow Taarna,' Nan-Kerr declared.

"'How?' Mombi demanded.

"'With this!' And after putting on protective gloves, Nan-Kerr produced a strange, bright-bluish, baseball-sized, crystal-like orb.

"'This is the most precious and powerful magical device I've ever acquired,' she said. 'It was a special birthday gift to me from Locasta when we were at fairy school.'

"'She gave you this? What will it do?' Mombi said calmly, concealing her hatred of Locasta as she reached for the orb.

"'Be careful! Don't touch it with your bare hands,' Nan-Kerr warned. 'When you present this orb to our dear Taarna and she touches it, she will turn into an ultra-powerful but totally harmless slave that will do your bidding,' Nan-Kerr said.

"'But why don't you do it; why come to me?' Mombi said.

"'Because she used very devious methods and a vicious zapping of my beautiful leg to prevent me from seizing power from her before, so naturally she doesn't trust me. After all, no witch trusts one whom she has deceived. But she knows nothing of your intentions; she will trust you.'

Chapter Ten

"'And how, pray, will I get her to touch that thing?' Mombi said, eyeing the thing suspiciously.

"'Oh, she knows already about this orb and its power to give her colossal magical powers; she just doesn't know about the becoming-a-slave part. She has long wanted to find this precious orb that my dear friend Locasta found in a dark cave one day, and entrusted to me, lest hardship ever befall me, which it has.

"'Taarna thinks the orb's power to give her infinite cosmic powers is a really great thing—little does she know...!' And Nan-Kerr laughed vindictively.

"So Mombi took the orb to Taarna, 'as a token of my esteem and affection,' she lied.

"'At last!' Taarna cried in joy, grabbing the orb with bare hands. 'The Great Cosmic Orb of All-Powerfulness that will turn me into...AN ALL-POWERFUL GENIE!'

"And at that moment, Taarna indeed became an All-Powerful Genie, and acquired absolute power—but she also became the slave of the spray can."

"Spray can?" Dan cried.

"Don't ask us what a modern aerosol spray can was doing in Ev at the turn of the century," Shacklet said. "It's just one of those things."

"It must have been an anti-fossil," observed Locasta.

"A what?" said Dan.

"Well, you know a fossil is a relic of something that got buried many years ago," Locasta explained. "On rare occasions, when something gets buried in a magical hot spot, it can get preserved backward in time, so that it shows up eons before it was laid down, as an anti-fossil."

"Well at any rate," Shacklet continued, "Taarna was a now a Genie, but she had just come to grips with her new cosmic powers when her wrists were bound with gold bracelets and she became attached to the spray can. Mombi became Taarna's first master, to whom by the rules of the Genie she had to grant three wishes."

"Disney will flip when they hear of this," Dan remarked.

"Please don't interrupt!" Shacklet said crossly. "These strange and incoherent remarks of yours put me off."

"Sorry," Dan said meekly.

"Anyhow," Shacklet continued, "Mombi's first wish to Taarna was for sufficient magical powers to conquer Oz. Now Taarna was pretty mad at having been tricked into a life of servitude, so she vowed to trick Mombi by interpreting her wishes in devious ways. So she gave Mombi just enough power to kidnap the rightful heirs to the Oz throne and to enchant everyone's memory so that they did not bat an eye. Now Mombi really wanted much greater powers than that, but, as Taarna observed, 'You didn't say that, master!'

"Mombi was furious, but she carried out the plan and proceeded to kidnap King Pastoria of Oz and to enchant everyone so that they remembered nothing about him or his family, thus setting the stage for the Wizard to arrive and be heralded as Oz's ruler.

"Mombi didn't realize the Wizard was a humbug, however, so she hid in the Gillikin Forest with the kidnapped royal family and bided her time until the climate was more favorable for an invasion of Oz.

"She remained skulking in the forest for many years until word reached her that the Wizard had left Oz in his balloon and that a girl named Dorothy from the Land of E Pluribus Unum had, with Locasta's aid, destroyed her sister witches.

"No longer fearing the departed Wizard, and vowing to put an end to Locasta's activist do-gooding in Oz, Mombi summoned Taarna. For her second wish, she wished for Locasta to be banished to a hot, humid, Lurline-forsaken desert. So Taarna sent Locasta to the Australian outback, which is hot, humid, and Lurline-forsaken, but is moderate compared to the Sahara or the Deadly Desert, and is also not far from Sydney."

"So although I was lost, no harm came to me, as Mombi hoped," Locasta interjected.

"Yes," Shacklet said. "By now Mombi was so furious at Taarna's moderate interpretations of her wishes that in a frenzied fit of fury she used her last wish to wish for Taarna to be locked inside her spray can and be buried deep below the Deadly Desert. After Taarna vanished to her fate, Mombi kidnapped Princess Orin of the Ozure Isles—"

Chapter Ten

"And she used the switcheroo incantation she got from Nan-Kerr to turn her into me and me into her!" cried Locasta with delighted realization. "And she must have done the same thing with Ozma and—"

"The boy Tippetarius, yes," said Shacklet. "So Orin was given the appearance of Locasta, so that no one would notice Locasta's disappearance. Mombi then deliberately lost a battle of magical wits with 'Tattypoo,' as this impostor Good Witch of the North was called, so that she could go back into hiding and formulate a plan to invade the Emerald City.

"But soon thereafter, Glinda, now by far the most powerful sorceress in all Baumgea, found Mombi out; rescued the Ozian heir, Ozma; forced Mombi to transform Ozma back into a girl; and then robbed Mombi of all her powers, thus ending her plans to rule Oz."

"And I was lost in the Collective Hunch for many years, before I met you, my dear friend," Locasta said affectionately to Dan, which made him blush.

"And meanwhile, after Taarna became a Genie, Nan-Kerr crowned herself Queen of Whaqoland," Shacklet said. "But by this time, all the goody-goody fairies were overrunning Baumgea, and soon Whaqoland dwindled in size like the Ottoman Empire until it was just a small forest as it is today. And Nan-Kerr's subsequent leadership was so ineffectual and uninspired that we grew tired of being wicked Whaqoland witches and organized a rebellion of voluntary goodness. The result is that we spend our days being kind and warm and helpful and hospitable...It's a dirty job, but someone's got to do it."

"Why was Nan-Kerr's leadership ineffectual?" Dan asked.

"Well, I think homesickness is a big part," Shacklet said. "After all, this sure isn't the Cloud Kingdom. And the fact that she clearly isn't evil doesn't help."

"Poor Nan-Kerr!" Locasta said sympathetically. "I've got to get her out of this place and help her find her kingdom again."

Shacklet sighed and said, "And we, the witches of this shack, now have a morbid desire also to be good and kind and warm and helpful. It just ain't like old times."

"And I suppose our next kind and warm and helpful deed will have to be to help you escape the demons' clutches," one of the other witches said, very disgruntled.

"Oh, I say, that's capital of you!" Locasta said.

Just then, there came a knock at the door. Shacklet opened it to Nan-Kerr herself!

"Eh, why, hello, your majesty," Shacklet said nervously. "We were just about to terrorize the prisoners."

"You don't have to pretend," Nan-Kerr said in a melancholy voice. "I know all about your rebellion—and I'm joining you! Oh, Locasta!"

And she came in and gave Locasta a big hug.

"Please forgive me," Nan-Kerr said. "I was taken in. I was forcibly brought here to Whaqoland to take up a life of evil. They promised me fame and fortune and gold medals in Magical Artistry and riches earned from celebrity endorsements of sneakers and chicken soup. But instead, they require me to be mean, rotten, viscous, nasty, and cruel, and I can't stand it anymore!"

"It's all right, my dear," Locasta said. "These kind witches have told us the whole story."

"You can't stay here in Whaqoland—there's no telling what those witches and demons will do to you tomorrow."

"What will we do?" Dan asked.

"You can leave right now, and I advise it," Nan-Kerr said. "I'd escort you myself, but if those demons found out I was working against them, they'd sell me to the Baumgean Navy!"

"Baumgea doesn't have a navy," Locasta said.

"It does now!" Shacklet observed.

"What?" said Locasta, puzzled.

"No time to explain," said Nan-Kerr. "You have to get out of here while you can. The demons sleep now, but they may awaken at any time. Take the opportunity and split."

"Oh, very well, but I wish you would come with us. Start a new life. Make a new beginning. Turn over a new leaf," Locasta implored.

"You were always a persuasive one, even at witch-school," Nan-Kerr said. "You were the smartest one in the class... Your magic always stank, but you were the smartest. All right—I'll come with you and 'turn over a new leaf,' as you brilliantly ad-libbed. I hereby wash my hands of Whaqoland, and I won't have anything to do with those monstrous demons ever again!"

"Bravo!" cried Locasta. I'm very proud of you."

"We just have to figure out how to outsmart the demons should we meet with them on the way," Nan-Kerr said. "I'm more powerful than any of them, but there are a lot more of them."

"The demons are mean and vicious and not quick to let anyone stroll out of Whaqoland unharmed," Shacklet observed. "However, if you all just use your wisdom and knowledge, and bear in mind that demons hate knowledge and wisdom, you'll find a way to circumvent them until you are safely through the great gate at the border of Whaqoland, through which the demons cannot pass. For beyond that gate is the Land of Op, ruled by the good Princess Gyma, whose vast knowledge of all kinds of magic and other things makes the demons recoil with fear."

"Is it a long way to the gate?" Dan asked.

"The journey is not inherently long" Nan-Kerr said. "It may become long if we meet any of the demons, though."

"We'll take the risk," Locasta proclaimed.

"But what if they plop us in the D Square?" Dan said anxiously.

"The D Square! You know what the D Square is?" Nan-Kerr said.

Dan and Locasta shook their heads.

"The demons think it is a magnificent instrument of torture," Nan-Kerr explained, "but actually, all I did was lay down some concrete in a square and then painted it red with a yellow D in the center. Don't worry—I'll see to it that you come to no harm."

"Thank you, my dear," said Locasta gratefully. "You were always a good friend."

"You'd best be on your way now," Shacklet said. She rose and saw them to the door. "Just go straight from our cottage and make a left at the post office."

"Thank you!" said Locasta.

"And you'd better take these..." As the witch spoke, she made a magic pass, and Dan and Locasta were each suddenly clutching a red and blue umbrella. "Our crystal balls predicted early morning cloud cover, turning to scattered showers by late afternoon."

"Thank you so much," Locasta said to the Witch ensemble. "You've all been very kind."

"I know," Shacklet sighed. "It drives us nuts!"

Escape from Whaqoland

DAN, Locasta, and Nan-Kerr crept slowly toward the boarder of Whaqoland. Eyes alert and umbrellas raised, they scanned their surroundings for a hag in black, or an ugly little man with horns and a forked tail. It was a hard journey, because they had to trudge through moss, weeds, and various rotting foodstuffs, and before long, Dan was puffing and panting and started to lag behind.

"Yoo hoo!" said a pleasant voice suddenly.

Dan jumped out of his skin.

"Over here!" the voice called serenely.

He turned around nervously and saw a sweet-looking teenage girl with reddish curls, a sweet smile, and bright blue eyes.

"Hi," she said sweetly. "My name is Tasmminy, and I'm an aspiring actress. Can you tell me the way to where the Rohsawft Very Little and Run-Down Theatre Troupe is currently performing?"

"Sorry," Dan said, and started to continue on.

"Oh, you're not leaving, are you?" Tasmminy appealed to Dan.

"Well, I have to," Dan said. "We're on our way to the Land of Op and—"

"Oh, please, kind sir, stay with me…"

As she spoke her voice grew low and seductive, and Dan's eyes became wide and glazed as he slowly and obediently walked toward her.

"Come on, stay with me…I'll make you happy…Just drive me places and cook my meals and do my laundry and let me cry on your shoulder, and I'll make you *think* you're happy…Because I'm the girl of your dreams…I'm self-centered, and I have no character or moral integrity, but I'm the girl of your dreams!…Come on…come closer…closer…"

Hypnotized, Dan was now coming up to Tasmminy, and being drawn into her power.

But just as Tasmminy's clawed hands begin to move slowly up to grip Dan like a steel trap, a sweet young woman's voice suddenly cried out: "Run, Danny! It's a trap! She's one of the demons of Whaqoland! Run, Danny, run!"

Dan snapped out of the spell, and with a gasp of fear dropped his umbrella and turned away from the demon. His eyes widened at the sight of the beautiful Princess Ozma standing before him.

"Follow me, Danny!" Ozma grabbed his hand and they raced off, with Jellia Jamb, Locasta, and Nan-Kerr following them.

With a snarl of rage, Tasmminy bared her long, sharp teeth—which she had kept hidden until now—and raced off in pursuit.

When she failed to catch up with Dan and his friends, she barked, "Calling all demons! Calling all demons! This is Tasmminy in region 38446-A in pursuit of hostile aliens! Calling all demons! Calling all demons…!"

As Tasmminy's message traveled through Whaqoland like bad news, the demons all crept out of their dark, dank, slimy holes, and crevices and began to give chase. In a few seconds, they found themselves pursued by the whole band of wicked witches and nasty, ghoulish demons of all shapes, sorts, and sizes.

Chapter Eleven

Leading the chase was Forg, the Chief of the Demons, holding a list of all the goody-goody people of Baumgea whom he longed to eradicate. Close behind was his colleague, a demon named Jess-He, who hated art, music, plays, and about everything else except good, grimy smoke like that which emanated from his pipe-like snout.

Racing alongside Tasmminy was a snake-haired gorgon named Saman-Nage who liked to tell unwary princes how nice and wonderful they were and then hit them over the head with a playbill, and beside her was cobra-headed Bo-Hub, who, with one snap of his fanged jaws, turned sweet children into mean bullies.

Stumbling right behind, and constantly bumping into things on account of his opaque glasses, was Scott Glib, a demon with a big mouth and no brain. Scott ran a radio studio in Whaqoland that broadcasted the "Scott Glib Show," which pretended to be an intellectual talk show but that was really meant to destroy Scott's unsuspecting victims.

As these and many other demons and witches joined in pursuit. Dan began to feel slightly desperate.

"Chin up, my boy!" Locasta said to Dan. "I'll get us out of this in two seconds."

She waved her arms and muttered an incantation.

Exactly two seconds later, Dan, Ozma, Jellia, Nan-Kerr, and Locasta found themselves bound in tight ropes and sitting helpless in the center of a circle of snarling and laughing demons.

"Oh, no!" Locasta cried. "That spell is for curing hiccups!"

"And it worked! The hiccups that I've had all day are all gone," sneered one demon, who looked like an octopus.

The other demons laughed fiendishly.

Then Skin-Droop, S-Slinger, and Reed appeared in the encirclement.

"Excellent work, demons!" Reed said.

"You picked a great moment to show your magical might," Nan-Kerr growled at Locasta. "I'd better take matters into my own hands..."

"You will do no such thing, *your highness!*" Skin-Droop snapped sarcastically.

"Quick, do something!" Jellia whispered to Ozma. "Use the Magic Belt!"

"I can't!" Ozma said despairingly. "I realize now that these are magic-proof ropes. I'm just as helpless as you."

"Quite right," Reed sneered. "The sweet Princess of Oz is now our prisoner."

"Nan-Kerr and those traitorous witches of the shack treated you with hospitably and gave you some friendly advice, did they?" S-Slinger snarled at Dan and Locasta. "Well, they will pay for their devious betrayal, I promise you. But I think you should write them a thank-you note." And she handed Dan a pen and paper.

Trembling with fear, Dan obediently took the pen and wrote. "Dear Witches of the Shack, Thank You for—"

"What in Baumgea are you doing?" S-Slinger snapped and snatched the paper from Dan.

"I was writing a thank you note!"

"Why aren't you writing your alphabet, like I told you?" S-Slinger screamed.

"But you said—"

"Idiot!" S-Slinger snapped and wrote on the paper. "Student is mentally incompetent; should be returned to kindergarten."

"What are on earth are you talking about?" Ozma demanded. "You witches are not Danny's schoolteachers!"

"There's a definite resemblance, though," Dan muttered.

"Reed, the boy is a half-wit. Would you sit on him please?" S-Slinger said.

"With pleasure!" And Reed went over and dropped her bloated body upon poor Dan, to the delight of the demons.

"Hello, everyone!" cried Scott Glib into a microphone—which was his tail—as he moved into the circle. "This is Demon Scott Glib of KHS Division Radio, bringing you all the hippest sounds in Whaqoland, including the score of Andrew Lloyd Webber's *Cats* played backward, which of course gives us a recording of Ronald Reagan's second inaugural address in Japanese!"

"MMMMMM!" cried a muffled and forlorn voice from under Reed's backside.

Chapter Eleven

"Do not adjust your radio, folks," Scott Glib said. "It's just Old Reed's chair!"

"Get off of Dan this instant!" Locasta demanded.

"Leave Danny alone!" Ozma cried.

"Shut up!" snarled Skin-Droop. "You're not queen here!"

"Well, that was relaxing," Reed said as she lifted herself up.

"Ah, here's our chief," said Skin-Droop as Forg approached. "We'll just leave these fools in your care, demons."

"Thank you, Skin-Droop," Forg sneered as he faced the terrified captives.

"Demons, as your queen, I demand that you free us at once!" Nan-Kerr cried.

"Silence, traitor!" Forg bellowed. "You are no longer our queen! I am hereby taking over as Ruler of Whaqoland under Article 184 of Whaqoland Law!"

"Hooray!" the demons and witches cried in chorus. "Down with Nan-Kerr! Hail, Forg! Hail, Forg!"

Nan-Kerr gasped. She knew about Article 184 and how it allowed the Chief of Demons to take over rule of Whaqoland if he thought the queen has become too much of a wimpo goody-goody. She helplessly watched as the demons and witches launched into wild chantings of "Hail, Forg! Hail, Forg! Hail, Forg! Hail, Forg!"

Scott Glib continued his apparent radio show: "There you have it folks! You heard it right here! We have a new ruler—Forg! This is a historic day! This show is being brought to you live on tape from Whaqoland Forest Clearing 37249-B, where we demons are preparing to inflict massive torture upon our ex-queen, a mortal from America, and three fools from Oz! That's right my friends, Oz! That rotten, stinking, wimpo, lovey-dovey fairyland ruled by this wild-eyed, ranting loony pinko!"

"How dare you attack me and my good people!" Ozma fumed.

"Very easily, with you tied up and at our mercy," Scott sneered. "Yes folks—Oz. That nation of nincompoops which is long overdue for conquering by us."

"Hail, Forg!" the witches and demons cried.

Chapter Twelve

"Now see here—!" Locasta began.

"Ah, I believe the fat Witch of the North wishes to comment before we plop her and her friends into the D Square, where they will languish in inconceivable agony," Scott Glib said as he pointed his mike at Locasta.

"I regard what you have said about us and Oz as preposterous and a hideous character smear!"

"'Preposterous'?" Scott Glib said, perplexed. "'Hideous'? 'Regard'?...Those are 'words of the Cosmos' that we do not comprehend."

The other demons were likewise scratching their heads in puzzlement.

"Look it up!" Locasta said. "They're in the unabridged dictionary."

"The Una—aba—what?" Scott Glib faltered.

The other demons looked perplexed and disturbed.

Ozma's eyes suddenly brightened. "Keep it up my dear," she whispered to Locasta. "You're getting to them."

Locasta smiled vehemently on the demons. "Well, how do you like these words then: Hyperbole?...Integration?...Anachronistic?"

The demons shuddered in horror and tried to back away.

"Narcissistic?...Deuterostome?...Microcosm?... Philophilosophos!" Locasta snapped.

The demons writhed with anguish.

"Hippopotomonstrosesquipedalian!" Locasta cried as a grand finale.

The demons responded to this colossal word by turning to solid marble, and the ropes that bound their prisoners melted away!

"We're free!" Locasta cried, delightedly jumping to her feet.

"Locasta, you're a genius!" Dan cried.

"Yeah, just so long as you don't do any magic," Nan-Kerr added.

"Now let's blow this amusement park for buzzards," Jellia cried.

Ozma grasped the Belt and in a twinkling they were at the great gate that led into Op. (Actually, it was an ordinary-looking gate, like in the fence of someone's house.) They opened the gate with ease,and walked through into an open and sunny countryside.

12

The Adepts' Journey

WITH indescribable elation, the Adepts traveled on a wave of their magical wind over the Deadly Desert. They were on their way to the Land of Ev, where they were confident they would at long last be reunited with their grandmama.

Lightly and gracefully, they landed on the grassy field in Ev just outside of Gump Forest, right at the spot where Dan and Locasta had first materialized in Baumgea. But now there was no sign of either of them.

"Where are they?" Sofia said. "Ozma's Magic Picture said that they were here."

"Maybe they were kidnapped by wicked witches," Zsuzsa suggested.

"As usual, Zsuzsa, you're looking on the bright side," Sofia said sarcastically.

"Well, maybe they went into the forest," Judit suggested.

Chapter Twelve

That seemed likely to Sofia and Zsuzsa, so they started toward Gump Forest. As they approached the forest's edge, they came to a sign planted in the ground which said:

WARNING
BEWARE STAMPEDES
OF MIGRATING GUMPS
(BEGINNING NOON, OCTOBER 1)

Zsuzsa glanced at her pocket watch. "Ah, well, wouldn't you know it would work out that way!"

"What?" Judit cried.

"It's just exactly noon...on October first!" Zsuzsa said.

"That can't be!" Sofia cried. "Yesterday was September thirtieth, so today must be September thirty-first!"

"Thirty days hath September!" Zsuzsa said in a low voice.

"What about leap year?" Sofia said.

Zsuzsa was about to explain it to her again when they heard a low rumble like thunder.

"What's that?" Judit gasped.

"I doubt that it's field mice!" Zsuzsa said.

The rumbling quickly grew much louder, and suddenly a stampede of what seemed like a million big, antlered creatures emerged from the forest and thundered straight in the direction of the Adepts.

"Now what should we do?" Judit cried.

"Run terribly fast?" Sofia suggested.

"No, fly! Quick, our wind!" Zsuzsa screamed. The Gumps were almost upon them!

The Three Adepts spread their arms and summoned the magical wind, which quickly blew them into the air and out of the stampede's path.

"Whew! That was close!" Judit gasped as they ascended. A second later, she bumped into a gray sea gull that was flying alongside them.

"Great Gatsby!" the sea gull cried in alarm. "How'd you all get up here?"

"I beg your pardon!" Judit apologized to the bird.

Chapter Twelve

"Who are you?" the sea gull asked.

"We are the Adepts at Sorcery," Sofia said.

"Of Oz," Judit added.

"Who are you, and where are you of?" Zsuzsa asked.

"Allow me to introduce myself," he said. "I am the celebrated author Eric Seagull, author of *A Lovebird Story* and *Veterinarians,* and now working on my new classic, *Rooster, Hen, and Chick.*"

"How's it coming?" Judit asked sweetly.

"Not good," Eric admitted.

"We're desperately searching for our grandmama, we've narrowly escaped being trampled by migrating gumps, we're aimlessly flying toward Lurline knows where, and she asks how his book is going!" Zsuzsa muttered in disgust.

"Zsuzsa!" Sofia scolded.

"How far have you got so far?" Judit asked.

"Just the title," Eric said. "Good title though, isn't it?"

"Terrific!" Sofia said enthusiastically.

"Oh, just lovely!" Zsuzsa snarled to herself.

"Maybe you could help me with the opening," Eric suggested. "How's this sound: 'It was the best of times; It was the worst of times...'"

"I'm afraid that opening's been used," Sofia said.

"Oh. Well, how about this: 'Call me Ishmael.'"

"That's been used, too," Judit said.

"Gee!" said Eric, frustrated. "Well, how about: 'Dorothy lived in the midst of the great Kansas prairies...'"

Sofia shook her head. "No, I don't think that one is taken."

"Great!" said Eric. Then, scratching his head with a wing, he said, "But it doesn't fit my plot line! I need a powerful opening to build momentum towards a powerful climax and a satisfying denouement..."

"Yes, a powerful opening and a strong plot line are very important!" Sofia agreed.

"Characterizations are important too, though," Judit observed. "No matter how good the plot is, the story will be unenjoyable unless the characters are interesting."

"Look, could we cut the literary seminar?" Zsuzsa exclaimed. "How in Oz are we ever going to find where Grandmama and Danny disappeared to?" They continued to glide, high over a strange, rather somber-looking landscape.

"Well, I hope to Henry Thoreau that they're not there; that's the Land of Im down there!" Eric said emphatically.

"Why? Is there something wrong with Im?" Sofia asked.

"Something wrong?" Zsuzsa cried. "You know what they say about Im's ruler?"

"Yes, King Graytfyl has a somewhat bad temper," Eric said.

"Somewhat bad temper?" exclaimed Zsuzsa. "I heard that just last month he threw a man into the dungeon for telling him that his tie was crooked, and that the month before that, he had his long-time chess partner beheaded for making off with his queen."

"He kidnapped the queen? That's terrible!" Judit said.

"The king's chess queen! He took it on move 37, and the king beheaded him, partly in rage, partly in order to win by default," Zsuzsa said in disgust.

"Very true," said Eric sadly. "Beating the King of Im in a game of chess is a grave offense, and taking his queen is capital...I believe that abducting the real queen is only a misdemeanor."

"Well, I'm not afraid of any small-brained kings," Sofia declared. "I'm worried about what's happened to Grandmama and Danny."

"Yes, let's land at once and decide what to do," Zsuzsa said, "and if the king comes into the picture...well, we'll just cross that drawbridge when we come to it,"

"Impossible," Eric said sadly. "Im is surrounded by an impenetrable ultra-magical barrier...landing now is out of the question, unless you want to get magictrocuted."

"Well, where should we go?" Judit said.

"Well," Sofia mused, "it seems to me that the best course is to go back to the Emerald City and look through Ozma's Magic Picture again. That will tell us where Grandmama is now."

"You're right!" her sisters agreed, and they began to steer toward Oz.

Chapter Twelve

"May I come with you?" Eric asked.

"Of course you may!" Judit said sweetly.

So the four of them started the journey over the scorching, poisonous Deadly Desert to Oz. Suddenly, their flight halted with a sharp and unexpected jolt and they tumbled like stones down toward the lethal sands below.

"What in the name of Lurline's fairy band is happening?" Judit cried.

"Our magic is malfunctioning, that's what's happening!" Zsuzsa screamed.

"But how can that be? It's quite impossible!" Sofia proclaimed.

"Dear sister, in about twenty seconds we're going to hit the scalding desert sands and be reduced to charred cinders; this is no time for logic!" Zsuzsa shouted over the whistle of the air as they fell.

"Will we, though? We're fairies. We should be able to survive even the sands of the Deadly Desert," Judit observed.

"Well, let's not chance it—Girls, let's put our heads together!" cried Sofia.

They grasped each other's hands and drew themselves together so that their foreheads pressed against each other. They muttered an incantation...but nothing happened.

"It's no use! Our magic is totally kaput!" Sofia cried in despair.

"So now what will we do?" Judit gasped.

"Try to land head first so that we don't feel a thing?" said Sofia.

"Hilarious!" snarled Zsuzsa.

Suddenly, to their astonishment, they were caught by a rowboat that just happened to be floating about a hundred feet above the desert floor, and they stopped with a thud.

"Whew! That was close!" Zsuzsa gasped, wiping her brow.

"What in Ibsen's *Peer Gynt* happened?" cried Eric, as he swooped down and landed in the boat next to them.

"I don't know. Our fantastic flying forces failed us," Sofia panted.

"It's lucky this rowboat caught us...Lurline knows where it came from, though," said Judit.

Suddenly, they heard a sneering voice laugh vindictively: "Awwww, did you fall down and go boom?"

The Adepts looked up and saw Forg and the nastiest of the demons of Whaqoland floating calmly alongside the boat.

"Did you make us fall?" Sofia demanded.

"Nothing personal," Forg snarled. The demons advanced menacingly toward them. "But we are going to invade Oz at long last, and we can't have any Adepts getting in our way."

"You'd better keep away," Zsuzsa said as she stood and threateningly raised her arms. "We know magic judo!"

"I wouldn't try that if I were you," Forg cried gleefully. "You Adepts are all very adept indeed at mechanical magic, but out here in the wide and stark desert, your powers are little more than those of a medieval fairy. You are helpless against us demons."

"What are you going to do to us?" Judit stammered.

"We're not going to teach you any big words, that's for sure!" Old Skin-Droop the witch declared. "Your queen, your dear grandmama, and the American boy would be now as helpless in our clutches as you if it hadn't been for their ridiculous megawords that temporarily turned us into stone."

"You mean you captured them and they escaped?" Sofia cried.

"To the wretched Land of Op," Forg cried. "But not for long. They would normally be protected there by Princess Gyma, but King Graytfyl of Im has disposed of her for us, and as soon as we've sold you into slavery in the navy, we shall march into and occupy Op as a stepping stone to our conquest of Oz."

"You're mere demons! How can you conquer Oz?" Zsuzsa scoffed.

"It may interest you to know, my three beauties, that we have located Ruggedo's whereabouts!" explained Old Skin-Droop.

"You have?"

"But we're not going to tell!" Forg sneered with glee.

"And we also have found the secret of the vast magic that has hidden Ruggedo from you and your cronies in Oz all these months," Skin-Droop declared. "With this vast magic, we shall depose not only Ozma, but Glinda and all the other magic workers in Baumgea, confiscate all your magical tools, neutralize all your native powers, and then enlist you all into the Baumgean navy!"

Chapter Twelve

"Baumgea doesn't have a navy!" said Sofia.

"Silence!" Forg snapped. "I won't stand any back talk; not when I'm on the verge of acquiring Final Knowledge!"

"What would Final Knowledge be?" asked Zsuzsa skeptically.

"The most fundamental magic in the universe! When we get to Op, I shall seek out Locasta and make her tell me the Magic of Everything, the knowledge of which will make me the most powerful being in Baumgea."

"I doubt that!" Zsuzsa said.

"Hold your tongue!" Old Skin-Droop snapped.

"With the Magic of Everything, I will have final and total knowledge of all magical forces and why they exist. I will know how to control everything."

"I've never heard anything so ridiculous," retorted Zsuzsa.

"But don't you know there's no such thing as final and total knowledge or having power over everything?" Judit said gently. "The universe is infinite and will always be greater and grander than any of us. No one can ever know everything or have command over everything."

"Silence!" cried Forg. "We shall conquer the universe, and we will begin by invading Oz and destroying all its goody-goody freaks. Especially that rotten shrew, Glinda."

"Why are you so against Glinda and Oz?" Eric asked.

"Glinda and I went to fairy school together," Forg sneered, "and during our final Fairy History test, she refused to let me copy her answers—which of course made me fail the test. So from that day, I swore that I would have revenge on Glinda and all her sick friends in that pathetic Land of Oz!"

"You should have studied for that test," Sofia observed.

"It is common sense that Glinda and her fairy pals are a bunch of goody-goody, lovey-dovey freaks, and the time has come for them all to be run into the ground!" cried Forg.

"But why do you want to hurt the innocent Oz people?" Eric said. "Aren't you satisfied with making evil in Whaqoland?"

"Of course not! Terrorizing a land that is already evil has no point," Old Skin-Droop asserted. "Witches and demons can only be productive if they are molesting good, honest people in sickeningly beautiful and peaceful kingdoms like Oz."

"We would have invaded and destroyed Oz long ago if it hadn't been for that rotten Nan-Kerr, who we were stuck with as a ruler for so long," Forg snarled. "Ever since she usurped the throne from Taarna the Terrible, her polices in governing Whaqoland were languid and ineffectual. Taarna was a much better leader than Nan-Kerr."

"That's right," said Skin-Droop, "but we have located Taarna as well, and after we have met with them and laid out our plans, she and Ruggedo will lead us into a grand invasion and destruction of Oz."

"And all of Baumgea and other goody-goody continents!" Forg cried with evil passion. "Taarna will lead us in an all-out war against all good things. With her now vast powers, we will sweep good from the face of the earth."

The other demons and witches cheered this speech. The Adepts and Eric were horrified

"And now," Forg hissed at the Adepts, "we will direct this rowboat to its mother ship, where you shall be recruited into the navy and be unable to interfere with our grand plans for Fairyland and beyond!"

"What are you talking about? What navy?" Sofia cried.

"The flying navy?" Judit gasped as she looked up and saw a big, brown, three-masted ship looming threateningly above them.

"Holy Hemingway!" Eric cried. "We're being attacked by the Flying Dutchman!"

13 The Princess of Op

IT was a beautiful country that Dan, Locasta, Ozma, Jellia, and Nan-Kerr now found themselves in, with clear blue skies, towering trees, delicate wildflowers, and dinosaurs.

"Dinosaurs?" Dan gasped in astonishment at the herd of brontosaurs that were gracefully tramping past.

"Oh, yes, Danny! My cousin Gyma rules over and takes care of this last community of dinosaurs on this planet," said Ozma. She took Dan's hand in hers. "Come, and we'll introduce you."

As they headed towards Gyma's palace, Dan now closely regarded Ozma for the first time. She was even more beautiful than he had imagined from reading the Oz books. Her rosy cheeks; her bewitching green eyes; her wide, sweet smile; the two big red poppies adorning the long brown hair softly tumbling down on either side of her bare shoulders; her graceful, slender figure; and her bosom, which was not particularly large, but definitely developed.

"So much for that debate," he thought as he recalled the clearly inaccurate descriptions of the lovely young queen as a "little girl after all."

Ozma turned and looked at Dan, who looked away like a flash.

"It's all right, Danny," said Ozma kindly. "I don't mind your looking at me. I think you're very sweet."

"How do you know my name? And why are you so kind to a slob like me?" Dan shyly asked the beautiful Queen of Oz.

"I've been reading your correspondences with the Adepts," Ozma replied. "And you are not a slob! You are a very good, kind-hearted fellow, and I am very grateful to you for the kindness you've shown Locasta. She could never have returned to Fairyland without you."

They hurried through the fields of Op until they encountered a herd of dinosaurs of varied sorts and sizes.

"This is remarkable!" Dan cried, as he beheld the majestic prehistoric creatures. "And I always thought dinosaurs were extinct."

"Gee, I always thought human beings were extinct," said the herd leader, a building-sized brontosaur with a long neck with fin-like frills.

"What do you think Princess Gyma is, a hippopotamus?" a five-horned dinosaur remarked to the brontosaur petulantly.

"She's a fairy. That doesn't count, does it?" said one dinosaur that had two rows of spikes down its back.

"I reckon I don't see why," said a pterodactyl the size of an airplane, as it swooped down and landed among the rest of the herd in front of Ozma and her party. "These beings look like the same species as our princess."

"I am Princess Ozma, Gyma's cousin from Oz."

"Who?" asked the brontosaur.

"Princess Ozma, the Queen of Oz!" the five-horned dinosaur said in a rude tone. "Use your brains! Both the one in your head and the one in your tail!"

"That is no vay to treat our herd leader!" reprimanded a man-sized two-legged dinosaur with curved claws. "Remember that this is Op, the land where dinosaurs und fairies live in harmony!"

Chapter Thirteen

"Actually, the full name of this land is the Land of Endosauropsida," said a dinosaur with a crocodile-like snout, "but we all found that too hard to pronounce, so we just say 'Op' instead."

"Maybe we should introduce ourselves," the great, frilled brontosaur said in a sweet, feminine voice. "I am Margie. This is—"

"What's the matter, don't you think I can introduce myself?" the five-horned dinosaur snapped, and said to the humans, "I'm Penty."

"I am Professor Veloski, scientist, philosopher, und Opian historian," the two-legged dinosaur said with a bow.

"I am Kent, Op's resident percussion musician," said the prickly dinosaur, rubbing his spikes together to make a sound that was irritating to Dan's ears, but that the dinosaurs seemed to like.

"I am Sir Bary, baronet of Boboland," said the one with a crocodile-like snout and a fin-like ridge on his back.

"And I am Quetz, Op's ten-gallon pterosaur, partner!" the great flying creature said, jovially slapping poor Dan, Nan-Kerr, and Locasta on their backs with his great wing and almost toppling them over.

"We're pleased to meet you, I'm sure," Dan said.

"Yes; can you take us to my cousin now?" asked Ozma.

"Alas, no!" Professor Veloski said with a sob. "Princess Gyma hass been kidnapped!"

"Kidnapped?" Ozma gasped.

"Yeah, kidnapped," Quetz said, "along with Princess Esu, by that two-bit varmint, Old Pascalabes."

"Old Pascalabes?" cried Locasta.

"Princess Esu?" said Dan.

"Gee, an echo just like the Alps," Penty snarled.

"I say, Penty, let's please control our temper," Sir Bary said.

"And let us not forget Old Pascalabes' devious accomplice, Old Ray-Shy," Kent said, angrily waving his spiked tail.

"I think ve should relate the sad tale from the beginning," Veloski said with a regretful sigh.

"Quite," Sir Bary said, and Dan and Locasta seated themselves comfortably on Margie's great tail, Ozma and Jellia sat on Kent's back (carefully avoiding the spikes), and Nan-Kerr leaned on Penty's indignant shoulder while the tale was told to them.

"Up until very recently," Kent began, "Princess Gyma ruled, nurtured, and protected us dinosaurs and other prehistoric creatures of Op, with the help of Princess Esu the Tyrannosaurus rex—"

"I've never heard of a dinosaur who was a princess!" Dan exclaimed.

"You've obviously been living a secluded life under the rafters for a very long while," said Penty haughtily.

"Don't mind him," Kent said to Dan and continued. "Princess Gyma was very good and wise, and knew all about all sorts of wonderful things, from the orientation of objects to the marvelous magic of the Wizard of Lisp; from how the Quicksort of Quok got so quick to what balances the Binary Trees of Boboland.

"Her greatest joy was to share her great wisdom with her subjects and to teach them about the wonders of magic and the fairy world. And she was a very good teacher—she believed in making leaning something fun, like a game, rather than a terrible ordeal as most teachers do. She and Esu taught us to learn to marvel, respect, and cherish the world around us, and we loved them for their wisdom and kindness.

"Then one day, our land was invaded by a wicked pirate named Old Pascalabes, who descended upon us in his flying ship like a black vulture and kidnapped Gyma and Esu and took them to the Land of Im, ruled by his brother, King Graytfyl."

"What then?" Dan asked.

"Ve don't know," Veloski sighed. "All ve know is that that was the last ve ever saw of our princesses."

"By Galileo! We'll rescue them!" Locasta cried. "How do we get to Im?"

"Well, just hold your hippocampuses there, ma'am," Quetz gently interjected. "It ain't as easy as all that. Im is surrounded by a magical barrier that only Old Pascalabes' ship can penetrate—"

"Then we'll get aboard the ship!" Locasta said.

"But you see, Old Pascalabes' ship, the SS *Able*, is in constant flight, hundreds of feet above the Deadly Desert," Quetz explained.

Chapter Thirteen

And when he does come down here," Penty said angrily, "it's only to plague our lives by shooting his magic cannons at us, or sending Old Ray-Shy chasing after us."

"When Old Pascalabes took Gyma and Esu from us," Sir Bary explained, "he assumed rule over us and immediately outlawed all teaching and conveying of information—and I don't mean he just outlawed the schools. He outlawed all means of acquiring any kind of information. He outlawed cookbooks that taught people how to make luscious dishes. He outlawed coaches from teaching experienced athletes new plays, and new athletes from learning the game at all. He outlawed maps that told people what direction the Op Theater of Performing Arts was in. He outlawed bus and train schedules that told us what to catch in the morning to get to the shopping bazaar in Ev."

"He outlawed these and many, many more," Penty growled.

"But how could anyone find out which train would get them to Ev, or how to make a perfect chocolate mousse?" Jellia asked.

"'Figure it out yourself,' he says. That is Old Pascalabes' answer to everytink," Veloski said sadly.

"And the old witch Ray-Shy is his enforcer and effectively his policewitch," Margie added. "She travels around Op on her broomstick, ensuring that no one is learning anything."

"Well, to be perfectly accurate, we can learn things, but she ensures that it is a totally painful and unbearable ordeal for all of us," Quetz said.

"But that's terrible—people can't just figure out everything on their own!" Dan cried. "They're not mind readers!"

"Don't you think we know that?" Penty snapped.

"But that's not the vorst of it," Veloski sighed. "Ray-Shy hates anytink that is mechanical because she is distrustful of it—so she outlawed all machines in Op."

"It didn't matter actually that the buses and trains had no schedules," said Penty, "because Ray-Shy outlawed buses and trains. She said she doesn't trust buses or trains."

"And we have no music, except my spikes," said Kent, "because she says she doesn't trust phonographs or musical instruments."

"And we have to carry our six bags of weekly shopping in our arms," said Sir Bary, "because she doesn't trust shopping carts."

"And we are always late for important appointments because we can't tell the time," Margie said.

"She doesn't trust clocks?" said Dan.

"Precisely," Veloski said. "Und when ve eat, ve have to eat with our hands off of the ground!"

"She doesn't trust forks, knives, spoons, tables, or chairs?" said Dan.

"Exactly," Veloski sighed.

"In any case, reaching Old Pascalabes' ship, the SS *Able,* is out of the question," said Margie, "except for those times when he comes down for his periodic terrorizing."

"Well, we'll just have to wait until the next time Old Pascalabes comes down," Locasta said.

"And this old witch Ray-Shy doesn't bother me," Nan-Kerr added. "My magical powers are great—much greater than dear Locasta's, bless her heart."

Locasta gave her a reproachful look.

"Well, in any case, if all else fails, my Magic Belt will protect us," Ozma reassured them.

"I have an idea," Veloski said. "Why don't you stay for dinner und spend the night with us?"

"Yes, then we can discuss what you plan to do to rescue our princesses," Margie added.

"Thank you very much," Locasta said.

"Much obliged," Dan added.

"But we really don't know when Old Pascalabes will bring his ship down here again," Kent said. "It's usually to carry away and enslave some poor soul who breaks the law."

"Well, if all else fails, we'll break the law," Nan-Kerr proclaimed.

What Happened to Ruggedo

AFTER Ruggedo was disenchanted and fled from Wogglebug College, he ran as fast as he could back to his old cottage and to the gravel pit where he had thrown Taarna's spray can many years before. He now sincerely regretted having thrown her there, and after all his failed attempts, he now realized that this All-Powerful Genie was his one hope of getting revenge on Oz.

Ruggedo fetched a rope from his dilapidated cottage and tied the rope to a rock. He then used the rope to carefully climb down into the gravel pit. Then he dug violently into the gravel with his chubby bare hands until he found a dirty, dented, rusty metal cylinder with dusty rubies and a slightly bent push button at the top.

Ruggedo pressed the button and, with a SSSSSSSSS-ing sound, Taarna once more emerged.

"Free! I'm free! I'm—Oh, it's you," Taarna growled.

"My dear Taarna," Ruggedo said with fake reverence, "I apologize for my shabby treatment of you."

"Oh good, and only...seventy-one years after the fact," Taarna snarled, checking her watch.

"I believe in letting bygones be bygones, and I am now ready to help you devastate the lives of all those sickening Oz people!" Ruggedo screamed.

"Well, I—" Taarna began.

"To torture them, torment them, and annihilate them!" said Ruggedo in an increasing frenzy.

"Yes, if I could just explain—"

"Taarna, I wish for all of Oz to—"

"You're not going to wish for the total and utter destruction of Oz, are you?" said Taarna.

"Why not? I want revenge on those fools!" Ruggedo cried.

"Well, if I may, I would like to point out three problems with executing so sweeping a deed. One, destroying Oz completely would mean destroying all the people in Oz. (For the full argument supporting this reasoning, see any decent introductory textbook on symbolic logic, page 82.) But the destruction of the Oz people is impossible because we Genies can't kill anyone, and the Oz people are virtually indestructible anyway. Two, even if the Oz people were destroyed, that would mean that you could no longer make them suffer. Three, if Oz and all its people were destroyed, then you would be unable to rule Oz as you've always desired. After all, as one learned philosopher once said, 'You can't very well be king of beasts if there aren't any.' "

"You're quite right," Ruggedo cried. "We should not destroy Oz, but just make it so Oz is forever trembling under my control. Now, how do we start?"

"I suggest that you go into hibernation," said Taarna.

"Hibernation!" Ruggedo roared. "What do you think I am, a bear?"

"You're sure reacting like one," Taarna observed with contempt, then said more affably, "If I were to magically put you into hibernation for a few months, you see, that will give me time to lay out a perfect and infallible plan of attack. Then when you awaken, spray the can to release me. I will then tell you my plan, and your second wish will be for me to execute the plan."

Chapter Fourteen

"Oh, very well!" Ruggedo cried. "How do you suggest I get out of this pit, though?"

With a disgusted look to the sky, Taarna pointed a magic finger at Ruggedo and levitated him out of the pit.

"That wasn't my second wish, was it?" Ruggedo said.

"No, that was a freebie," Taarna explained. "And I'm also making a barrier around your house so that we can formulate our plans without either Ozma's Magic Picture or Glinda's Book of Records detecting a thing."

"Great! I didn't know I was allowed freebies!" Ruggedo said. He strutted jovially into his neglected cottage and lay down on his couch.

"Just don't ask me for any more," Taarna warned.

"Of course not," Ruggedo said. "Just think, in a few months' time, I will rule all of Oz, I will again have the Magic Belt and all my powers, and Ozma and Dorothy and the lot of them will be slaves or ornaments in my throne room!"

"Pleasant dreams," Taarna said sweetly, and she retreated into the spray can to begin formulating her plans.

In her great palace in the Quadling Country, Glinda sat in her Library of Knowledge searching her Great Book of Records for a clue to Ruggedo's whereabouts. Ozma and Jellia had, as you know, been trying for several months to find him, but there was no sign of him wherever in Oz they searched. Neither did Ruggedo show up in Ozma's Magic Picture, which usually shows her anyone she wants to see and what they are doing at any time. Glinda realized that some black magic was masking Ruggedo from the view of the Magic Picture, and apparently from the Book of Records, as it had nothing to say about Ruggedo.

Glinda decided that stronger magic was called for, so she and the Wizard began executing a series of incantations to try to exorcise the black magic that was apparently interfering with the Picture and the Book.

Whatever spell it was, it was apparently very powerful, and Glinda had to use the greatest magic she knew to break it. Finally, in the Book of Records appeared the words: "The Nome King is in his old cottage just outside the Emerald City, where he is plotting to conquer Oz (yes, again)."

Glinda realized that the Nome King had to be captured before he did anyone any harm. So she and the Wizard traveled in her magnificent swan-pulled chariot to the Emerald City to make sure the Magic Picture worked now and showed the Nome King. And since she also know how the Great Book could be at times not entirely accurate, she wanted to ascertain that what the Book said about him was entirely true.

When Glinda arrived in Ozma's throne room, she wanted to send for Ozma, but she was still in the Ozian countryside with Jellia, and the Scarecrow didn't know their exact location. So Glinda, along with Dorothy, the Wizard of Oz, the Cowardly Lion, and the Hungry Tiger, proceeded to the room where the Magic Picture hung.

Glinda stood before the Picture and said, "Show me Ozma!"

They saw an image of Ozma and her friends, including Locasta, having a quiet dinner in Op and planning to rescue Gyma.

"Shall I bring them back?" asked Glinda.

"No, let them be," advised the Scarecrow. "I'm sure your magical might will be sufficient to quickly defeat Ruggedo on your own."

"All right," Glinda said, smiling at everyone's faith in her. Then she turned back to the Magic Picture and commanded, "Show me Ruggedo!"

Immediately, the Picture displayed an image of Ruggedo sound asleep on his couch, and a strangely jeweled spray can sitting on a neighboring table.

"He looks peaceful enough," said Dorothy.

"Dreaming of making us his slaves, no doubt," said the Hungry Tiger with an angry snarl.

"I vote we tear him apart," growled the Cowardly Lion, baring his claws, then quickly retracting them, frightened by their dangerous size.

"We must bring him here, and get him to tell us what he is planning," said Glinda gravely. "Afterward, we will decide how to punish him, but we must not hurt him."

"Oh, why not?" said the Tiger, disappointed.

Chapter Fourteen

"Ozma will not abide cruelty," said Glinda firmly, "not to any living creature."

"Look!" cried Dorothy, pointing to the picture. "He's waking up!"

In the picture, they saw Ruggedo stretch his arms and let out a colossal yawn.

"Ah, that was a good sleep," he snickered, and hopped to his feet.

"And now," Ruggedo cried gleefully. "Let the destruction of Oz commence!"

But then, just an instant after they noticed that Glinda was doing a silent incantation, those who were gazing at the Magic Picture saw Ruggedo get bowled over and carried off by gust of wind.

"Ruggedo is now in the royal prison," Glinda announced.

In the Emerald City prison, Ruggedo realized with rage that he was a captive. Nevertheless, he couldn't help his astonishment at his surroundings, for this room he found himself in was quite unlike any other prison in the world. The walls were beautifully wallpapered and ornamented by paintings by Rembrandt and Turner. It was furnished with soft reclining chairs, long glass tables, and numerous shelves of books.

A door appeared in the wall. Glinda, Dorothy, the Wizard, and the Scarecrow of Oz came in. The door then closed itself and vanished.

"Are you taking me to prison or to dinner?" remarked Ruggedo sarcastically.

"Sit down," was all Glinda said.

"Oh, please, a game of Parcheesi first?" Ruggedo mocked.

Glinda glared at Ruggedo, and without his knowing why, he found himself obeying her.

"Well, what do you want of me?" he said to Glinda (the only Ozian he slightly feared). The others quietly took seats behind the Great Sorceress.

Ruggedo expected Glinda to address him severely, but instead her voice was soft and patient.

"What are you planning to do to harm Oz and its people?" she asked.

"I wish you no harm!" snapped Ruggedo in an I-wish-you-a-universe-of-harm sort of voice.

"Behold my pearl!" said Glinda, holding out the beautiful piece of jewelry she clasped in her hand.

"A black pearl?" said Ruggedo in disbelief.

"This magic pearl is white as long as the truth is told to me, but it turns black when someone is lying to me," explained Glinda.

"Do tell!" Ruggedo snapped defiantly.

"You were punished for your previous wickedness by being turned into a cactus," Glinda reminded him gravely. "If you do not tell me the truth, I will surely do much worse to you now."

Ruggedo trembled at these words, but he racked his brains to devise a way to avoid lying, and yet not tell Glinda the whole truth.

"I believe someone must be helping you," said Glinda. "Who is or are your confederates?"

"Jefferson Davis and Robert E. Lee!" Ruggedo asserted.

The pearl turned blacker than the hole in Calcutta.

"Who are your confederates?" said Glinda sternly.

Ruggedo tried desperately to think of an evasive answer, but as he was a former monarch and not an elected official, he finally had to give up and say truthfully, "Taarna the Terrible."

"Who?" Dorothy said.

"The Queen of Whaqoland?" Glinda asked.

"Former queen, to be exact," Ruggedo sighed, now fearing all was lost.

"What is Whaqoland?" Dorothy whispered to the Wizard sitting next to her.

"The most evil country in all Baumgea," the Wizard replied with a shudder. "Oh, my sainted aunt, what a terrible place!"

"We'll have to ensure that Taarna stays in Whaqoland where she belongs, with all those disgusting other witches," said the Scarecrow.

Suddenly, an idea entered Ruggedo's head. He realized that they didn't know that Taarna was now an All-Powerful Genie.

"Where is Taarna now?" Glinda asked.

Chapter Fourteen

"In my house," Ruggedo said carelessly, "concocting a plan to invade and overrun Oz."

"We saw no one with you in the Magic Picture," Dorothy said, although Glinda's pearl indicated that he spoke truthfully.

"Well, you didn't look very hard then, did you?" Ruggedo taunted. "She's probably at this moment almost ready to put her plan into motion."

"Come on, everyone," said Dorothy to the others. "We have to stop her!"

"Just one second, my dear," Glinda interjected. "Where exactly is Taarna in your house?" she asked Ruggedo.

"Well...in the spray can on the table in my living room," admitted Ruggedo reluctantly. The pearl, of course, remained white.

"In the spray can?" Dorothy exclaimed.

"How'd she get in there?" asked the Scarecrow.

"That can is of the most immense magical importance to Taarna," Ruggedo slyly half-explained.

This time the pearl became off-white.

"I suspect you are withholding something," Glinda said in a voice low but firm. "Now tell us the truth—What is the connection between Taarna and that can?"

"Well...," Ruggedo searched for a strategic answer. "In point of fact...Taarna...lives in it!"

The pearl nearly shone with whiteness.

"Lives in the can?" Dorothy asked.

"Quite so," said Ruggedo triumphantly. "But don't you go fetching the can with the idea of getting her out. Her powers render the can implacable to all magical forces you might try. Only I know how to release her."

This was close enough to the truth that the pearl remained white, but the Scarecrow was becoming quite suspicious.

"Something is bothering me," he whispered to Glinda. "I think he's twisting the facts around to deceive us."

"What would you suggest that we do?" Glinda whispered back.

"Ask Ruggedo if he has told us the truth, nothing but the truth, and the whole truth," said the Scarecrow.

"Ruggedo, have you told us the whole truth?" Glinda asked

"As much as you need to know," Ruggedo said, stating his personal opinion and thus causing the pearl to turn a noncommittal gray.

Glinda tried again: "Are you deliberately withholding information from us?"

"I'm telling the truth!" Ruggedo evaded. "Taarna is in my house and—"

"Look!" Dorothy exclaimed. "The pearl is blue!"

"When it turns blue, it means he's told a falsehood unknowingly," Glinda explained.

"Last time he said Taarna was in his house, it was the truth," the Scarecrow observed.

"Taarna's not there now?" Ruggedo said in genuine astonishment.

"She's escaped! We have to stop her!" the Wizard exclaimed.

"I'd like to see you try!" Ruggedo taunted.

"We'll deal with you later!" the Scarecrow cried, shaking a straw-stuffed finger at the Nome.

He along with Glinda and the others bounded out of the prison, and then the chamber sealed itself off.

"Heh heh heh!" the Nome Ex-King snickered after they were gone. "Didn't think to ask me if she was a Genie or something, did you? That bought me time!"

Then Ruggedo grew uneasy. "But where is Taarna? She might have been Genie-napped!"

He searched the chamber for an escape, but found none. He couldn't even detect a seam where the door had been.

"Now what do I do?" Ruggedo snarled to himself. "When they come back, they'll cast me to the bottom of the ocean or turn me into an amoeba or something! Thunderation!"

Ruggedo sat in the big reclining chair and was irritated to find that it did not rock. He stood and paced furiously, trying to think of how to get out and find Taarna before they did. After a few minutes' unsuccessful thought, he groaned in despair and moved to plop his fat little body back on the chair...and then was astonished a second later to find himself falling through the air.

15

The Grand Plan

"WHERE am I?" Ruggedo said. He had landed with a thud and found himself in a dark and somber castle, surrounded by a nasty crew of ugly and fiendish-looking beings.

"Welcome to Whaqoland!" Forg said jovially. "I am your new confederate!"

"I'll choose my own friends, thank you!" Ruggedo blustered as he stumbled to his feet. "Who in thunderation are you, and how did I get here? Just a minute ago, I was just sitting down in the Emerald City prison, and the next thing I know, I'm here!"

"I am Forg, king of the witches and demons of Whaqoland, and co-master of your Taarna! Shall we overrun Oz?"

With these words, he produced the spray can that he had nimbly and stealthily stolen from Ruggedo's cottage. He sprayed it.

"It's about time, Ruggedo!" Taarna said with an irritated yawn. "I had gone into hibernation myself for a while there. Now, for our plan, I think we—" She stopped, stunned, as she saw the tribe of demons leering up at her.

"Forg!" Taarna cried in alarm.

"Hello, your ex-majesty. I am your master now!" Forg cried with glee. "Now you will help me with my plans."

"I am not in the habit of having a shabby, grimy, snarling demon for a master," Taarna said contemptuously.

"I think you will find in the Genie Union Code Book," said the demon Scott Glib, producing the volume, "on page 745, section C, paragraph 1A, that there is nothing forbidding a Genie from having a nonhuman master provided it is intelligent enough to rub the lamp or spray the can, and has a voice to make wishes."

"Look, Ruggedo is already my master," Taarna protested, "and I—"

"In the Genie Union Code book, page 1124, section K, paragraph 2B, it states that the *current* lamp rubber or can sprayer is the Genie's current master...unless the current master consents to allow the previous one to be a joint master," Scott Glib stated.

Taarna conjured up her own copy of the Genie Union Code Book and consulted it.

"Well, it appears you're right," Taarna conceded. "It appears that you and Ruggedo are both my masters, and that you have five wishes between you, since Ruggedo has used up one wish."

"Excellent! Excellent!" Forg cried, leering. "So, my dear Ruggedo, as we all have the common goal of wreaking revenge on Oz, I suggest we work together to give those wretched Ozians their comeuppance."

"After all, you don't have to be a demon to be a good citizen of evil," the demon called Jess-He remarked, and added, "though it sure helps."

"Come now, Ruggy boy," the demon Tasmminy said sweetly, "we can all be evil together, can't we?"

"If not, we turn you into a block of wood and feed you to the termites!" Old Skin-Droop added cordially.

Chapter Fifteen

"Very well, Taarna," Ruggedo said doubtfully. "These demons may take part in our plans."

"I knew you'd see reason," Forg said. "And now, Taarna will tell us her grand plan to invade and conquer Oz."

"Yes! Yes! Something slow and painful, I hope," Ruggedo said eagerly.

"Now, first of all," Taarna began, "there can be no doubt that, if we simply invade Oz and attempt to overthrow Ozma, she would be defended by that wretched Wizard, that gruesome Glinda, and those appalling Adepts—"

"We've already disposed of the Adepts. We sold them into slavery!" Forg chortled, leering.

"Splendid!" Taarna hissed. "But the others would definitely come to the defense of Ozma and Oz."

"That is quite true," Ruggedo said. "How can we possibly fight all of the greatest magicians of Oz?"

"Yes," Forg agreed, "snuffing out the Adepts' pitiful powers was so easy it was a joke!" Forg sneered gleefully, then added soberly: "But Glinda is something else again."

"Ha! I can take away her powers! I am an All-Powerful Genie!" Taarna proclaimed with a grim smile. "We will travel to Oz and set up a radio talk show where we will say very mean things about Ozma and Oz! This will lure Glinda to come to us in Ozma's defense! Then, when we have her, I will slowly drain her of her pathetic powers, soon making her as helpless as a housefly."

Forg and the other demons snickered malevolently.

"But what about the others?" asked Tasmminy.

"Disarming the Wizard is just a matter of stealing his Black Bag, and with Ozma we need only relieve her of the Magic Belt," said Taarna.

"And after they're all robbed of their powers, can we then do to them what we did to the Adepts?" Forg said eagerly. "Shall we hand Glinda, Ozma, the Wizard, and any other magical person that may try to help them over to Old Pascalabes, too?"

"Yes!" Taarna sneered. "Old Pascalabes the Sand Pirate, who kidnaps fairies and, after their powers are disposed of, makes them slaves on his flying ship; or, if they're of no use to him, he hands them over to his brother, King Graytfyl of Im, who has an especially grim fate in store for those who fall into his hands." Taarna punctuated this speech with a sadistic laugh in which the demons heartily joined.

"And when Old Pascalabes and King Graytfyl have rid us forever of Ozma and Glinda and any others who might be faithful to them, and those silly Oz people are trembling with despair in our merciless shadow, you, my dear Forg, shall assume the throne of Oz!" Taarna concluded dramatically.

"Splendid!" Forg cried, clapping his claws. "A brilliant plan!"

"I don't think it's so brilliant!" Ruggedo protested. "When Forg is King of Oz, where, pray, does that leave little old me?"

"Oh, you shall get back your Magic Belt, then swoop over to Ev, turn the Evian Royal Family back into ornaments, and assume rule of both Ev and your old Nome Kingdom."

"Good, but not good enough," Ruggedo said. "I want to rule Oz...In fact, come to think of it, I want to control all of the Nonestic Archipelago—Oz, Ev, Ix, Mo, Merryland, Rinkitink, Wonderland, Looking-Glass Land, Orkland, Snark Island, the Kingdom of Wisdom, Living Island, Lidsville, the Land of the Lost, Tranquillity Forest, the Jewelled Mountains, the Seven Deserts—the whole enchilada!"

"Sure you don't want Mars, Saturn, and the Andromeda Galaxy, too?" Taarna ventured to say.

"The lands that I've listed are the least I'm entitled too!" the Nome screamed.

"Really trumped-up and self-important aren't we? Ever considered a career in modeling?"

This rebellious remark from Taarna caused her bracelets to glow with threatening brilliance.

"See! You can't order me around; I am your master!" Ruggedo gleefully observed.

"Quite right!" Taarna hastily agreed. "Forg, let's let Ruggedo have Oz, okay?"

Chapter Fifteen

"I'll make a deal with you," Ruggedo proposed. "Let me have Oz, and I'll let you have the rest of the Nonestic fairylands beyond Oz."

"I'll make a deal with *you,*" Forg said in his most amiable voice. "Let me have the fairylands beyond Oz, and I'll let you have a pig's eye!"

"Why? I think that's a very good offer," Ruggedo snarled.

"I want to rule Oz, and I want the Emerald City for an express purpose," Forg explained. "I want to equip the Emerald City with my magical machinery so that I may open a weapons factory."

"Whatever for!" Ruggedo growled.

"So that Oz may arm in preparation for a great celestial war that will lead to my controlling the entire world, and eventually, the entire universe!"

"Modest planner, isn't he?" Taarna whispered to Ruggedo.

Forg continued: "And I can't think of a better way to enslave the Oz people than to make them into grimy, sweaty, smelly workers in my factory for weapons of mass destruction. And I'll be a slimy boojum if I'm going to let any lowly Nome rob me of that pleasure!"

"Ahem! Your majesty!" Skin-Droop coughed.

"Excuse me—a private conference with my subordinates," Forg said, and huddled in a circle with the highest ranking witches and demons.

"By rickety! I wish I knew what they were saying!" Ruggedo hissed as he strained in vain to pick up the muffled whispers.

"I am an All-Powerful Genie and I hear all," Taarna hissed back. "They're plotting to make a deal with you that sounds good, but they mean to cheat you out of everything worth anything to you, and they mean eventually to dispose of you."

"Taa—rna!" Ruggedo stammered nervously. "I'd like to make my second wish—I wish for Forg and all these demons and witches to be cast in an airtight and implacable vessel to the deepest crack in the deepest trench at the bottom of the Nonestic Ocean!"

"Believe you me, nothing would please me more, master," Taarna murmured regretfully. "But like it or not, he is my master, too, now, and I can do him and his 'people'—I use the term loosely—no harm!"

"Well, hang it all, what am I going to do?" Ruggedo moaned.

"Don't worry, and just keep calm, master," Taarna said reassuringly. "If a Genie feels less than compassionate toward her master, she can frequently trick him—and you can be sure that our friend Forg is definitely going to get the full treatment from me!"

"You don't like these Whaqoland characters either, then?" Ruggedo said.

"No doubt about it," Taarna said with a discernible shudder, "in the time since I ruled Whaqoland, they have all grown so radically evil that they give evil a bad name. I frankly could never bring myself to rule over them now—"

She cut herself off as Forg ended his "conference."

"Here is my proposition, Ruggedo," Forg announced. "You shall have the western lands of the Nonestic Archipelago: Ev, Op, Im, Rinkitink, the Kingdom of Wisdom, Agrabah and so on; I'll take the eastern lands: Ix, Mo, Merryland, Burzee, Wonderland, Snark Island, Living Island, Lidsville, Tranquillity Forest, et cetera, et cetera; and we shall both have joint control over Oz."

"You mean you propose that we share Oz? Forget it!" Ruggedo roared.

"Then you will be king of Oz, and I'll just be your Grand Vizier! That's my final offer; take it or leave it!" said Forg.

"And what if I leave it?" Ruggedo said defiantly.

Forg said nothing, but raised his long-clawed hands into the air, and out of the knife-sharp claws sprang an electricity-like bolt of black magic that shot out the castle window and reduced a nearby encirclement of trees to a charred crater filled with black ashes.

"It's a deal," Ruggedo sighed, and shook hands with Forg.

"Now that's settled," Forg said. "Now make your second wish— wish for us to conquest the fairylands."

"Why should I waste my precious wishes?" Ruggedo demanded. "You haven't used any of your wishes yet—Why don't you wish?"

With a look of malevolence, Forg pointed his evil fingers at Ruggedo.

"Okay! Okay! If you insist," Ruggedo stammered.

"I do!" Forg stated flatly, the claws locked on their intended target.

Ruggedo looked at Taarna, who gave him a reassuring wink, and then he said, "Taarna, my second wish: I wish for us to conquer Oz and the rest of the Nonestic Archipelago as laid out in our plans here today."

Chapter Fifteen

"To hear is to obey, oh master of time and space!" Taarna proclaimed.

"Just one thing," Forg interjected. "Before we commence this great enterprise to conquer Oz and beyond, shouldn't we compose a good name for it?"

"I already have," Taarna said. "I'm calling it 'the Campaign to Take Back Our Fairyland.'"

"Terrific!" said Forg gleefully. "I can't wait until Oz is 'taken back' and belongs to the Forces of Evil once more!"

Locasta Breaks the Law

LOCASTA and her companions had a pleasant dinner that evening—in spite of having to eat off the dirty ground with their hands—with many of the dinosaurs, pterodactyls, crimson crocodiles, and mammal-like reptiles of Op. They all expressed their gratitude to the Ozites for their determination to find Gyma and Esu, and they said to Ozma that if her people in Oz ever needed their assistance against wicked invaders, they would gladly lend their help.

The next day, they started to discuss what to do to conquer Old Pascalabes.

"One thing's for certain: We have to get aboard that ship," said Dan.

"Oh, my dear boy, surely you don't propose to come with us on what promises to be a very perilous journey," said Locasta.

"I'm not allowing my friends—the best friends I've ever had—to go off and face danger while I sit around and twiddle my thumbs. I *must* go with you," proclaimed Dan. "Besides, I have a thirst for freedom and adventure. I've been cooped up in orphanages and unhappy foster homes the whole of my life. I need to break free and feel the warm sun on my brow and the cool wind on my face."

"What are you, weird?" Nan-Kerr muttered.

"Freedom—that's all I've ever wanted. And to help my new friends [he looked from Locasta to Nan-Kerr to Jellia, and finally to Ozma], I will put my new freedom to the best use I can, whatever dangers may lie ahead."

"You know what I think?" Locasta said to Nan-Kerr. "I think I should explain to you about the Magic of Everything."

"What good would that do?" Nan-Kerr cried in surprise. "After all I've done, associating myself with those horrid demons, I hardly deserve to know it. I'm sure I would never understand its intricate complexities, anyway."

"I think in these dangerous days, it is best that as many good sorceresses have the knowledge as possible, and as an old school chum, I trust you more than anyone outside of Oz," Locasta said. "Also, if I told you the Magic of Everything, it would be in violation of Op's law against conveying knowledge, wouldn't it?"

"And it would bring Old Pascalabes' ship down to us; yes, I see," Nan-Kerr said. "But still—"

But Locasta assured Nan-Kerr that it was all for the best, and so she told her the Magic of Everything. She told Nan-Kerr about the Grand Scheme of All Things Magical. In the few minutes it took to tell Nan-Kerr that simple set of incantations, every spell and bit of hocus-pocus in the magical universe made perfect sense to her.

"It all so wonderful, so miraculous!" Nan-Kerr cried. "Now if only I knew how to use it."

"And the most marvelous part is that it's not final knowledge," Locasta said. "The knowledge of the universe is as infinite and unending as the universe itself, and can never be all known. What I've given you is the fundamental of every known spell, but we have not an inkling of an idea of how to derive all new, unknown spells, which is what the Magic of Everything claims to do..."

"So in a way the Magic of Everything is a fraud?" Nan-Kerr said. "Because it doesn't provide final, complete knowledge, as many, like Forg, think it's supposed to do?

"Yes," Locasta said, "but 'fraud' is an unduly harsh word, for what it does tell us about the way magic works is the most precious bit of knowledge in Fairyland."

"Well, now that I know the M.O.E., I do feel as if everything made sense to me as never before. Oh, this is a wonderful day!" Nan-Kerr cried with joy.

"This is not a wonderful day; this is a terrible day," Penty snapped at Nan-Kerr and Locasta. "You have broken the law, both of you."

"Ja," Veloski said sadly to Locasta. "You told dat Magic of vatever-it-vas to her, und any minute now dat awful Ray-Shy vill come und—"

"Heeheeheehee!" cackled a voice. "Did I hear someone take my name in vain?"

They turned and saw a hideous old hag standing in the shadow of the big, black umbrella she held (even though it was a sunny day). She had brown, curly hair, sharp cheekbones, a tiny nose and mouth, and big round glasses so thick that you couldn't see her eyes at all. She wore camo-colored pedal-pushers and a muddy-looking cloak with a badge that read, "I motivate."

"Er, dat's Ray-Shy," Veloski explained.

"What does she motivate, I wonder?" Ozma whispered.

"Nausea—total disgust—Am I close?" Jellia muttered.

"So, you dare break the No-Knowledge Law, eh? Well, your punishment shall be great and terrible," Ray-Shy cackled. She produced a big whistle and blew it, producing a deep, horn-like sound that echoed throughout Op.

Then they all saw a dark, brown, forbidding ship descend from the sky, like a three-masted storm cloud. It was the SS *Able,* the same ship that the Adepts had confronted. When in a few seconds it was directly overhead, Ray-Shy spoke an incantation, and Ozma, Locasta, Dan, Jellia, and Nan-Kerr were levitated aboard the ship.

"Good-bye. Farewell," the dinosaurian citizens of Op cried to them sadly.

Chapter Sixteen

"Don't worry; we'll release your princesses, and we'll stop these foul invaders," Ozma promised as they disappeared into the evil craft.

A second later, Ozma and the others found themselves on the deck of the ship. Ray-Shy appeared next to them. "Welcome aboard the SS *Able*," she said in an evil tone,

"Why is it called the *Able?*" Dan asked.

"Well, what else would we call it, since it is manned by Able seamen?" said Ray-Shy, leering. "And now you will be among our Able seamen as well!

"And using your meager powers against me is useless," she added as she saw Nan-Kerr staring at her intensely and muttering an incantation. "I shall now remove your powers."

With an evil flourish, Ray-Shy drew from her cloak a small jar, and quicker that it takes to say it, she unscrewed the jar, reached in, shoveled up a fistful of a strange powder from it, and tossed it over Nan-Kerr's head. The powder rained down as shimmering raindrops. As Nan-Kerr finished her spell, she found that nothing happened.

"Why aren't you a monitor lizard now?" she demanded of Ray-Shy.

"Because I took away all your powers," the hag sneered. "You are no longer a witch; you are now a magic-less private fairy citizen.

"And you are next," she continued, leering at Ozma. "Now stand by while I remove your powers."

Ozma clasped the Magic Belt and whispered a command to it, but for the first time ever, it did not obey its wearer. Instead, the Belt shuddered and made some rude noises, and then dropped from Ozma's waist.

"Yes!" chortled Ray-Shy. "Not only has my magic-removing powder erased your native fairy powers, but it has short circuited the Magic Belt just long enough for the Forces of Evil, for whom the Belt was originally manufactured, to repossess it. So if you would be so kind, Princess Ozma, the Belt, please." And Ozma watched helplessly as Ray-Shy took the Belt and fastened it to her own waist.

"Let's see—who else has powers that need removing?" the wicked witch said as she scanned her prisoners. "I can tell that you two are mortals," she said to Dan and Jellia, and then, leering at Locasta: "So I shall now remove *your* powers."

"Speaking as one witch to another, you can't make me a private fairy-citizen," Locasta proclaimed. "I am a powerful and influential cit-Oz-en."

"Not anymore," Ray-Shy sneered, and she reached for another handful of her magic-removal powder.

"You'd better not," Locasta said with a noticeable twinkle in her eye. "My powers are so vast I can make this ship disappear."

Locasta than waved her hands and turned the muddy brown ship to red and blue plaid.

"Oops!" said Locasta. "But I *can* turn you into a beetle."

She waved her arms. Ray-Shy's head, wrists, and ankles were immediately decorated with big, pink bows.

"Oh dear, I guess I'm a little rusty," Locasta said. "But I can do this—" She drew out a deck of cards, fanned them out, and said, "Pick a card, any card," and immediately dropped the cards all over the deck.

Chapter Sixteen

"Oh, I don't have time for such foolishness," Ray-Shy said in disgust. "You are obviously a humbug like that idiot Wizard in Oz. No need to waste my precious magic-removing powder on you!"

She closed the jar and thrust it back in her cloak. And after she indignantly restored the ship's former ugly shade of muddy-brown, she said, "I will tell the captain you're here," and vanished.

"That was brilliant!" Dan cried in admiration.

"Yes, you are very wise, Locasta," said Ozma. "With you with us, I just know that these monsters can be defeated."

They looked around at the ship. It looked like a three-masted ship of old, but everything was an ugly muddy color, and all over the deck were numerous fairies of various sorts and sizes, all wearing sailor suits and engaging in various chores, such as scrubbing the deck, shoveling sand, and forging iron. They all looked very fatigued and forlorn.

As the five newcomers watched this heart-breaking sight, four fairies dressed in officers' uniforms approached.

"Hello," the apparent leader said, as she sadly shook Locasta's hand. "I am the first mate of the SS *Able,* Lieutenant Janus Rhincodon Typus."

After greeting Ozma, and the others as well, she then introduced the other officers: "This is Lieutenant Wilbur Granchio, Ensign George Bandersnatch, and Ensign Susan Wifea."

"I'm delighted to meet you," Locasta said, as though they were at a party.

"We're not delighted to meet you," Ensign Wifea said.

"You're not?" Locasta said, a little hurt.

"It's nothing personal—it's just that we are always very sad to see new faces on board this ship." Ensign Bandersnatch said, and shed a bitter tear.

"What our highly emotional ensigns mean," Lieutenant Granchio said, hastening to explain, "is that everyone who comes aboard this ship becomes the slave of the captain as we all are, and we hate to see any more nice people become slaves."

"We sure do," sobbed Mr. Bandersnatch, now in near hysteria.

"You see, we are all fairies from various parts of Baumgea," Janus explained, "and Old Pascalabes has made a diabolical career of kidnapping fairies. So he kidnapped us and made us his sailors and slaves."

"And Old Ray-Shy, whose powers are much greater than any of ours," Mr. Granchio added, "took away all our fairy powers so that we couldn't escape or rise up in rebellion."

"And you're all forced to do hard work aboard this ship? That's terrible!" Dan cried.

"And now it is our painful obligation to show you to your duties," Mr. Bandersnatch whimpered.

"Just as soon as those other new ones get up here...Ah, here they are," Janus said.

And with joy, Locasta's eyes fell upon her three granddaughters.

"Judit! Zsuzsa! Sofia!"

"Grandmama!"

A second later, the space within Locasta's arms was filled by the Adepts at Sorcery, who hugged their Grandmama as tight as they could.

"Oh, my darlings! I'm so glad to see you!" Locasta cried.

"Oh, us too!" Judit said.

"We missed you so bad," Sofia added.

"From now on, we're not letting you out of our sight," Zsuzsa promised.

After the Adepts greeted their grandmama, she introduced them to Dan. To Dan's surprise and delight, they each gave him a colossal hug.

"So here's our computer pen-pal," said Zsuzsa.

"The genius who found our grandmama," said Judit.

"You're even handsomer in person, Danny," said Sofia.

"Wow," Dan murmured, his lonely heart quite elated by how much affection the girls of Oz were showering upon him.

"Oh, my darlings, I'm so happy to see you, but what are you doing here?" Locasta asked her granddaughters.

"Same as you and all of us—they were kidnapped," Lieutenant Janus R. Typus said. "As we said, the entire crew of this ship are fairies whom the captain has captured and enslaved."

"Well, we must set you all free at once. Is Princess Gyma here?" Locasta said.

"No, her powers were too great for Ray-Shy to nullify," said Janus Typus, "so she handed her and Princess Esu over to Pascalabes' brother, King Graytfyl of Im...and he has no doubt locked them away in his magic-proof dungeon."

"Why?" Dan asked.

"To get her out of the way, so she couldn't fight against Pascalabes," Janus said sorrowfully.

"Well, in any case, we shall certainly free you all!" Locasta said.

"How?" Nan-Kerr asked. "I don't think we can manage with your, shall we say, obsolete brand of magic?"

Before anyone could speak in Locasta's defense, Eric Seagull swooped down from somewhere and landed on Judit's shoulder.

"Oh, let me introduce the renowned writer. Eric Seagull," Judit said. "He's become our friend, and he's acting as our lookout."

"Lookout for what?" Dan asked. "Storms? Sharks?"

"No—the captain," Eric cried, just as the crew all cowered at the sound of heavy footsteps.

"Shiver me timbers," a gruff voice bellowed.

They all turned and saw Old Pascalabes, captain of the SS *Able,* emerge from his cabin, followed by Old Ray-Shy. He had black, unkempt hair, a bushy mustache, and a dirty face (pirates are not big on personal hygiene), one baggy eye (an eye patch covered the other), and one wooden leg (the real one had been bitten off by the Deadly-Desert-dwelling monster known as the sandy, savage, snarling See-plus-plus), and he walked with the aid of a big cane made from a whale's tusk. He stood at the door to his cabin and eyed his captive crew with irate repugnance.

"All right, you clowns," he yelled at them. "Fall in for inspection!"

"Inspection?" Dan gasped.

"You're in the army now," Zsuzsa said.

"The navy, actually," Judit observed.

They and the other fairy-sailors assembled into several neat rows on the deck.

"Don't worry, Danny," Sofia said reassuringly.

"Silence!" Pascalabes snapped. "One more word from any of you and you're on report!"

"What report?" Locasta whispered. "The weather report? A report on what I did this summer?"

"Shhh," Lieutenant Granchio hissed.

"That includes shushing, Mr. Granchio," Pascalabes snarled, and then he paced slowly and malevolently before the front row of sailors, which included the officers, Dan, Ozma, Locasta, Nan-Kerr, Jellia, and the Adepts. As he paced, he scrutinized them from head to foot.

Suddenly, Dan sneezed.

"Put that sailor on report!" Pascalabes roared, pointing at Dan.

"Sorry, I couldn't help it," Dan said.

"Oh, you couldn't help it, hey?" Old Pascalabes sneered. "It seems you need to learn to be a model sailor."

"How may I be a model sailor?" Dan asked, trying not to cringe in reaction to the pungent fumes emanating from Pascalabes' grimy, bath-forsaking body.

"Figure it out yourself," Captain Pascalabes snapped. "And if I catch you in any way not being a model sailor again, I'll cancel your shore leave for the next twenty years, and all your privileges to attend the Saturday night movie as well."

"It doesn't matter, Danny," Judit whispered to him. "He defines shore leave as fifty laps around the Baumgea beach, and the only thing he allows to be shown at the Saturday night movie is reruns of *Cheers.*"

"As for the rest of you pathetic pampered pixies," Pascalabes growled at the crew as a whole, "you'd better all shape up, or I'll hand you over to my brother, King Graytfyl, who will send you to a superlatively terrible and horrible fate in his dungeon."

"What's he talking about?" Dan whispered, but Lieutenant Janus R. Typus hastily shushed him.

"But before we cast off, I thought this would be a good time for us all to have a little chat," Pascalabes continued nastily. "In other words, I shall have a little chat and you shall have a little listen.

"Apparently some sailors onboard this vessel still think they can pull the wool over my eyes. I went to my private pantry to get four scoops of strawberry ice cream, and it had been *stolen!* Apparently you sailors aren't satisfied with eating scrap metal, eh?" He looked right at Sofia on this last sentence.

"Eh, well—it's not what we're used to," Sofia stammered.

"We have trouble digesting metal," Judit added.

"The aluminum foil is especially bad," Zsuzsa shuddered. "Reminds me of cold cereal."

"Well, get used to it!" Pascalabes roared. "And whoever stole my ice cream better confess or I'll put him in solitary confinement for three months."

"Beggin' you pardon, sir," said a pretty little fairy-sailor meekly, "but how will you put the thief in solitary confinement when you don't know who he is?"

Pascalabes hesitated, then cried, "Then I'll put you *all* into solitary confinement!"

"I took it," Locasta said, to everyone's astonishment.

"How can you have taken it? You just came on board," Old Ray-Shy snarled.

"Ah!" Pascalabes said with a wicked leer. "These are my new recruits then?"

"Yes, but this one is either an idiot or a wise-guy," Ray-Shy said, indicating Locasta.

"Excellent," Pascalabes said as he examined Locasta and her companions. "I love having new additions to my crew of beautiful fairies." With a glance at Locasta, he added, "Ugly ones, too."

"She is not ugly!" Dan cried.

"You will address me as 'sir' or you'll be peeling potatoes in the kitchen!"

"Beggin' your pardon, sir," said Ensign Wifea meekly, "but there ain't no more potatoes, sir. We ran out three months ago."

"I'll make him peel them anyway!" Pascalabes roared.

"You can't talk to Danny that way!" cried Ozma passionately.

"Oh, you like this teenage delinquent, do you?" the captain snarled.

"Yes, I do!" said Ozma emphatically.

"She likes him!" Old Ray-Shy shrieked gleefully. "When the Law of the Forest by which all fairies are bound strictly forbids a fairy from falling in love! It's the scandal of the century!"

"Wait—wait!" cried Dan. "The word 'like' is open to interpretation. I think she meant she likes me as a friend. I'm sure she could never fall in *love* with me."

"Then she's committed perjury!" crowed Ray-Shy. "The Fairy Tribunal will string her up for this!"

"She did nothing of the sort!" cried Jellia. "You were the ones who misunderstood—"

"Silence!" Pascalabes snapped. "We could not have misunderstood! We are infileable."

"Infallible," Locasta corrected.

"That's what I said, you terrestrial insect!" the pirate snarled, and then to the crew in general, he exclaimed, "Shiver me timbers!"

"Beggin' your pardon, sir," Mr. Bandersnatch said, "but why do you always say, 'Shiver me timbers'?"

"Because that's what pirates are supposed to say, you lily-livered lout!" Pascalabes roared. "Now back to work, all of you. And Ms. Typus, you will now show the new recruits to their duties." And he lumbered back to his cabin.

"Come," Janus said sadly. "We must indeed show you to your duties."

"I already know our duty," Ozma cried. "Our duty is to save you all from that—that—"

"That not-at-all-nice person," Sofia offered, and pointed toward the captain's cabin.

The Demons Invade Oz

"GOOD evening, all you fellow Likewise-Brains and hostages of Führer Ozma. This is Scott Glib of KHS Division radio, bringing you all the goings on in Fairyland and all the antics of our fairy kings and queens. And our first scandal comes from Oz, folks. Yes, it's true; ol' Ozma is at it again, folks. It seems that the Tart in the Emerald City has taken in a wounded buzzard and is nursing it back to health. So like her. We're trying to make an honest living, and she's feeding illegal immigrant buzzards..."

"Can you believe this?" Dorothy whispered to Ozma's courtiers. They had been listening to this radio show for about an hour.

"What is this strange radio show? Why are they saying these things?" the Wizard asked uneasily. No one had an answer, so they continued to listen.

"And speaking of illegal immigrants, Dorothy Gale from that evil empire, Kansas, made imbecile history today by allying herself with those lunatic tree-huggers who want to keep pollution out of Oz. Well, let me tell you, my friends, it seems to me that pollution is vastly underrated..." Glib said. "And now for the big news of the day, folks. There is new evidence that King Evoldo, the father of King Evardo of Ev, did not commit suicide, but was murdered by order of Ozma."

"This is awful, what they're saying about Ozma," the Scarecrow said.

"What lies they're telling!" added the Tin Man.

"I think what they are say–ing is ve–ry log–i–cal," Tik-Tok droned in his mechanical voice. "They make per–fect sense to me. I a–gree with them."

"Tik-Tok!" cried Dorothy, understandably shocked by the clockwork man's advocacy of these Ozma-haters.

"His thinking's run down," Dorothy observed, and she grabbed Tik-Tok's key from where it hung on a hook on the mechanical man's back and wound him under his left arm. Immediately little LED lights at the top of Tik-Tok's head began to wink on and off, indicating that he was now thinking again.

"Ma–ny thanks," said Tik-Tok. "For a se–cond there I was in great dan–ger of be–com–ing like them."

"That just goes to show—always keep your thinking wound up," said the Scarecrow.

"I'm beginning to suspect that some devious sorcery is behind this radio show, and that someone is plotting to do harm to Oz," the Wizard said.

"And they're using political ploys to weaken our resistance," the Shaggy Man added. "Not unlike the United States."

"Very clever!" Dorothy fumed. "They're trying to turn everyone against Ozma so they can take over Oz themselves."

"What shall we do?" cried Betsy.

"Oh, it's all swill," Captain Bill remarked as he puffed on his corncob pipe. "No one's gonna turn the Oz people agin Ozma. Everyone loves her. I think someone's just tryin' to skeer us."

"All the easier to invade us," the Cowardly Lion growled.

"You don't think Ruggedo has anything to do with all this, do you?" Dorothy asked.

"Well, whoever these people are, we can't let them do anything to us," said the Wizard.

Chapter Seventeen

Scraps, the Patchwork Girl, sang as she danced wildly about the room:

"Hippity Hoppity Heen!
Someone's acting mean.
One of us should go
On this awful show,
And well defend our Queen."

"You're quite right, dear Scraps," the Scarecrow said. "I think someone should go over to this radio studio and find out who these people are."

"And denounce all these bad things they're saying about our beloved Ozma," the Tin Man added.

"Yes," the Shaggy Man said. "I'll do it."

"I think I should go," the Scarecrow said. "My great wisdom would make me say all the right things."

"I could do it," the Wizard said. "I've often worked by Ozma's side and know all the good she's done."

"If I did it, I could tell all about how Ozma made me," Jack Pumpkinhead said, as he let the little girls Betsy and Trot examine his head to make sure it was not overly ripe.

"As Ozma's closest friend, I think I should be the one who speaks in her behalf," Dorothy proclaimed.

"I could do it," the Cowardly Lion said. "I'll tell them the truth about Ozma, and if they don't believe me, I'll tear them apart."

"Or I could eat those vicious, hate-mongering villains, and my conscience wouldn't bother me a bit!" said the Hungry Tiger.

"Well, I think Glinda should do it," Betsy said. "She is very wise and very kind, and I think she could state Ozma's case better than anyone."

"Thank you, my dear. I am very flattered," Glinda said with a smile.

"And if these people really are devious sorcerers, who but she could stop them?" the Scarecrow said. "I agree; it should be Glinda."

"I move we make it ominous!" Jack Pumpkinhead cried.

"You mean 'unanimous,'" the Shaggy Man gently corrected.

"Boy, you do know all about politics, don't you?" said Jack in awe.

"All in favor of Glinda's going on this radio show to defend our gracious Queen, say aye!" Dorothy cried.

"Aye!"

"Well, if you all insist, I will," said Glinda, "but I want you to come with me, Oscar."

"Of course I will," the Wizard replied.

"Glinda, you don't think they can really make people not like Ozma, do you?" said Dorothy anxiously.

"Don't worry, my dear," Glinda said softly.

"I think they just want to make us unhappy about these bad things they are saying, and so take the fight out of us so that they can invade us," said the Wizard, and added, with a friendly glance at Glinda, "but they don't know with whom they are dealing!"

"Hello again friends, this is Scott Glib of KHS Division Radio welcoming you to *Chessboard*—our forum for an open and mature debate on the issues. This show is brought to you live from Darkest Gillikin Country in Northern Oz. Tonight on *Chessboard* we have two very special guests: on the Black, Toni H. Ardent, an ordinary pompous talking head, and on the White, Oscar Z. Diggs and Glinda T. Good, Joint Chiefs of Sorcery in the Ozma Administration. Tonight's topic: 'Ozma's Regime: Isn't Ninety-eight Years Enough?' Toni, I yield to you for an opening statement."

"Thank you, Scott," said Toni H. Ardent (who was really Taarna disguised as an ordinary person). "Good evening, my fellow Ozites. Is Big Brother watching you?"

"I beg your pardon?" Glinda said.

"Did you, my fellow Ozites, know that Ozma has a Magic Picture, with which she can spy on you, any time, any place?" Toni hissed, as Scott put "He knows when you are sleeping, he knows when you're awake" on the tape player.

Chapter Seventeen

"And Glinda here," Toni continued in a threatening voice, "has a Book of Records with which she reads about everything you do, the very instant you do it!"

"Not nearly everything," Glinda explained calmly. "Just important happenings that enable Ozma and I to better help people. And in regard to the Magic Picture—"

"Privacy is dead, thanks to Ozma," Toni interrupted. "And her wimpo defense policy nearly destroyed Oz."

"How?" the Wizard inquired defensively.

"She refused to fight the Nome King when he was going to invade Oz with the Phanfasms, Whimsies, and Growleywogs," Toni barked.

"But she ended the threat peacefully," Glinda tried to explain. "You see—"

"And she's so soft on crime!" Scott said. "She puts them in a fun prison, and then almost immediately forgives them."

"But—" Glinda said weakly.

"And the way she and you insist on wasting precious magical resources in helping insignificant peasants and degenerate riff-raff!" Toni continued.

"Right on! Let them drink Ozade," Scott proclaimed.

"End Ozma's loony, fanatical, hoodlum regime! Have her prosecuted by the Fairy Tribunal!" Scott cried.

"Have Ozma prosecuted? On what grounds?" the Wizard demanded.

"Word has just reached us that she has fallen madly in love with a mortal man from the Collective Hunch. Clearly a High Crime and Misdemeanor in the eyes of the Fairy Tribunal. And if they won't convict her of that, there's always those magical secrets she's been selling to the evil forces of the Nonestic Archipelago."

"That's absurd. She has not done anything of the kind, and never would," declared the Wizard.

"It is irrelevant whether she has or not. Ozma is an evil, vile, sick blob of degenerate pond scum, and by golly, we'll find *something* to convict her of!" Toni screamed.

"Why are you talking like such maniacs?" Glinda said. "I thought this was going to be a honest discussion."

"Ah, shut up! We all know you ate chocolate in high school and that half of your court kisses in public!" Scott snarled.

"Everyone loves and respects Ozma, and she does them," Glinda said firmly.

"Oh, do they?" Scott said aggressively. "Well, let's go to the phones now and let the Oz people speak for themselves. Our first call is from Munchkinland. You're on the air."

"Hi, Scott and Toni," the voice said. "When Oz had an election, I voted for Ozma, and I now see what I fool I was. Our crops have all shriveled up, our clocks and phones don't work, the trains are running a half-hour late, we had a rainstorm last week, the Mets didn't make the World Series, I've gained ten pounds, and it's all Ozma's fault!"

"How could those things be—?" Glinda began.

"You are absolutely right, my friend," Toni said. "Everything is Ozma's fault, and it's time to get rid of her!"

"Our next call is from Winkie Country," Scott said a minute later. "Hello, you're on the air."

"Hello. I just want to say that Ozma is a good and honest ruler and always has been."

"Oh, well, is there anything else you want to convey to us besides your phenomenal stupidity?" Scott said rudely.

"Look, I am Gloma the Good Witch of the West; and Glinda, I have to tell you that Oz is in great danger. As we speak there is a vast army of demons and other malevolent beings marching into Oz."

"Good grief!" Scott whispered to Toni. "This is a real Oz citizen, not any of the negative, anti-Ozma calls you pre-orchestrated!"

"Well, hurry and cut her off, you idiot," Toni hissed, "before they start a substantive, intellectual discussion."

"Well, thank you very much for calling," Scott interjected out loud into the dangerously mindful dialogue that was breaking out between Glinda and Gloma.

"But I'm not finished talking with Glinda!" Gloma's voice cried.

"Yes, there's a bad connection. What did you say about danger to Oz?" the Wizard said anxiously.

Chapter Seventeen

"Thank you very much, Roma!" Scott cried.

"Gloma's my name."

Scott snarled, "Do you really expect an exalted Investigative Reporter like me to pronounce a name like G—Gl—"

"Gloma."

"Whatever. Good-bye, Paloma." And he hung up.

"Why did you hang up? She was trying to warn us about something," Glinda demanded.

"She was a fool," Scott proclaimed.

"A biased imbecile," Toni agreed.

"She was not. She was trying to tell us something important," the Wizard said. "I believe that Oz is in grave danger."

"Aw, don't be such a Gloomy Gus," Scott snarled. "The only danger to Oz is from that schnook, Ozma. Now back to some real calls. Our next is from Oogaboo. Hello, you're on the air."

"Hello Scott, Toni. I called to say that I'm sick of intellectual snobs telling me that Ozma is some kind of great leader when she's so out of touch with normal people."

"Ozma works hard every day for the benefit and well-being of her people, and you sit there and tell me she's out of touch?" Glinda said. "And what, pray, does 'normal people' mean?"

"People who aren't elite sorceresses like you!" Toni explained.

"A while ago you criticized Ozma because she helps the unfortunate, and now you criticize her because she is liked by the 'elite'? I think you talk through both sides of your mouth!" Glinda said angrily.

"Why doesn't she just leave everyone alone?" Scott snapped.

"Because she shows compassion for the weak and helpless!" Glinda said.

"See, what you're saying right now proves that you're out of touch. One only has to listen to the calls we've had to see how fed up people are of you and Ozma's nicey-nicey, goody-goody, lovey-dovey claptrap!" Scott screamed.

"I don't even believe these callers you've had are real," Glinda said. "I think you have helpers whom you told to call and say cruel and untrue things about our gentle ruler."

"Well, Glinda," Toni said with mock respect, "maybe you can answer this question: Isn't it true that Ozma has a fundamental credibility problem—That she is liked by elitist intellectuals?"

"Yeah, what Oz needs is more stupid people," Scott observed.

"You're both bananas!" Glinda said, by now completely forgetting her usual dignified decorum.

"Intellectuals are a dangerous threat to civilization!" Scott Glib said.

"If it were not for intellectuals, there wouldn't be any civilization," Glinda said. "And if you knew the good people of Oz at all, as I have come to know them over the past century or two, you would know that our people are good and kind and respectful of others, the world around them, and the wisdom of people like Ozma. You're the ones who are out of touch!" But Glinda was drowned out and couldn't get a word in.

"It's only a matter of time before the Oz people come to their senses and run Ozma out of town on a rail!" Toni cried. "She's a traitor!"

"A liar!" Scott cried.

"A coward!" Toni yelled.

"A raving radical!" they screamed in chorus.

"I demand that you cease your persecution of our queen!" Glinda demanded.

Toni laughed, then calmly rose and said, "Well, my dear Glinda and Wizard, I now have a real scoop for you. The time has now come to say good-bye to Toni H. Ardent, the Political Commentator—and to say hello to *Taarna, the All-Powerful Genie!*"

As she uttered these totally unexpected words, the radio studio vanished (being no longer needed), and Taarna assumed her true Genie form and grew to the size of a skyscraper.

The Wizard tumbled backward in alarm, but Glinda quickly helped him regain his feet. But before they could take any magical action against the mammoth monster that now towered over them, Taarna grabbed Glinda and the Wizard in an evil fist.

"Before you meet your end," Taarna said, wickedly leering at them, "you shall behold the demons of Whaqoland as they march into Oz!"

"You can't do this!" Glinda cried. "We will fight you!"

Chapter Seventeen

"You will do no such thing," Taarna gloated. "During the time that you were attempting to answer my statements about Ozma, I drained you both of all your magical powers. You and the rest of Oz are now entirely within my powers, thanks to the 'magic' of negative media coverage. Now, hapless fools, turn and witness your country's fall!"

Because Glinda and the Wizard couldn't turn, being held firmly in Taarna's grasp, Taarna turned the fist that held them fast. Over the neighboring hills of Gillikin Country, they saw the most terrifying army imaginable advancing.

At the head of the procession was Forg riding atop a giant woolly mammoth. He looked like a proud, mighty Eastern emperor as he malevolently gripped a large and formidable-looking mallet. Just behind came Ruggedo, gleefully riding a frumious bandersnatch.

Next came all the witches and demons of Whaqoland—Reed, S-Slinger, Skin-Droop, Tasmminy, Jess-He, and many others.

After the Whaqolanders, Glinda and the Wizard were very, very alarmed to see an army of Phanfasms, Whimsies, and Growleywogs— Oz's enemies of yore whose erased memories Taarna had restored as she had Ruggedo's— and Oz's most horrible foes of all, the Mimics of Mount Illuso. They all marched with the demons and were prepared now at last to invade and conquer Oz. Queen Ra, the Chief Whimsie, the Grand Gallipoot, and the First and Foremost gleefully led them, carrying a banner over their heads that read in bold, malevolent letters: "SAY GOOD NIGHT, OZMA."

And finally, at the very tail of the hideous procession, lumbered Keyel— a fifty-foot-high cyclops from the High Mountains of East Baumgea and the look of whose big, bulging eye could make marble and emerald crumble into dust, whose heavy feet could crush a building, and whose crab-like claws were built for molesting the kind, gentle, honest, law-abiding citizens that he despised.

As these nightmarish ogres reached a clearing at the foot of the hill, Forg's mammoth turned. Its trunk accidentally knocked Ruggedo off his "steed" and the Nome landed on the ground in an indignant heap.

Forg blew on a long horn, signaling his army to halt. He faced the hideous warriors and proclaimed: "My fellow Whaqolanders and other creatures of darkness, I have just signed a royal edict outlawing Oz forever! Black-magic bombing begins in five minutes!"

The monsters all cheered, and Ruggedo joined in after he brushed himself off.

"The Campaign to Take Back Our Fairyland will now allow the wicked witches and other beings of evil to once more seize control of what shall soon be the ex-marvelous, ex-beautiful, ex-merry old ex-Land of Oz!" Forg said.

The horrible warriors cheered even louder.

"So get out of the way, Ozma and Glinda, 'cause we're comin' through!" Forg proclaimed.

The monsters cheered louder than ever and chanted, "Hail, Forg! Hail, Forg!"

Forg pointed his mallet toward the Emerald City and, with the cry of *"Charge,"* began to lead the evil marchers down the Red Brick Road leading to Oz's capital.

Glinda tried desperately to free herself from Taarna's grasp, but Taarna just leered and evilly scolded: "Ah Ah Ah! No one escapes from Taarna!"

With those words, she produced a bottle and stuffed Glinda and the Wizard inside, corked it, and hurled it into the air. The bottle took off in a cloud of smoke like a rocket and careened toward the dark and dreadful Land of Im.

"Bye-bye, sick sorceress and fat wizard!" Forg cried. "Oz is ours at last!"

The *Able* Mutiny

THAT evening the crew of the S.S. *Able* and the Ozites met in secrecy in First Mate Janus R. Typus's cabin. They immediately vowed to find a way to stop the evil beings of Baumgea, starting with a total mutiny against Old Pascalabes.

"I say, though, there's no chance Ray-Shy can overhear us in her crystal ball or something, is there?" Jellia whispered anxiously.

"Oh, no—Old Ray-Shy would never use a crystal ball!" Janus said.

"She doesn't trust crystal balls," Dan surmised.

"The only way we could ever mutiny against Old Pascalabes is if we got rid of Old Ray-Shy," Mr. Granchio observed. "Her magic is what protects him. Without her, he's helpless."

"Get rid of Ray-Shy!" Locasta cried. "Of course! Nothing easier! We'll just melt her with a bucket of water, like Dorothy did the Wicked Witch of the West. Quick, someone fetch a bucket of water!"

But Janus shook her head sadly. "That is impossible. We have no water. The captain wouldn't allow it. We have to use sand for everything."

"No water!" Dan cried. "But how do you scrub the deck?"

"With sand," Janus said.

"How do you water the plants?"

"With sand," Mr. Granchio said.

"How do you quench your thirst?" Ozma asked.

"With sand," sighed Mr. Bandersnatch.

"That's ridiculous!" Dan exclaimed.

"Not to mention incredibly cruel!" Ozma added.

"Yes," said Janus. "I admit that washing the deck with sand is very inefficient, but the captain figures it keeps us busy."

"You mean to say there's no water on this ship, not a drop?" cried Jellia, who was feeling thirsty already.

"None," the officers all sighed at once.

"And as this ship always flies over the Deadly Desert, there's no hope of ever getting any," Janus added.

"Well, never mind," Locasta said brightly. "There's more than one way to liquidate a witch."

Everyone brightened in anticipation.

"Darned if I know I what they are, though," she added, and they sank into despair again.

"Well, let's think about it a minute," Sofia said. "How else have witches been killed in the past?"

"The Witch of the East was killed when Dorothy's house fell on her," Ozma said.

"Ah, there we go!" Sofia cried. "Now if we could find a falling house somewhere, direct the ship right underneath it, and...and..."

Sofia became aware that everyone was looking at her funny, and she stopped speaking.

"We all admire your selfless generosity, Sofia, but isn't giving away your brain a bit extreme?" Zsuzsa snarled.

"Well, look, does she have any other vulnerabilities? Is there anything else harmful to her?" Ozma asked.

Chapter Eighteen

"Not that we know of," Mr. Bandersnatch said despairingly, and gently sobbed into his handkerchief.

"I'd like to know why she always carries that umbrella around with her in this desert," Zsuzsa said.

"Unless it's not an umbrella—Maybe she uses it as a parasol," Ozma said.

"Hey, what about her name, 'Ray-Shy'? Does that mean she's afraid of the sun's rays?" asked Judit with a bolt of insight.

"I don't know...I never thought about it before, but perhaps you're right," Janus said.

"Of course she's right—Judit's a genius!" said Sofia.

"Yes—wicked witches' skins are so dry and shriveled as it is," Zsuzsa observed, "that perhaps just a few rays of direct desert sunlight would dehydrate her to death. So what I suggest is that we steal her parasol and—"

"I'm afraid stealing her parasol is impossible," Janus said. "She'd turn you into a salamander in a second."

"Well, couldn't we wait until she's asleep?" Judit asked.

"When Ray-Shy is asleep," Janus said, "her room is guarded by a *flying cat* that can tear a mortal man apart!"

"I'm not a mortal man; I'm an immortal witch," Locasta proclaimed. "And I happen to know of a magic formula that can send any ferocious cat to sleepy-bye-bye-land in sixty seconds."

"Okay, so we put the cat to sleep. Then what?" Mr. Granchio said skeptically. "Her room will still be locked."

"I will sneak in the porthole!" Eric Seagull cried. "I'm small enough to fit, and I can just swoop in, grab the parasol, and swoop out again."

"And what if she wakes up while you're in there?" Janus protested. "And stealing her parasol in the dead of night is no help—she'd be able to use her magical charms to conjure up a new one before dawn."

"We will have to steal it just before dawn," Ozma said.

"She wakes up just before dawn," Mr. Granchio said.

"By George Orwell, I don't care," Eric said. "I am prepared to risk life and wing. Anything for Ozma and Oz!"

"Thank you, Eric." said Sofia, and she gave Eric a hug.

"Ah, shucks." he said.

So early next morning, while everyone else on the ship slept, Nan-Kerr and Eric looked on while Locasta stood in the ship's kitchen with a mortar and pestle mixing her put-a-flying-cat-to-sleep concoction, so that Eric could then use the porthole in the front door to enter Ray-Shy's otherwise windowless cabin.

"Ten burning matches; one cup desert sand," Locasta said as she added the ingredients. "A pinch of sea salt; one teaspoon chalk dust—"

"That's a tablespoon," Nan-Kerr said flatly.

"Oh, of course. How idiotic of me," Locasta said gaily, and fetched the right spoon.

"She's going to blow us all to Snark Island!" Nan-Kerr muttered to herself.

But Locasta successfully mixed the concoction. Just as the very first early morning glow appeared on the eastern horizon, Locasta took the mixture, which was now letting off weird, multicolored sparks like sparklers on the Fourth of July, and with Nan-Kerr and Eric, advanced toward where the flying cat guarded her mistress's cabin.

The cat sat as erect and noble as a cat from ancient Egypt. It was larger than an ordinary cat, about the size of a German Shepherd, and it had white and orange stripes and a pair of white, birdlike wings.

Believing that a courteous introduction was in order, Locasta removed her hat, bowed respectfully, and said, "O Cat."

"Cut the snow job. I'm not gonna let you in," the cat snarled.

"What makes you think I want to go in and see that terrible witch?" Locasta asked.

"You want to destroy her. And I won't let you. I'll tear you to shreds first." And the cat extended her claws and showed her sharp teeth.

Locasta quickly drew the smoking mixture as close as she dared to the cat and wafted the colored steam in the cat's direction.

Chapter Eighteen

"You are getting sleepy," Locasta said in a soothing tone. "Sleeeepy...Sleeeeeeeeepy."

The cat growled and advanced menacingly.

"I don't think you're swaying her with your logic," Nan-Kerr said.

Suddenly, the cat spread her wings and took to the air, swooping like a dive bomber toward Locasta and Nan-Kerr, who ran like crazy.

Eric's first impulse was to go help them, but he figured Locasta's magic would prevail, so he carefully slipped through the porthole and found himself in Ray-Shy's room. She was asleep on a little sofa with her thin legs sticking out into the air. She was hugging the parasol like a teddy bear.

Eric silently inched toward the slumbering witch. Then he carefully climbed up onto her tummy. With nerve-wracking slowness, he grasped the parasol and slid it out of the witch's arms. To his horror, the witch stirred and mumbled in her sleep, but fortunately she did not wake. When Eric had the parasol firmly in the grip of his wings, he inched back to the door.

I'm home free, he thought as he reached the porthole. He was about to slip the parasol through when something suddenly grabbed his tail like a carpenter's clamp. Then he was yanked from the porthole and found himself dangling by his tail from a bony hand, and looking into evil, bloodshot eyes.

"Oh, please! Don't go so soon," Ray-Shy sneered.

Meanwhile, the cat chased after Locasta and Nan-Kerr until they were trapped at the edge of the ship.

"Now there's no place for you to go," the cat snarled as she hovered malevolently over them, "except down to the scorching desert sands below. You really thought you could vanquish Old Ray-Shy?"

"No, no, of course not!" Nan-Kerr cried in a panic.

"Yes, we did!" Locasta cried boldly. "And we still do. Eric Seagull is probably at this moment stealing her parasol."

"What?" said the cat.

"He's stealing the parasol—the only thing protecting her from the rays of the sun that would make her shrivel up like a dry leaf," Locasta said.

"What? You mean you *do* know how to destroy her?" the cat said, now with no trace of malevolence in her voice.

"You sound pleased!" Nan-Kerr said in astonishment.

"Of course I am! You don't think I want to work for that old hag do you?" the cat cried.

"Well, we—" Nan-Kerr began.

"I hate her. She's a monster. I only do this because if I don't she'll turn me into a doodlebug or something," the cat explained. "But if your friend is 'disarming' her—Well, what are we waiting for? Let's help him, as sure as my name is Trudi." And she flew off toward the cabin.

"Don't get me wrong," Ray-Shy hissed as she shook poor Eric by his tail. "I love little birdies...especially with ketchup and mustard."

Just then came a knock at the door.

"Who is it?" Ray-Shy snarled.

"It's Trudi, with two prisoners," the flying cat called.

Ray-Shy went and opened the door. Trudi burst into the room, grabbed Eric with her front paws, snatched the parasol with her tail, and with a "too-dle-oo," sailed out again.

"Traitor!" Ray-Shy screamed. "Come back with my parasol!"

In a rage, she thoughtlessly raced out of her cabin into the very first rays of the rising sun.

"AAAAARRRRGH!" Ray-Shy screamed. "You cursed cat! Look what you've done! The sun's rays! I'm shriveling! I'm crumbling! I'm crumbling! OOOOOHHHHH!"

And that's what she was doing. Her form was crumbling away like a cracker. By the time the crew had emerged from their cabins to find out what all the screaming was about, Ray-Shy had been reduced to a fine powder, and only the button saying "I motivate" remained.

Chapter Eighteen

"The witch is dead!" Locasta proclaimed as she picked up the "I motivate" button and stuck it in her cloak. (For some reason, her magic slate advised her to do so.) Ozma grabbed the Magic Belt and re-fastened it to her slim waist.

"Old Ray-Shy is dead!" Janus cried triumphantly. "Let the mutiny commence!"

The crew cheered and headed to Old Pascalabes' cabin. They banged on the door with forks, ladles, and other objects. The door finally creaked open and revealed a sleepy pajama-and-bunny-slipper-clad captain.

"What do you want?" Pascalabes yawned. "Reveille *is* at 4:00 A.M., but I get to sleep 'til noon."

"Not anymore, you don't," Mr. Granchio cried.

"Seize him!" Janus commanded her crew. "To the plank with him!"

The crew surrounded the captain and tied his hands behind his back.

"What are you doing?" Pascalabes cried in terror.

"Retiring you," Mr. Bandersnatch explained.

"Ms. Typus is our captain now," a fairy-sailor said.

"We don't like you," another added.

"You fools!" Pascalabes threatened. "You'll all be punished for this mutiny!"

"By whom?" Zsuzsa taunted.

"Old Ray-Shy! She'll protect me."

"Old Ray-Shy is dead. You haven't a friend in the world, buster," said Jellia.

Pointing sharp swords at him, the crew directed Pascalabes out onto the deck and toward the plank. Eric and Trudi circled tauntingly over the evil pirate's head and Pascalabes himself was sobbing for his mommy.

When they reached the plank, Janus vengefully touched the ex-captain's chin with the sharp point of her sword and said, "Walk!"

Sorrowfully, Pascalabes climbed onto the plank and began to walk it, to the elated cheers of the crew. Janus prodded him on with her sword, and when Pascalabes reached the edge, he hesitated and looked down at the scorching, deadly sands below. He whimpered.

"Come on, come on, we haven't all day," Janus demanded, shaking her sword aggressively. "One more step for you, and all of our problems will be gone!"

"Please, please!" Pascalabes sobbed. "Have mercy on me! I'm too young to die! I have a wife and kids and a doggie!"

"You should have thought of that before you treated us so bad," Mr. Granchio said.

"Come on now, captain," Janus snarled. "One more step."

"No!" cried a voice.

They all looked and saw that it was Ozma who had spoken.

"Old Pascalabes may have been cruel to you all, but that does not justify our being cruel to him in return," Ozma said.

"It doesn't?" Zsuzsa cried.

"Ozma is right," Sofia said. "He deserves to be punished for his wrongdoing, but not in a brutal way."

with apologies to N. C. Wyeth

"Instead of frying him in the sands of the Deadly Desert, why don't we just cast him adrift in an open sand boat and let him wander the desert forever—alive but alone?" Judit suggested.

"That's a terrific idea!" Janus cried. "All right, mates, prepare the lifeboat."

So they dumped Old Pascalabes in one of the lifeboats and lowered it down onto the searing desert sands. As the new captain, Janus, started to steer the *Able* away, leaving Old Pascalabes there in the endless wasteland, Pascalabes shouted up to the ship. Though his words were lost in the noise of the crew's celebration, he cried, "Cast me in an open sand boat, would ya, nearly fifty miles from Im's port of call, doomed to my fate, and without so much as my teddy bear and my *Cheers* tapes for company? Well, you ungrateful fools, Forg will find out what you've done, and he'll get you. I'll see you all hanging from the highest crab apple tree in Whaqoland for this!"

The Riddles of the Sfinks

LATER that day, Janus, now captain of the *Able,* recorded in the ship's log:

> *Let it be known on this day that Lieutenant Janus Rhincodon Typus did forcibly relieve Captain Joshua Ahmed Pascalabes of his command of the SS Able, and that the witch Old Ray-Shy was turned to dust by means of the courageous intervention of Locasta the Good Witch of Northern Oz, Eric Seagull, and Trudi the Flying Cat. Let it be further known that the crew of the Able, now liberated from the tyrannical slavery of Old Pascalabes, are now committed to an expedition to the Land of Im for the purpose of liberating Ozma's cousin Gyma and subjugating the evil demons and witches of Whaqoland.*

As the ship glided towards Im, everyone celebrated their freedom from Pascalabes. At dinner that evening, Ozma, Locasta, Jellia, and the others happily talked over the events of the day. Dan listened unhappily. He was dying to talk with Ozma—alone. Locasta had advised him to talk to her about what pleased him most—computers—but his shyness seemed insurmountable. And it seemed absurd to him that a kind and gentle Fairy Princess like her could possibly feel any warmth toward a clumsy, awkward mortal commoner named "Dan." He could imagine the abject horror that the very idea would strike into the hearts of many who loved Ozma dearly. And yet he could not totally dismiss the thought that just perhaps his affection toward Ozma was not futile, and that he was just sitting there like a dolt and doing nothing about it...

The conversation reached a quiet lull, and Dan seized the moment.

"Ozma?" Dan said, in a voice that obliged him by coming out high and squeaky.

"Ahem!" he firmly and decidedly cleared his throat and tried again.

"Ozma?" he said huskily.

"Yes, Danny?"

She gazed at him with her bewitching eyes. The others were looking at him too...looking rather like a firing squad he thought.

"N—n—nothing."

Ozma turned back to ask Jellia for another amusing anecdote, but her loyal maid whispered to her in a playful, sing-song voice, with a nod toward Dan, "He li-i-i-ikes you!"

Meanwhile, Dan glanced at Locasta in despair. The little witch smiled back, as if to say, "You'll get another chance, my boy—And you'll do it this time."

Dan nodded confidently and turned to Ozma.

"Well, I guess it's getting late," she stated before he could speak. "Shall we turn in?"

"Yes...er, but first...c–c–could I speak to you in private?" he said, struggling to suppress his bashful stammering.

"Certainly. Meet me on the bridge at 10:00 P.M. sharp."

Dan's heart beat like a tribal drum, and he scampered off to his cabin to prepare for the tête-à-tête.

Chapter Nineteen

When he came onto the bridge at ten, dressed in a striking green suit that one of the fairy sailors had loaned him, he beheld in the soft moonlight a slender, feminine figure dressed in a long, silky, strapless gown of blue (Dan's favorite color).

"Hi, Danny," the figure said sweetly.

"Er...um...hi."

"You really look nice."

"So do you."

"So—was there some important point in the affairs of state you wished to discuss? Or am I right in assuming that you mean for this to be our first date?"

"Well—I—I—That is—I—er, I—" Dan stammered.

Ozma giggled. "You cutie! Let's take a walk together. It's a beautiful night."

"You—you mean—You really want to take a walk...with just me?"

"Just you." And Ozma linked her arm in his and they took a promenade around the deck of the ship.

"Beautiful night, isn't it?" said Ozma.

"Yes," Dan agreed, as he gazed up at the three moons. (Two of the moons are fairy moons, and are invisible from the Collective Hunch.) Literally thousands of stars brilliantly sparkled in Baumgea's light-pollution-free skies.

"Listen, Ozma..." said Dan nervously. "I've gotta be open and honest with you. When I was a kid reading the Oz books, I fell in love with you... you were so sweet and kind and beautiful...and now to find out that you're a real person and not just an ideal conceived by L.Frank Baum and John Neill, it has just overwhelmed me. But I know I have no chance...I'm little more than a boring computer geek."

"You are not boring, and you are not a 'geek,' whatever that means," Ozma said emphatically. "Your love of computers is something to be proud of. And I find them fascinating, even though I know nothing about them."

"You do?" Dan cried. "Most girls make for the hills when I tell them I like computers."

"I don't see why—Of course, as I say, I know so little about them... What are computers for?"

This was such a simple, straightforward question that Dan was stymied by it.

"Er, well—" he began. "They're for—they're for—"

"Yes?" said Ozma encouragingly.

Dan thought a moment. He knew how some other computer people would answer Ozma's innocent query: "What a stupid question"... "Were you brought up in a cave?"... "Get this technophobe out of here."... "That's the sort of naive, down-to-earth question that women always ask."

To which us men frequently have no answer, Dan thought with a little smile. He had always been angered by the impatience and condescending attitude computer "experts" frequently had toward novices (especially women novices), and he had always vowed that if he ever had the opportunity to share his knowledge of computers with someone who knew nothing about them, he would treat them with the respect they deserved and give intelligent answers to their questions, which were never stupid.

So Dan thought for a moment, then replied. "Well, they were invented to do mathematical calculations, but then they were applied to other things, like writing and drawing."

"You can write with a computer?"

"Oh yes... And it's so great because you just click the mouse and erase errors or move text around or anything."

"That sounds wonderful!"

"Of course what I really want to do is programming...Knowing how to program a computer is like knowing how to fix your own car, you know?"

Ozma looked blank.

"Or...," Dan tried to think of something relevant to Oz. "It's like being able to perform magic. I know it probably sounds silly to you."

"Not at all."

"It's so hard to explain... Oh, if only I had a computer of my own so I could show you myself!"

"Well, maybe you could—When things have quieted down a bit, I'll bring a computer here for you with the Magic Belt."

Chapter Nineteen

"Could you?"

"The Magic Belt is smart about summoning just what I want."

"Obviously it doesn't run under Windows."

"What?" The joke was of course lost on her.

"Nothing. But you mean you'd really like me to show you about computers?"

"Indeed I do—What is important to you is important to *me*, too," Ozma said with sincere emphasis, so that Dan dared to believe that she really meant it and was not just humoring him.In a joyous burst of gratitude and of impulsiveness that he never knew he had, he leaned over gave the Queen of Oz a *very light* peck on the cheek.

He waited to see if she would slap him and call him a vulgar, sex-crazed bull moose. But she didn't; she only smiled. Dan smiled back—an innocent, endearingly goofy sort of smile that sweet-natured young men get at that wonderful moment when finally their gentle and innocent love is appreciated and *returned.*

They walked some more along the ship's deck and talked and laughed.

Just as Dan was elated to find that Ozma was interested in computers, she was delighted to find that Dan shared many of *her* interests—art, nature, Jane Austen, and other things. They had a lot in common.

They parted at Dan's cabin and he retired to with new hope in his lonely heart. He had friends now. He was living in Fairyland, forever out of the reach of those who had hurt him for most of his life, and he was actually making headway in his relationship with a beautiful girl. His life was turning around for the better with such rapidity that it made his head spin.

He soon nodded off into the most peaceful sleep he'd had in years.

His dreams that night of running along the sunny beach hand-and-hand with Ozma were rudely interrupted by a voice whispering, "Wake up, Dan! It's morning."

"Mmmmmm?"

"Wake up, Dan." Jellia urged.

"Errrrmmmmm. Go away," Dan mumbled with mindless drowsiness, and stuffed his head under his pillow.

"Dan," Jellia whispered in his ear with a mischievous twinkle in her big, dark eyes, "Ozma is at the foot of your bed taking her clothes off!"

Dan bolted upright and saw only Jellia, laughing hysterically.

"You devilish scamp!" cried Dan, gently tossing the pillow at her and joining in her mirth in spite of himself.

"I'm, sorry—I couldn't resist," she said presently when she had collected herself. "You're really nuts about her, aren't you?"

"What makes you say that?" Dan said innocently.

"Oh, just something about the way you keep looking at her with those longing eyes," said Jellia. "I know just how you feel, too, believe me. I may be a maid, but I have suffered love too."

"I'm sorry," said Dan. "I hate to think that you've suffered."

"You and Ozma have a lot in common," Jellia observed with a smile. "You're both gentle and quiet in temperament. I think I'd like to see you married to Milady."

Dan's heart skipped a beat. He hadn't dared imagine that much felicity.

"Of course Milady is not one to make rash decisions or to rush into anything—I'd say you have an excellent chance, but it'll take time. Many suitors come seeking Ozma's hand, and who knows who might show up filled with an ardent will to win Ozma's love and devotion?"

Dan sighed dismally at this prospect, so she added hastily, "But I'm sure you will prove to be the kind, gentle man she wants in the end, or my name isn't Jellia Jamb. Ozma will marry you; I know she will. And if she doesn't, *I'll* marry you."

"Let's face it—We're both good people and we'll both find someone worthy of us."

"That's the spirit, Dan. And no matter what happens, you and I must be good friends and confidants—always."

"Of course!" And he took Jellia's hand and softly kissed it.

"Oh gosh," she blushed.

Chapter Nineteen

After breakfast, Ozma announced her strategy. "At Locasta's recommendation, she, the Adepts, and Danny will see to the rescue of my cousin, while Jellia, Nan-Kerr, and I protect the fairies onboard the ship."

"You're staying here?" said Dan.

"I feel I must. The special Evil Detector on my Magic Belt is picking up strong waves of hate and malice emanating from Whaqoland. I'm certain that they'll try to avenge Pascalabes, and I feel I must stand guard if they do."

"Don't worry, Danny," said Sofia, totally misinterpreting his reluctance to be separated from Ozma. "I'm sure we can rescue Gyma ourselves. The death of Ray-Shy nullified her magic neutralizing powder, so we have our powers back. And our powers are quite substantial, you know."

"He knows that," Zsuzsa remonstrated, and whispered, "Don't you know a would-be Romeo when you see one?"

"How will you ever get into Im, though?" said Eric Seagull. "Im is surrounded by a magic-proof barrier."

"And the main gate into the kingdom is guarded by ferocious monster," Trudi added as she groomed her wings with her whiskers.

"Don't worry. My magic will protect us," Locasta assured them.

"Whoopee. Just the sort of ultra-heavy-duty sorcery you're going to need," Nan-Kerr said sarcastically.

"Locasta's more powerful than you think," said Dan in defense of his friend.

"Thank you, my boy," said Locasta. "After all, I do know the Magic of Everything."

"And no one dares hurt anyone who has received your magic kiss," added Sofia.

The *Able* swept over the border of Im and landed in front of the grand gates leading into the country. The Adepts, Dan, and Locasta climbed out of the ship and faced the "gates" to Im, which were, in fact, a pair of ordinary-looking double doors, on which hung a sign:

WELCOME TO THE LAND OF IM
NOW GO HOME

"Is everyone in Im that hostile?" Dan asked, knocking on the door.

"Who is it?" sang a sweet-sounding voice from the other side of the door.

"Locasta and company."

"Just a minute while I...EAT YOU!" The voice turned suddenly deep and gruff, and between them and the door suddenly materialized a hideous monster. It had a bulky body with heavy, pillar-like legs and long, sharp claws. It had a crocodile-like head, and on its back and lizard-like tail were rows of tall, dark whachamacallits.

"Allow me to introduce myself," snarled the monster. "I'm the Sfinks of the Gate of Im."

"You don't look like a sphinx to me," Zsuzsa said boldly.

"I am not a sphinx!" the creature said indignantly. "I'm a Sfinks, with an *f*. And you presume to pass me and enter the Land of Im, do you?"

"Yes," said Locasta firmly.

"Well, I'm guard of the gates," the Sfinks said, "and it's my job to see that you don't get in. So hold still please while I rip you limb from limb—"

"We are among the most powerful sorceresses in all of Baumgea," Sofia asserted, "and if you attempt to harm us, we'll...we'll...turn you into an acorn....or something...whatever...I'm scattered this morning. Those hard ship bunks, you know."

"We shall use elaborate and subtle quantum-fluctuation sorcery to create anomalies in space-time to circumvent any implacable impediments to ingress and egress sustained by the local matter field," Judit stated.

"Exactly," said Sofia blankly.

"Sorry, no sorcery can penetrate my special mechanisms for protecting Im from unauthorized entry," the Sfinks taunted.

"You're the only one who can open the doors?" said Dan.

"Of course," said the monster, and laughed sadistically. "There's no way for you to get into Im...unless you can solve my three riddles."

"Riddles?" they echoed.

"A man!" Dan cried out.

"What?" the Sfinks snapped.

Chapter Nineteen

"A man. That's what has four legs in the morning, two legs at noon, and three legs in the evening," said Dan.

"That was the sphinx's riddle; I am the Sfinks!" the creature roared.

"Oh yes—Sfinks with an *f*—I forgot," said Dan meekly.

"And my riddles are much more difficult!" the Sfinks assured them.

"We're not afraid of a challenge," Locasta proclaimed.

"Oh," said the Sfinks, disappointed. "Well, the rules are these: If you answer each of my three riddles correctly, I will let you enter the country."

"And if we don't?" asked Zsuzsa.

"If you don't—" the Sfinks began ominously, then asked sharply, "Did you say you were sorceresses?"

"Yes—and those that aren't are immune to bodily damage on account of Locasta's magic kisses," Dan said.

"Then I'll only be able to hurl you back whence you came," the Sfinks said sadly, then brightened. "But maybe your magic will fail and you'll tumble into the sand dunes of the Deadly Desert and you'll all burn up!"

They trembled in anxiety as the Sfinks laughed fiendishly.

"Now listen carefully; this is your first riddle," said the Sfinks with a nasty leer. "I'll be a nice guy and start you off with an easy one: A train started off in New York with eight passengers. At Albany, four got off and one got on; at Boulder, three got off and two got on; at Charlotte, five got off—"

"That leaves minus one passenger," Judit observed.

"Five got off," growled the Sfinks, obviously not wanting to be interrupted, "and six got on. At Dallas—"

"It's an awfully roundabout route so far," Sofia remarked.

"At Dallas," snapped the Sfinks, "one got off and three got on; at Eureka, five got off and five got on; at Fiji Islands—"

"That's not in the United States," Dan remarked.

"Who said it was?" snapped the Sfinks. "At Fiji—"

"Presumably the train could do the backstroke," Zsuzsa observed.

"At Fiji Islands," the Sfinks snarled malevolently, "one got off and three got on. At Greenville—"

"Which one?" Dan asked. "I think there are several."

"At Greenville," hissed the Sfinks, "six got off and nobody got on. At Hartford, four got on and two got off; at Independence, ten got on and seven got off; at Jacksonville, twelve got on and six got off; at Khartoum—"

"There's no such place!" Zsuzsa cried.

The Sfinks gave her a withering look.

"Er, well, this is—I never heard of it before," she said nervously. "But then you...uh...don't hear of a place, do you, until you...er...hear of it..."

"At Khartoum," snarled the Sfinks, "three got on and four got off; at Louisville, one got on and two got off; at Manchester, five got on and one got off; then the train arrived back at the terminal in New York—"

"Ha!" cried Judit. "That wasn't so hard. Sixteen passengers left on the train."

"That's not the question!" roared the Sfinks.

Chapter Nineteen

"Oh."

"The question is this: How many stops were there in all?"

They exchanged nervous glances.

"But that's not fair!" Sofia protested.

"We weren't keeping track of *that!*" added Zsuzsa.

"Oh, weren't you?" the Sfinks sneered triumphantly.

The sneering turned out to be premature, however, for a moment later Locasta, who had been considering the matter, asked, "Do you count the terminal in New York as a stop?"

"No," said the Sfinks soberly.

"Thirteen!" Locasta exclaimed.

"That's correct," admitted the crestfallen Sfinks, but then added, "But that might have been a lucky guess. Can you tell me how you got that answer?"

"Certainly," Locasta said. "I admit I didn't count the stops, any more than the others, but I noticed that the names of the places where the stops were all started with a subsequent letter of the alphabet: Albany was *A,* Boulder was *B,* Charlotte was *C,* and so on. The last stop before arriving back at the terminal in New York was Manchester with an *M. M* is the thirteenth letter of the alphabet; therefore there were thirteen stops."

"Hooray!" Sofia cheered exuberantly.

"All right!" the Sfinks growled, repressing a tantrum. "But that was just the first riddle; two more remain. Now listen to the second: I know of a magical place which spins around in circles, and is the meeting place for many lines. If you are there, no matter which way you walk, you will be walking in the same direction. And this place is located in a country with no cities, towns, streets, or even a flag or a national anthem. What is this place?"

Everyone's faces clouded.

"Don't know it, do ya?" leered the Sfinks.

"I've got it!" Locasta cried. "The South Pole!"

The Sfinks flinched. Its tall, dark whachamacallits became malevolently erect. "May I inquire how you arrived at that?" it hissed.

"Delighted," said Locasta. "The earth always spins around its axis, which lies at the poles, so the South Pole is always spinning. On a globe of the world, the vertical lines, the lines of longitude, intersect or 'meet,' as you say, at the South Pole. And since the South Pole is the very southernmost point on the earth, any direction you walk from that one point will take you north. Everything I've just said also applies to the North Pole, but then you said that it lies in a country with no cities, towns, streets, flag or national anthem. Only one country in the world meets that description—Antarctica."

"Brilliant!" Dan cried.

"That is also correct," admitted the Sfinks. "But there is still one more riddle to go, and no one has ever answered this one right." (Actually, some people had, but the Sfinks just wanted to scare them.)

"Now listen," the Sfinks continued. "An owl was soaring over an open field, searching for a bat who was wanted by the police."

"Why was a bat—?" Dan began.

"Don't interrupt!" snapped the Sfinks. "Now I have to start all over again! An owl was soaring over an open field, searching for a bat who was wanted by the police. The bat was completely black and there was no—"

"Aaaachoo!"

"Bless you, Dan," Locasta said.

"Gazoondyke," said the Sfinks through its teeth.

"Thank you."

"An owl was soaring over an open field, searching for a bat who was wanted by the police," the Sfinks repeated. "The bat was completely black and there was no moon, no stars, and no artificial light of any kind. Yet the owl was able to easily see the bat and catch him. How was this possible?"

There was a tense pause.

"Er...could we have a private conference to discuss this one?" Zsuzsa asked nervously.

"Of course," the Sfinks said, confident of his victory. "You have sixty seconds."

They all quickly huddled in a circle, as in football, and discussed this final riddle.

Chapter Nineteen

"What do you think? How could an owl see a black bat in complete darkness?" said Dan.

"Owls have acute hearing," Judit observed. "Maybe the owl heard the bat."

"Yes, but he definitely said—" Dan paused and looked over his shoulder at the Sfinks and verified: "You did most definitely say, in no uncertain terms, that the owl could see the bat, didn't you?"

The Sfinks nodded. "You have forty seconds left," he said smugly.

"Don't some owls have night vision?" Zsuzsa said. "Can't they see in ultraviolet light or something?"

"That's true. Did the owl have night vision?" Sofia asked.

"No, he was entirely stricken with night blindness," said the Sfinks smugly, and added, "You have twenty seconds. Nineteen, eighteen..."

"All right, all right; wait a minute!" Dan cried, racking his brains.

"Seventeen, sixteen..."

"No night vision, no moon, no stars, no artificial light!" Zsuzsa cried despairingly. "There's no way he could see the bat!"

"Fourteen, thirteen..."

"Don't despair," said Judit gently. "Remember what they taught us at Fairyland High: 'Never assume.'"

"Seven, six, five..."

"Well, the only thing we're assuming is—" Dan stopped, and a smile came to his face. He whispered four words in Locasta's ear.

"That's it! Thank you, my dear. I love you to pieces!" Locasta cried, and gave Dan an enormous kiss.

"Oh, Mister Sfinks..." she sang.

"Yes? Do you have a last request before I hurtle you to your doom?"

"Let me just recap the riddle," said Locasta. "'An owl was soaring over an open field, searching for a bat who was wanted by the police.' Okay so far?"

"Verbatim," the Sfinks said.

"'The bat was completely black and there was no moon, no stars, no artificial lights, and the owl had night-blindness. Yet the owl was able to easily see the bat and catch him. How was this possible?'"

"That's the riddle, and I'm deeply sorry you found it too much to handle," the Sfinks cried triumphantly. "And I assure you that your destruction will be swift and—"

"The owl was able to see the bat," Locasta said slowly, "because—it was broad daylight!"

The Sfinks turned purple with rage. It viciously rolled and unrolled its tail and the tall, dark whachamacallits quivered in fury.

"Although that question was wholly unfair," said Locasta. "I don't think owls can see in the daylight. But then as my granddaughter rightfully said, 'Never assume.' I say, is something wrong?"

The Sfinks was beside itself. It let out a scream of rage and, with a great leap of its strong, pillar-like legs, it shot up into the sky like a rocket, and that was the last they saw of it.

"And Judit; she didn't assume!" cried Dan, and hugged her.—"Oh, I'm sorry!" he said, feeling that he may have been presumptuous.

"No, we here in Baumgea prefer hugs to bombs and machine guns," Judit observed, and all Three Adepts embraced Dan.

Suddenly a fanfare trumpeted from an unknown source, and the doors into the Land of Im swung slowly open.

King Graytfyl

THEY walked down the path that extended through the little country of Im until they came to a medieval-looking castle surrounded by a moat. At the bank of the moat was a string-operated bell with a sign that said:

PLEASE RING BELL FOR ADMITTANCE
(IF THIS SIGN IS NOT HERE, PLEASE KNOCK)

"This must be the place," Judit said, and rang the bell.

After a minute, a drawbridge descended and slowly laid itself across the moat. Then two figures emerged, one a young man with brown, unkempt hair, and the other a young woman with black, unkempt hair. They were both dressed in chef's uniforms.

"Welcome to King Graytfyl's castle," said the man. "I am Jay, and this is Bernadette. We're the king's two chefs."

"We're also the butlers, the footmen, the housekeepers, the chauffeurs, the gardeners, the jailers, the night watchmen, and the VCR programmers," Bernadette said. "But chefs is our chief employment."

"Oh, really? I thought programming the VCR was," said Jay, astonished.

"Won't you step this way?" Bernadette said, beckoning them to cross the bridge and enter.

They stepped across the bridge and the chefs led them into the castle. They went down a long corridor and then they reached the throne room.

King Graytfyl was seated on his throne reading a comic book. In the throne next to him was his wife, Queen Hungrie, who was eating a large pie while her ladies-in-waiting, Lady Shannon and Lady Cassie, were combing her royal hair and filing her royal nails. Seated at a desk across the room was Andrea Seymour, the King's prime minister. Various courtiers were also in the room, standing around looking important.

"Hey, King." cried Jay as they entered the throne room.

"Call me 'your majesty'!" demanded the King, for apparently the five hundredth time.

"Sorry, we'll try to remember next time, King," Jay said.

"King," Bernadette announced, "may I present the Good Witch Locasta, the Three Adepts at Sorcery, and Daniel Maryk of the Land of E Pluribus Unum."

"No, you may not present them!" the King snapped. "I am engaged in urgent business." And he went back to his comic book.

"Locasta? The famous Good Witch of Oz?" Andrea stood and came forward and shook her hand. "This is an honor, your honor...er...your grace... uh...excellency...er...that is—"

"Just 'Locasta' is fine," she smiled.

"Rex, this is Locasta of Oz," Andrea said to the King.

"Rex?" said Dan. "I thought his name was Graytfyl."

"That's my full name—King Rex Graytfyl," said the king, not looking up from *The Fantastic Glob Man.*

"Rex," said Andrea, "these are emissaries from Oz, and I really think that we should give them an audience."

THE
MAN

"Go ahead; I'm all ears," said King Rex Graytfyl, his mind currently focused on pulling apart two pages that had stuck together.

"Please sit down," the queen said through a mouthful of blueberries.

"Thank you," said Judit in an authoritative tone as they sat on a large silk sofa. "Your majesties, Prime Minister Andrea, courtiers of Im: As you all probably know, our ruler is Princess Ozma, whose parents were Queen Lurline of Burzee and King Pastoria II of Oz. Pastoria had an uncle Ozeme who married a baroness in Ev named Evina. They had two daughters and three sons, one of whom, Ovez, moved east and served in the court of Queen Zixi of Ix until he married Zixi's great grand-niece Gymella, who was the maternal great-granddaughter of Zixi's third cousin Ixixa, who had substantial fairy blood on account of being a descendant of a renegade member of Lurline's band who had married a nobleman of Mo, one of whose children went on to marry the Rose King, and founded the lineage that gave rise to Ozma's other cousins Ozga and Ozana, four times removed. And so it is Ovez and Gymella's daughter who, upon coming of age, traveled to Op and became the Caretaker of the Dinosaurs, and it is by this lineage that she is the cousin of our queen."

There was a pause.

"Er...do you think we could have a diagram?" said a perplexed Queen Hungrie.

"Yes, thank you, Judit—I couldn't have explained it more incoherently myself," said Zsuzsa.

"May one ask what your point is?" the king said, as he cut out the comic book ad for a free with $20.00 user fee authentic imitation Tottenhot arrowhead.

"The point is," said Locasta, "that Ozma's cousin Gyma ruled Op benevolently for years until she was kidnapped and brought here and made a prisoner."

"No, no, not a prisoner! She's a guest," King Graytfyl said, drawing from his vast arsenal of deceptive euphemisms.

"Well, whatever she is, we wish to see her," Zsuzsa insisted. "You have no right to keep her from us."

Chapter Twenty

"Ah, I see," said King Graytfyl, smiling cordially. "Your situation is now quite clear."

There was a pause.

"Well?" said Judit.

"I'm glad you could stop by," King Graytfyl said. "Good-bye, and don't slam the drawbridge on your way out."

"Look, Rex, what's the problem?" Andrea said. "Why can't these good Oz people see Ozma's cousin?"

"Gyma is a major celebrity and she never lets her fans meet her," King Graytfyl snapped.

"You talk about Gyma as though she were a folk singer turned rock singer turned Gilbert and Sullivan singer turned Gershwin singer turned opera singer turned Spanish singer!" Sofia cried.

"Whatever," grumbled the king as he eyed her suspiciously.

"Could you say that again?" the queen asked, and in doing so inadvertently spit pickle relish in her face.

"Now you listen here," said Zsuzsa irately. "You are holding Gyma captive, and we demand that you release her. Now!"

"Who are you to order me about?" snarled King Graytfyl ominously,

"Emissaries from Oz," Andrea asserted.

"Oz is of no concern to us," the king said coldly. "We are a neutral state."

"But the demons and witches of Whaqoland present a dire threat to the whole of Baumgea—including here!" Dan cried. "They are cruel, vicious monsters."

"Of course they're planning to invade me. Everyone is always trying to invade me. I'm surrounded by enemies," the king stated, and added, like a scientist a little too confident of his theories, "but the magic-proof wall surrounding my kingdom will protect me. It is made of the strongest magic in the universe, I kid you not."

"Come on, Rex, let's help these guys," said Andrea. "Besides, I've been meaning to ask you about Gyma—I haven't seen her for some time, and she's been here quite a while to be a 'guest.'"

"She staying in the guest room," the king explained.

"The upstairs guest room is vacant," Andrea observed.

"Gyma is in the *downstairs* guest room," the king hissed malevolently. "Perhaps you'd like to join her?"

"Look, I don't understand what's going on, but we're not leaving here until you help us," said Judit.

"Well, I'm not ever going to help you," the king stated, "which must mean that you will stay here for good..." The king's face brightened. "Which must mean that I'm going to make you my personal guests, too—in my dungeon!"

"Brilliant reasoning, Rex," Andrea said acidly.

"Now, wait just a minute," Queen Hungrie cried, swallowing and speaking out at last. "Oz is known for its beauty; its good, jolly people; its pristine environment—"

"You mean we could sell them some pollution?" the king said eagerly.

"We have an obligation to help these people!"

"We certainly do," Shannon concurred.

"And we shall fight those vile demons," the chefs added.

"Yes—call out the Imian army at once!" Cassie cried, patriotically waving her nail file in the air.

"Okay, that settles it," said Andrea. "Good people of Oz, we will help you. So chefs, fetch Gyma here at once."

"How dare you contradict me!" snapped the king.

"You're an idiot, that's how we dare," Andrea growled. "Rex, we can't let Gyma—"

"Will you all stop talking back to me! Isn't there anyone in this kingdom who is loyal to me?" the king cried.

"We're loyal to you," Shannon and Cassie said. "We just don't happen to agree with you."

"Chefs, will you please go down at once and—"

"SILENCE!" boomed the king. Everyone froze.

"Who has the last word in this realm?" the king snapped.

"You do," said the queen meekly.

"Whose word is law?"

"Yours," Andrea bitterly snarled.

"What is the Golden Rule of Imian Loyalty?"

Chapter Twenty

"Agreement with the king," Cassie growled.

"'My tyrannical totalitarian regime, right or wrong,'" Shannon snapped.

"That is correct. Chefs, take the prisoners to dungeon number three," the king commanded.

"Who, us?" Sofia cried.

"No, the Greek statues in the garden," snarled Zsuzsa.

"Yes, you!" the King told the Ozites. "And don't even think about escaping; Im's Dungeon is totally magic-proof and no one ever escapes from it and lives to tell the tale, I kid you not. Chefs, take these fools away at once."

"Yes, your majesty," hissed Jay bitterly, and before Locasta or the Adepts could "make some magic," the chefs had bound them in magic-proof ropes (similar to those of the Whaqolanders). As they reluctantly dragged them off to the dungeon, the king congenially waved bye-bye.

The Underground Passage

THE chefs sadly dragged them down 77 dark and moldy flights of stairs and dumped them into a dark, hard, wet cell and shut the heavy metallic door on them with a thud.

"Oh, now what will become of us?" Sofia cried, on the verge of tears.

"Don't worry," said Zszusa, barely able to conceal her anger at the King of Im. "We'll think of something."

"Of course we will!" Locasta exclaimed. "Chin up! Put on a happy face! We may be bound up, but I still happen to have a few verbal spells up my sleeve."

"Actually, you can't have something verbal up your sleeve; you can only have it down your throat," Judit explained. "Unless, of course, you had a tape recorder hidden in your sleeve or—"

"Thank you, professor," growled Zsuzsa.

"Now I'll show you what words alone can do," Locasta proclaimed. "Humuhumunukunukuapuaa!"

Chapter Twenty-one

Immediately, the room shrunk to half its size, squeezing everyone up very close.

"Oh dear!" she lamented. "I sure got that one wrong. Maybe it was—"

"Never mind, Grandmama," Judit said patiently. "Let's leave things as they are."

"Yes, lest your next incantation materializes a herd of stampeding elephants," Zsuzsa muttered, and got an elbow jog from Judit.

"Well, I always believe in looking on the bright side," said Sofia.

"And what bright side would that be?" Zsuzsa asked.

"Prisons are good places for wholesome spiritual meditation."

"Okay, High Lama—meditate us out of here."

"I wish your slate would help us," Dan said to Locasta. "Now would be a perfect time for it."

Locasta took out her magic slate. It was blank.

"What should we do? Tell us! Tell us!" Zsuzsa cried.

The slate remained blank.

"What's the matter, cat got your chalk?"

"Danny, I'm really sorry about all this," Judit said sadly. "If my sisters and I had known all this was going to happen, we would have left you in Los Angeles and kept you safe and out of it."

"Are you kidding?" Dan cried passionately. "My life was miserable there! I was so sad and lonely, I couldn't take much more. And I wouldn't have wanted you to suffer while I was 'safe.' You're my dearest friends, and I'm so grateful to you! I want to be with you and helping you all I can. I wouldn't leave you if I was offered riches and a happy life forever. You all are who I care about, and I'm sticking with you whatever the consequences. All for one and one for all!"

"Your devotion is touching but unhelpful," Zsuzsa remarked, and got another jog from Judit.

"You are a very good person," Judit said to Dan, "and I promise you that, if we ever get out of this, you will have a rich and happy life forever, as much as it is in my power to bestow it on you."

"And in my power as well!" Locasta added emphatically.

"And mine...and Zsuzsa's too, I'm sure. Her bark is worse than her bite," Sofia observed.

"Ha!" snorted Zsuzsa, but mentally she concurred with her sisters.

Dan smiled gratefully. "For the first time in my life I have friends, and that makes this the happiest day of my life."

"We're imprisoned in a dark, cold dungeon, facing a grim future and very likely certain death and he's giving us a Polyanna routine," Zsuzsa grumbled.

"Hey, look! Danny's ropes are broken!" Judit suddenly cried.

"You're right—I'm free! But how?"

"I used telepathic magic to undo your Gordian Knots. I told you meditation would do it!" said Sofia triumphantly.

"Hooray for Sofia!" Dan cried triumphantly, and taking a jackknife from his satchel, he proceeded to sever the magic-proof ropes binding his companions.

"There's that hurdle overcome. Now how do we get out of this cramped cell?"

The words were hardly out of Zsuzsa's mouth when Judit cried out with joy. Her keen eyes had spotted that one of the ugly black stones in the wall was not quite flush with the rest. With all his strength, Dan pushed against the stone until it finally gave way and fell to the ground. As Judit suspected, this stone was apparently a secret switch of some kind ("Evil lands such as this are just wrought with hoary clichés," she explained), for then one whole wall of the dungeon cell swung open like double doors revealing a long, dark passageway. A voice from somewhere said pleasantly, "Please enjoy your day in this dungeon."

"Well, come on, everyone. Best foot forward!" Locasta proclaimed.

"Wait, everyone," Zsuzsa cautioned. "It might be a trap...I'll go last."

Slowly and carefully, Locasta led them into the dark, cold, damp passageway.

"What exactly are we looking for?" Zsuzsa asked.

"The nearest exit," her grandmama said.

"Yes, I know that," Zsuzsa said. "But my questions is, would we know one if we saw one?"

Chapter Twenty-one

"Well, we came into this dungeon, so there must be a way to go out," Sofia observed.

"Don't be too sure," said Zsuzsa. "I keeping think about what Old Pascalabes said about the 'superlatively terrible and horrible fate' that awaited those trapped in Graytfyl's dungeon."

"Oh, don't be so pessimistic," Sofia told her.

They turned a corner and saw something that made them halt in horror. It was a hideous, dragon-like monster with two heads, armed with long, sharp teeth curved like a scimitar.

"Where did that come from?" cried Dan.

"What the hippikaloric is it?" Sofia gasped.

"Well, I'm just making an off-the-wall, stab-in-the-dark wild guess," said Zsuzsa in a weak voice, "but I think that it just might be a Superlatively Terrible and Horrible Fate!"

The monster regarded the company and snorted, releasing a smelly steam from its nostrils.

"Do you think it's safe?" asked Dan.

"Oh yes, *it's* quite safe," Zsuzsa observed. "It's just *us* who are in trouble!"

Both heads of the monster drooled visibly, and then the left head said to them cordially, "Hello, tasty dinner."

"Who, us?" Zsuzsa stammered.

The right head looked straight at her and said, "Yes, you. And you look especially plump and juicy."

Zsuzsa shook like a ringing alarm clock. The beast's heads then scrutinized the rest of the group, and decided that they were all delectable looking morsels.

"What do you think, Thom? Which one should we eat first?" said the left head to the right.

"We could lash out at them at random, Chris," the right head suggested.

"Good. I love mindless and senseless violence."

"Me too."

The party made an impulsive move to skedaddle, but the monster swung its massive tail around and blocked their exit.

"Sorry," the left head sneered. "We're not going to let you escape like we foolishly did that other one."

"What other one? Princess Gyma?" said Locasta.

"None of your business!" snarled the right head. "Your only business is that you goody-goody fairies will shortly be blobs of dead matter fermenting in our stomach."

"That's ridiculous!" Sofia said. "Fairies never die. You can't eat us."

"Well, actually there are special cases where a fairy can be utterly destroyed," admitted Locasta.

"Allow us to introduce ourselves—we are the 'special cases,'" both of the monster's heads said in triumphant chorus.

"What?" Dan cried.

"We are the Chris-mey-thom-veg!" the monster bellowed.

"And we have been specially magically engineered by Taarna the All-Powerful Genie to digest fairy matter," the left head hissed.

"And now...*lunch time!*" cried both heads, which then lunged out at the group. They shrunk back and screamed out in fear and despair as the monster's vast, gaping jaws descended upon them.

They next thing they knew, they were in a dark, damp, smelly cavity.

"Where are we?" asked Judit.

"We're in the stomach of that beast. It ate us!" Zsuzsa cried.

"Then why are we still alive?" said Dan.

"Are you sure that we are?" shuddered Zsuzsa.

"I know why!" cried Sofia in a joyful tone, as though she were at a birthday party. "It was Grandmama's kiss! It's protecting us from all harm."

"Being trapped in a monster's stomach isn't harm?" Zsuzsa cried.

"It's an inconvenience," Sofia explained.

"Oh, well, thanks for clearing that up."

"We're protected by my kiss from all physical harm," observed Locasta proudly. "Even from the claws, teeth, and gastric acids of this monster."

"So what do we do now, though?" Zsuzsa cried, as she nervously fondled one end of Judit's tunic.

"Shhh," said Locasta. "Remember, this monster thinks we're getting digested."

Chapter Twenty-one

"I think I have an idea," Dan said. "We want to find Princess Gyma—"

"Yes," Sofia said.

"—And only this monster could tell us where she's imprisoned."

"Granted," Zsuzsa said.

"So, let's make it tell us," Dan said.

"How?" Judit asked.

"I'll show you." Dan paused, and then started making a low, moaning sound. "Oooooooooooooooooooooooooooooo."

"What in the Nonestic Archipelago is he doing?" asked Zsuzsa.

"Can't you tell? Our Danny's a genius," Sofia whispered with delight.

Dan continued to moan, and Locasta and the Adepts, catching on to his charade, joined in.

"Oooooooooooooooooooooooooooooo," they moaned repeatedly, getting louder and louder. Suddenly, the voice of the monster echoed through the cavity of its stomach: "Who are you?"

"We are the ghosts of the fairies you ate earlier today," said Dan in a deep, dark voice.

"Wha—What do you want of us?" the monster cried in terror.

"Revenge!" moaned the "ghost." Sofia struggled to suppress a giggle.

"No! No! Please! Don't hurt us!" cried the cowardly monster.

"You hurt *us!* Why should we be any more merciful?" Judit hissed, joining in the fun.

"No, please. Spare us. We'll do anything!" the monster cried in a melancholy squeak.

"Tell us where Princess Gyma is," Sofia demanded sharply.

"Yes! Yes! Right away!" the monster said, and it lumbered as quickly as it could down the passage until it reached a deep pit in the floor.

The Chris-mey-thom-veg carefully descended the steep sides of the pit, and reached a door in the wall at the pit's bottom. Next to the door was a gold bell controlled by a string.

"She lives here," the monster stammered.

"Oh, dear, now what do we do?" Zsuzsa asked.

"That's right—we still have no way out of this creature. I should have thought that out better," Dan realized. "Damn—Er, I mean hippikaloric!" (He didn't want to bring profanity into Fairyland.)

"Never mind, my boy...You did your best," Locasta said.

"Yes, Danny, it was still a good idea," Judit added.

"Are you gone yet?" the monster said, addressing the ghost.

There was no answer.

"Hurry," the right head said to the left. "Let's get out of here before it comes back."

"We are still here!" Sofia cried, but in desperation she forgot to disguise her voice.

"Wait! You're no ghost!" the left head snarled.

"Er—Ah—of course we are. Ooooooo—"

"We've been tricked!" the right head growled. "What shall we do, Chris?"

"We go tell King Graytfyl, Thom," the left head hissed. "He will get in touch with Taarna. She will annihilate these fools once and for all."

The two heads laughed so heartily it felt like an earthquake to the helpless prisoners in their stomach. But doing some quick thinking, Dan grabbed Ray-Shy's "I motivate" button from Locasta's robes, unhooked it so that the sharp point of the pin was exposed, and pierced the wall of the monster's stomach with it.

"AAAAAAAHHHHH!" the monster howled in pain. So widely did the monster open its mouths in its agony that a ray of light came down its throats and lit the inside of its stomach—very dimly, but just enough to allow Dan to read what, in the dark a minute before, he had heard Locasta's magic chalk writing on the slate: PYRZQXGL

"Thank you, slate. The one thing we really needed at this moment was gibberish," Zsuzsa snarled.

"It's not gibberish," Dan said. "It's that magic word of transformation."

"Of course!" Locasta cried. "I've heard of this magic word, of course—but I don't know how to pronounce it."

They felt a rhythmic series of jolts as, in pain and rage, the monster began to lumber away toward a passage leading to King Graytfyl's apartments.

Chapter Twenty-one

"But if there's any chance you can figure out how to pronounce it, Grandmama, for Lurline's sake, please try."

"Pyr...pyrz...pyr—quez—glu...Pyrz...Erm..."

The monster laughed vindictively as it lumbered toward the king's apartments, and reveled in the imminent destruction of those goody-goodies in its stomach. Then suddenly, it heard a voice from within its body say, "I wish for you to become a harmless flower and for us to be peacefully resting in your blossom. Pyrzqxgl."

The monster felt itself shrinking and shriveling. It grew leaves and thorns and rooted itself in the cavern floor. The monster whimpered pathetically until its facial features all disappeared. Its two heads became two beautiful yellow blossoms, and an enormous red blossom opened where the monster's belly had been. Locasta and the others were inside.

"Oh, thank Lurline," breathed Zsuzsa with relief.

"No, thank Locasta," Dan cried, and they all hugged one another.

"Say, what's this...? It must have been in its stomach too." And Judit held up a small, corked bottle.

"That's no ordinary bottle—that's a Genie's bottle!" Locasta asserted.

"You mean Taarna made it?" asked Sofia.

"Or is in it," worried Zsuzsa.

"No, she's a slave of the spray can...I think she's holding something in this bottle." And Locasta pried it open.

A steamy mist emanated from the bottle and resolved itself into Glinda and the Wizard of Oz.

"Oh, thank you, Locasta," said Glinda, and added, "Welcome back to Baumgea."

"Thank you, my dear...but why were you in that bottle?"

"Taarna imprisoned us. She and the demons of Whaqoland have marched into Oz and conquered it," the Wizard explained.

"Oh, no! It's even worse that we thought!" Judit cried.

"Much worse," added Zsuzsa.

"But why didn't you fight them?" asked Sofia.

"Taarna took away all our powers," said Glinda sadly. "But obviously she didn't yours."

"Nor Gyma's...and she is the one we should go to for help." And Locasta approached the door to Gyma's cell and rang the bell.

"I hope Gyma is at home," Sofia said innocently.

"She's a prisoner, so I fear she's bound to be 'at home,'" said Glinda.

With a loud creaking, the door slowly opened into what looked like a little cottage, with soft chairs and a sofa, eighteenth-century portraits on the brightly papered walls, and a quaint little table set for tea. In the doorway appeared an attractive young woman with long, curly brown hair adorned with a big orange bow, and wearing a long, golden-colored gown.

"Howdy," she said warmly. "I am Princess Gyma. I believe you wanted to see me?"

Princess Gyma

"HI!" Judit said, somewhat perplexed. "Is the beautiful room we see behind you your dungeon cell?"

"Alas, yes," Gyma sighed. "My only rescue from a totally boring existence in a dark, dank, dungeon cell is the extent to which my magic has been able to make my surroundings seem like home. It's actually only a very elaborate illusion. But it doesn't matter. *You're* here now. Won't you come in?"

Quite impressed with this wonderful witchcraft, Judit led the others into Gyma's cottage.

"I'm delighted to see you all. I imagine you must be Glinda, and you the Wonderful Wizard of Oz."

They nodded.

"I'm Locasta, the Good Witch of the North."

"And I'm Dan, and these are Oz's Three Adepts at Sorcery."

"Hmmm...I'm sorry to admit that I've never heard of you before," Gyma said to the Adepts.

"Don't feel bad about it," Judit said. "We don't enjoy the fame and recognition in the Ozian community that Glinda and the others do."

"Yeah, we're not even mentioned in the *Oz Scrapbook*," Zsuzsa added.

"Am I right in assuming that you are victims of those horrible Whaqoland demons as well?" Gyma asked.

"Yes, that's part of why we're here," Glinda said. "The demons of Whaqoland have attacked and taken control of Oz."

"Oh, dear!" Gyma said. "Why didn't you stop them? I'm sure your powers are great enough to overcome mere demons."

"They're being helped by Taarna, an All-Powerful Genie," Glinda said. "In fact, it was she who took away all our powers."

"Not quite all," Dan observed. "Locasta still has her powers, as do the Adepts; and now it appears that *you* have your powers."

"Yes, this Genie was obviously not around when Old Pascalabes captured me—I say, does he have anything to do with all this?" Gyma said.

"Oh, yes; he was an integral part of the plan," Zsuzsa said sourly. "He made us slaves on his ship."

"How terrible!" Gyma said. "As you probably know, he kidnapped me and Princess Esu and handed me over to King Graytfyl."

"What happened to Princess Esu?" Locasta asked.

"Old Ray-Shy enchanted her," Gyma said sadly. "When Esu tried to defend me against her and Pascalabes, Ray-Shy turned her into a button."

"Like this?" And Locasta pulled out Ray-Shy's "I motivate" button.

"That's it!" Gyma cried joyfully. "Oh, if only I could change her back!"

"I can, now!" Locasta cried, and said to the button: "I want you to resume your natural form. Pyrzqxgl!"

Everyone was bowled over as the button exploded into a *Tyrannosaurus rex* nearly the size of the dungeon cell.

"Gyma!" Princess Esu cried as her tail accidentally knocked over a table, a bookcase, and a Greek statue. "What happened.?"

"Old Ray-Shy turned you into button that said 'I motivate,'" Gyma cried, joyfully hugging Esu's left leg.

Chapter Twenty-two

"'I motivate,' indeed!" Esu growled. "Old Ray-Shy couldn't motivate anyone to do anything. I think she was jealous of you, my dear Gyma, because you're such a fine magician and terrific teacher!"

"You're a teacher?" Glinda asked Gyma.

"Oh, yes! Back in Op, Esu and I teach people about magic, fairy history, the flora and fauna of Baumgea—all sorts of things," Gyma said.

"But Gyma is the very best teacher in the world," Esu said. "She teaches in a way that makes it enjoyable for everyone."

"Well, it makes sense that you were kidnapped by Pascalabes," said Dan. "He hates knowledge, as do the demons."

"How ever did you escape from his ship?" Gyma asked.

"We mutinied, destroyed Old Ray-Shy by crumbling her up in the sun's rays, and cast Pascalabes adrift in an open sand boat," Judit explained.

"Good show!" Gyma said. "Now maybe that sandy, savage, snarling See-plus-plus will get him."

"Snarling *what?*" Dan asked.

"The sandy, savage, snarling See-plus-plus. That's the creature who dwells in the sands of the Deadly Desert—one of the very few creatures that can withstand those lethal sands—and the creature that bit off Old Pascalabes' leg. He and the See-plus-plus are mortalest of mortal enemies."

"Oh, good!" said Zsuzsa. "Let's hope this sand beast scares the willies out of that pirate for ever after!"

"Fortunately," said Gyma, "my powers and magical expertise are such that Pascalabes and Ray-Shy were unable to take them away from me, so I was able to use them to fashion a somewhat more hospitable prison for myself, and await the day when someone might come to rescue me, which you did."

"But why couldn't you rescue yourself?" asked Dan.

"The King's dungeon is extremely resistant to magic, and I have never been able to break through the barriers of magic which hold me here...but with you here, we can help each other."

"But that horrible Taarna stole away Glinda's and the Wizard's powers!" Dan cried. "An incredible feat, since they're supposed to be the most powerful sorcerers in Baumgea."

"Yes, I know," Gyma said sadly. "You see, the reason Genies are so powerful is because they can see much farther into the deep, multidimensional magical fabric of the universe than anyone else. They can thus manipulate atoms and galaxies in a way that leaves the rest of us puny witches and wizards in the dust."

"But there must be a way to vanquish her!" cried Zsuzsa. "Can't you force a Genie to retreat back into its abode by destroying its masters—in this case, Ruggedo and Forg?"

"No, because their ruthless army would surely protect them," said Glinda. "And I'm sure Ozma would never allow us to do harm to them."

"She most certainly would not!" Sofia said in firm agreement.

"And the only other way to stop a Genie is to destroy it altogether by destroying its abode," said Judit stated. "But destroying Taarna's aerosol spray can, and thus releasing massive amounts of environmentally detrimental chloroflurocarbons is something that I would never consent to!"

"Isn't there any other option?" Dan asked Gyma. "Genies aren't totally, absolutely, utterly invincible, are they?"

"Well…uh…yes they are."

They all bowed their heads in despair.

"But your knowledge, courage, and goodness are strong," said Gyma. "If you all follow your hearts, right may yet triumph over might."

"How?" asked Sofia.

"I don't know," Gyma admitted. "But that's what the movies all say."

They sadly bowed their heads again.

"Unless, that is, I taught you to see into the cosmic network of multidimensional magic the way All-Powerful Genies do," Gyma added suddenly.

"Can you teach us?" said Sofia eagerly.

"No."

"For Lurline's sake, stop telling us what you *can't* do and tell us what you *can!*" Zsuzsa cried.

"I was just about to," Gyma said with a patient smile. "What we *can* do is use the Magic of Everything to peer just enough into the multidimensional magic to negate the Genie's influence over your powers, because, you see, she didn't really *steal away* your powers—she just *disabled* them—sort of gave you a temporary amnesia. The Magic of Everything—which is a magic so powerful that it controls other kinds of magic—provides the means to bring your powers back to life."

"But even with all our powers, we're still not powerful enough to defeat that Genie," the Wizard protested.

Gyma thought for a moment. "I'll tell what I can do," she said. "Who here besides me knows about the Magic of Everything?"

"Just Locasta," Glinda admitted. "I know the Magic of Everything, but I don't understand its workings and implications the way she does."

"Well, I'm sure I can manage," Gyma said. "Having control over those fundamental magical forces allows you to do things like restore lost powers and foil the supposedly infinite powers of Genies."

"Well, let's get started at once!" Glinda cried.

"Yes," agreed the Wizard. "What do we do?"

"Well, first I'll restore your powers," said Gyma. "Then we'll start dealing with stirring up the cosmic forces we'll need to defeat the Genie."

"How will we defeat Taarna?" Sofia asked.

"Once you have your powers back," Gyma replied, "I will send you back to Oz to protect your people from immediate harm from those demons. Meanwhile, Esu, Locasta, and I will use the Magic of Everything to summon the necessary cosmic magic-netic fields that will retard Taarna's ultra-powerful magic. Then we will join you in Oz and vanquish the Genie and all the demons."

"But I thought you couldn't escape from here," said Dan.

"I can now that you've bravely defeated the Chris-mey-thom-veg. With that monster gone, and with Esu here to help me, I can now break through all of King Graytfyl's barriers. Now to restore your powers," said Gyma. "Do any of you have any pots or beakers on you?"

"I do," Locasta sang, and drew a number of tall glass flasks from her robes.

"Excellent!" Gyma said. "I'll need four of them. I'll also need something to write with."

Locasta's magic chalk leapt up and wrote on the slate: "What about me?"

"Oh, wonderful!" said Gyma as Locasta handed her the slate. "This slate is itself enchanted—that makes it all the better."

Gyma proceeded to set up four candles on her coffee table and light each of them. Then she placed the flasks upon the candles and suddenly cried, "Oh, no!"

"What is it?" Locasta asked.

"One little problem," said Gyma with a bitter laugh. "I have everything I need to do this except the necessary magical elixirs!"

Everyone sank into despair again, but Locasta, doing some quick thinking, glanced around the cell. Her eyes fell on a glass pitcher filled with a dark brown liquid.

"What's this?" she said, taking the pitcher.

"That's my daily supply of prison water," Gyma said. "But I don't advise that you drink it. It's dirtier than the East River in New York."

But Locasta smiled and said, "What magical formulae do you need?"

Chapter Twenty-two

"Elixirs AG-47, QXP-199, JJ-76, and ABBA-4, a quart of each in each of these flasks," said Gyma. "Then to each of these I need to add one pint of Yakov's Golden Elixir."

Locasta poured some of the brown water into the first flask and said, "I want you to become a quart of Elixir AG-47. Pyrzqxgl."

Immediately the dark brown liquid changed to a bright orange.

"She knows that magic word, even as I've forgotten it!" the Wizard cried with glee.

"Oh, Locasta! What would we ever do without you?" said Dan joyfully.

She proceeded to do the same with the other three flasks, filling each with the water and then turning them into Elixirs QXP-199, JJ-76, and ABBA-4. Then she said to the remaining water in the pitcher, "I want you to become four pints of Yakov's Golden Elixir. Pyrzqxgl." And she poured a pint of the now dark red concoction into each of the flasks, where it mixed with the other liquids.

Gyma then took a spoon and mixed the strange potions until they bubbled and started releasing a strange steam of many hues. Then when the steam was nicely circulating around the room, she wrote several strange symbols on Locasta's slate and held the slate to her forehead, closed her eyes, and chanted a section of the Magic of Everything's field equations. The multicolored steam quickly filled the room like fog, and after Gyma uttered one more magic word, the steam vanished with a loud bang.

"End of phase one," Gyma said. "You now have your powers back. Now you can go and defend Oz."

"May I come with you?" said Dan.

"And risk setting you at the nonexistent mercy of those horrible demons? No way!" cried Zsuzsa.

"I agree with sister," Judit said. "I really don't think you should, Danny. We don't want to put you in any more danger."

"But like I said," Dan said emphatically, "I love you all, and I want stick with you and fight our foes by your side."

"Of course you may come with us," said Sofia tenderly.

Glinda then tested her restored powers by working a spell that turned the door of Gyma's prison into a magic portal that led directly to the Land of Oz.

Dan gazed in awe through the enchanted doorway and saw the beautiful Land of Oz before him. "You're wonderful!" he said to Glinda

"And so are you!" the Wizard said to Gyma.

"I know, I know," said Gyma with a modest smile.

"And so is Danny!" the Adepts cried. "He's our hero." And the trio leaned over and added to the increasing amount of lipstick on Dan's blushing face.

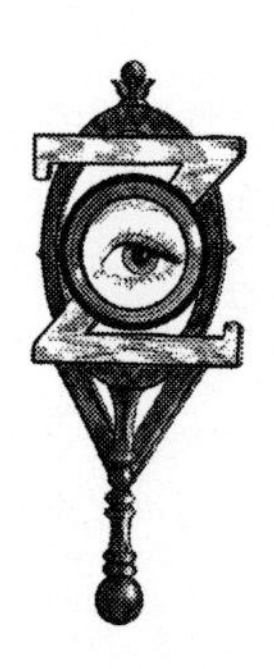

23
The New Order

THINGS were not going well in the Land of Oz. After Glinda and the others had been disposed of, Taarna, Forg, the Whaqolanders, and their allies marched into the Emerald City and captured all the citizens. Then Forg used his demon-sorcery to turn Ozma's palace into a weapons-of-mass-destruction factory, and he set the captured Ozites to work operating the factory's magical machinery.

The citizens of the Emerald City, used to living a carefree and joyful existence, now found themselves panting and perspiring from endless hours of pushing giant mills, turning massive cranks, and pumping cumbersome bellows.

"This is a sad state of affairs, isn't it?" the Scarecrow said to Dorothy.

"I don't see how this could happen!" said Dorothy angrily, as she shoveled coal into a scorching furnace. "After all Ozma has done to make our lives happy and bountiful, and we just let these people come in and take over!"

"We're genuinely sorry," said one of the captured citizens of Oz. "We were intimidated and scared by that radio show."

"It doesn't matter," said Taarna as she and Forg gloated over their prisoners. "I am All-Powerful, so I would have overcome you anyway. That talk-radio bit just made it that much more fun."

"And now we destroy the rest of Oz, right?" the First and Foremost said eagerly.

"And destroy the self-respect of all the men," purred Tasmminy.

"And make bullies of all the children," hissed Bo-Hub.

"And censor all the art," snarled Jess-He.

"And steal away everyone's bodies!" cried Queen Ra of the Mimics.

"And destroy all knowledge in Oz," snarled Scott Glib. "Especially Glinda's wretched Library of Knowledge and her rotten Book of Records."

"All in good time, my pets," Taarna said soothingly. "First we decide the special fates we have in store for Ozma's pathetic courtiers. Have you got the Magic Belt, Ruggedo?"

"I'm just putting it on now," Ruggedo said gleefully. "At last the Belt is mine again!"

"Shall we begin with little Princess Dorothy?" Forg hissed.

"I know what to do with Dorothy!" Taarna cried. "The killer of my mother, Old Sand-Eye the Wicked Witch of the East, and of my auntie, Old Snarl-Spats the Wicked Witch of the West—make her into an ice sculpture! Then she'll know how it feels to be melted!"

Ruggedo commanded the Belt, and Dorothy became an ice statue of herself, which slowly began to melt in the heat of the nearby furnace.

"Excellent! Excellent!" Taarna laughed vindictively.

"Except that now I don't have anyone to shovel the coal," Forg observed.

"Get the Scarecrow to do it. He'll just love being in such proximity to fire!" said Old Skin-Droop with a vicious snicker.

"Terrific!" Forg cried. "And now for—"

Just then the witches Reed and S-Slinger bounded in with anxious looks.

"Your majesty," S-Slinger said, "something terrible has happened!"

Chapter Twenty-three

"You didn't salute!" Forg snarled at them.

"Sorry—Hail, Forg—Something terrible has happened," Reed said.

"Well?" Scott Glib hissed.

"Glinda and the other Ozite sorcerers are back in Oz!" said S-Slinger.

"*What?*"

"Yes," said Reed. "We saw them in the Magic Picture. They somehow managed to defeat Old Pascalabes and Old Ray-Shy and liberate the crew of the SS *Able*, and then they somehow vanquished the Chri-mey-thom-veg and escaped from King Graytfyl's dungeon, and now they've come back here to stop us!"

"So, they prefer to meet a painful end, do they?" Taarna sneered. "Well, we aim to please."

"But they seem to have their powers back," S-Slinger said.

"Haw! Haw! Haw!" laughed Taarna contemptuously. "I'll just take their puny powers away again...and then they'll get the full treatment from me!"

"What do you mean?" Ruggedo asked.

"A means by which we shall rid ourselves forever of Glinda and those abhorrent Adepts!" Taarna proclaimed.

"How? I thought the Oz people couldn't be destroyed," said Ruggedo.

"They can't—but I will turn them into beams of light—pure energy," Taarna said, "an extremely painful state for a meat person to be forced into."

They all laughed gleefully at the prospect of the sorcerers of Oz in eternal agony.

"And now, my dear Ruggedo, I have a special job for you," Taarna said. "I want you to go to Quadling Country to supervise the burning down of Glinda's palace and the destruction of all the books and other hideous knowledge inside."

"Are you sure that's a good idea?" Ruggedo said. "The knowledge in all of Glinda's books might be of use to us sometime—"

"We demons hate knowledge!" screamed Forg. "Knowledge is for wimpo pervert nerds!"

"But must we really burn all of them?"

"If the books are in accordance with our Contract With Oz, our new manifesto for evil," Old Skin-Droop assured him, "then they are redundant and may be burnt, for in that case the Contract With Oz more than suffices. If, on the other hand, they are not in accordance with our Contract With Oz, then they are vile heresy and there can be no reason to preserve them."

"Suit yourself," said Ruggedo doubtfully. "But what about the Magic of Everything? I thought you wanted knowledge of that."

"The Magic of Everything is a set of incantations; that doesn't count as knowledge," Forg asserted.

"Whatever you say," Ruggedo said, even more doubtfully.

"So here is a magic ball of flame encased in glass," said Taarna, and she placed a big glowing sphere in Ruggedo's hands.

"Oo—oo—hot—hot!" cried Ruggedo as he wildly shifted the weight of the ball from one hand to the other, like a hot potato.

"Now, when you get to Glinda's palace, throw that ball—"

"Gladly!" Ruggedo cried.

"—into a window of the palace," Taarna directed him, "and soon three-quarters of all the knowledge of Oz will be consumed in flames."

"What about the other quarter?" demanded Forg.

"It's at the Wogglebug's college," Taarna explained.

"Good!" leered Forg. "We'll burn down the college, too, and I'll feed the Wogglebug to Whaqoland's resident giant praying mantis."

They all laughed viciously at this suggestion.

"Which brings me back to the destruction of the other Oz people," Forg hissed. "What shall I do with, say, Scraps the Patchwork Girl?"

"Make her a punching bag for the Whaqoland Demon Boxing Team," Tasmminy suggested.

"Good! And the Tin Man?"

"Melt him down for swords and spears," Scott Glib asserted.

"Excellent! And the Shaggy Man?"

"Make him your court jester," Old Skin-Droop said. "Tie strings to him and make him dance to your tune."

"That's what I'm doing to all the Oz people anyway," said Forg with an evil laugh.

"Gee, aren't those things you're suggesting kind of cruel?" Ruggedo said.

"Well, yes; that's the idea," Forg said.

Chapter Twenty-three

"I don't think I like any of this," Ruggedo said.

"What in Whaqoland are standing there jabbering about?" Taarna cried. "Get to Quadling Country and destroy Glinda's palace. At once!"

And with a wave of her arm, she made Ruggedo disappear to Quadling Country.

Ruggedo found himself in front Glinda's grand palace with its majestic pillars and marble halls. Some of Glinda's girl-guards appeared at the front entrance and froze in horror as they saw the dreaded Nome King standing there with a ball of flame in one hand. They shrank away in fear from Ruggedo's angry stare. He regarded them for a minute, and then said in a low, ominous voice, "Do you have a sitting room?"

The guards nervously curtsied in affirmation and led him inside to Glinda's private sitting room, with its great fireplace.

Ruggedo regarded the fireplace somberly and said, "Open the flue and put on some long-burning logs."

One of the guards obeyed, and then after a pause, Ruggedo tossed the fireball into the fireplace. The glass shattered and the logs began to burn, creating a very serene, homey fire in the hearth.

Ruggedo sat himself down in Glinda's big, comfortable easy chair, and was starting a long, thoughtful stare into the fire when his magic wireless Oz-o-phone rang. He reached into his pocket, drew it out, and said "Hello?" into the mouthpiece.

"Is Glinda's palace burning?" Forg's voice came over the speaker.

"Yes!" screamed Ruggedo, and stuffed the phone back into his pocket.

"Excellent news!" said Forg to his fellow demons. "I just talked to Ruggedo, and that rotten Glinda's palace is in flames."

"Hooray!" cheered the Whaqolanders. The Oz people, who were still slaving nearby at Forg's machinery, sank in despair.

"Stop shirking, you clowns!" Forg snarled at them. "Get back to work at o—"

Forg was interrupted by a sudden a gust of magic, and Glinda, Ozma, the Wizard, Jellia, Dan, and the Adepts stood bravely before the demons and the great Genie, who at her present size, towered several stories over their heads.

"All right, Taarna," Sofia cried up to her, "the jig is up!"

"Ah, Glinda and company! I'm delighted to see you," said Taarna fiendishly. "On behalf of the demons of Whaqoland, we're all so glad that you could join our little party."

"On behalf of the people of the Land of Oz, we demand that you surrender," Glinda declared.

"The Land of Oz no longer exists," Taarna assured them. "There is a New Order now. So get used to it."

"What New Order?" Zsuzsa demanded.

"The New Order of Evil!" cried Forg.

"We have our powers back, and you don't intimidate us now," Glinda proclaimed.

"And you're outnumbered—there's six of us great 'sorcerons' and only one of you," added Judit.

"I'm more powerful that a whole planet full of you!" Taarna snarled.

"I'll fix you in two seconds," the Wizard announced. "I wish for all these demons and other evil creatures to become acorns. Pyrz...Py...er...um... P-P-P—"

"Something slip your mind?" jeered Taarna triumphantly.

"I forgot it again!" cried the Wizard.

"I made you forget it again!" sneered Taarna. "And all your other magic, too!"

"You underhanded scoundrel!" cried Zsuzsa.

"You fools cannot defeat me with your cute conjuring tricks," Taarna announced. *"I am all-powerful."*

Chapter Twenty-three

"All-powerful?" Glinda said doubtfully. "No one is all-powerful. Everyone has weaknesses."

"Nobody's perfect," said Sofia.

"I am," Taarna insisted. "I could destroy the entire universe if I chose."

"And that would be being perfect?" Jellia asked.

"Ah, she's talking through both sides of her fangs," Zsuzsa scoffed.

"Oh, I am, am I? Perhaps you'd care for a demonstration of my infinite powers?" Taarna said with evil sweetness. "Shall I blow up one of the three moons, for instance? Or level the Tharsis Mountains of Mars perhaps?"

They all started trembling with fear.

"So? The Great 'Sorcerons' are nervous, are they?" Taarna sneered. "Well, I'll give them something to tremble about!"

"Why do I have the feeling that we should have stayed with Gyma?" Jellia whispered to Dan, who made no reply but stood firmly and waited to take the coming torture along with his comrades.

Taarna raised up her arms, and suddenly a gigantic, dark-bluish, oval-shaped cloud loomed in the sky and blocked out the sun, and a hideous gale blew through Oz knocking down trees, buildings, and the Ozites who dared challenge Taarna the Terrible.

In her great anger, Glinda was about to cast a terrible incantation upon all the demons and witches of destruction, but Taarna turned, extended an evil finger, and knocked Glinda down with a zap of magic.

"Ha ha ha!" the wicked Genie guffawed. "They just don't make sorceresses like they used to, do they?"

"They're called 'sorcerons' now," Scott Glib said mockingly.

"Hello, great sorceron," Forg jeered at Glinda.

"Ooo, we tremble at your power," sneered Scott Glib.

"Even as now your palace and all your books are being burnt to charred cinders," Tasmminy snarled.

"What?" exclaimed Glinda.

"You monsters!" Zsuzsa cried.

"Destroy them," Forg commanded, pointing at Glinda, Ozma, the Wizard, and the Adepts. Taarna raised her malicious hands and aimed her cruel fingers at them. They shrank away in horror, now fearing that all was lost.

"Oh, just one little thing," Taarna sang sweetly. "This special elimination of the six sorcerers of Oz will cost you one wish, please."

"Are you crazy? You think I'm going to waste a wish?" exclaimed Forg.

"Eliminating Ozma, the Adepts, the Wizard, and especially that little twit Glinda who always stood in your way in Fairy school? Would that be a wasted wish?" said Taarna.

"Maybe you could just wish for more wishes," Scott Glib whispered to his lord and master.

"That's true— Hey, Taarna! Can I wish for more wishes?" Forg cried.

"Sorry, the Amalgamated Union of Genies caught on to that game a long time ago," said Taarna firmly.

"Rats!" growled Forg. "But I refuse to waste a wish! Ruggedo must be the one who wishes for their elimination!"

"Oh, very well," Taarna said. "We'll go find him. And we'll take the victims with us."

"That's good!" hissed Forg. "Then Glinda can see for herself the destruction of her palace and of all the knowledge of Oz!"

24

Ruggedo's Remorse

IN a flash, Taarna transported herself, Forg, many of the witches and demons, Glinda, and her companions to the exterior of Glinda's palace. To Glinda's relief, the palace was not burning. Ruggedo was sitting sadly on the palace's front steps with his head on his hands and an expression of melancholy on his face.

"What's going on? Why isn't Glinda's palace in flames?" Taarna demanded.

"This is all wrong, what we're doing," said Ruggedo.

"What do you mean?" Forg demanded.

"I've been thinking about things, and I've realized that all those years after I lost my memory from drinking from the Fountain of Oblivion, Ozma and the other Ozites were good and kind to me—even after all my previous wicked deeds," Ruggedo explained. "And ever since I got my memory back, I've repaid them by more wicked deeds."

"So?" Scott Glib snarled.

"All this time I've wanted to conquer Oz," Ruggedo continued, "and now that I've finally succeeded, I realize that I was really happier before with my simple life in my little Emerald City cottage smoking my pipe. I'm tired of doing bad; I want my old life back."

"Well, you can't have it!" snapped Forg. "Don't you see what—"

"I've made a big mistake!" Ruggedo cried. "And if only the good people of Oz will forgive me, I promise to be a good Nome from now on. And for my first deed, I'm going to wish for everything to be put back the way it was."

"Everything?" said Taarna calmly. "And what would 'everything' be?"

"I mean, everything. Oz, the Emerald City, Ozma, Dorothy, Glinda—"

"I know what you mean!" Taarna shrieked.

"I knew he'd go funny on us," Skin-Droop whispered to Forg.

"I'm tired of all this torturing and tormenting of everyone," said Ruggedo.

"Torturing and tormenting everyone doesn't make you happy?" said Taarna with a snarl of amazement.

"Maybe it did once, long ago, when I was a different person," Ruggedo said. "But then when I lost my memory, I became an ordinary Nome who was content with his quiet life in the Emerald City for the few years before you came and ruined it. Well, now you shall *un*-ruin it. Taarna, I wish—"

"You can't do this!" Taarna screamed. "I haven't even finished carrying out your second wish for revenge on the fairies! Only when all of Baumgea is conquered can I turn my attention to your third wish. And I'll be a putrid boojum if I'll let you use it to just put things right back again!"

"I am your master, and you will obey me!" cried Ruggedo.

"You rotten, conniving little traitor!" Forg snarled in rage and lunged at Ruggedo, but he bounced back when he hit an invisible barrier.

"The Magic Belt is protecting me," Ruggedo said defiantly. "I've just used it to create a protective barrier around me and all my true friends, the Oz people."

Taarna, Forg, and the demons were beside themselves with rage. Glinda and the others were experiencing a mixture of gratitude and sheer bewilderment.

Chapter Twenty-four

"And now, Taarna, I wish—" Ruggedo said slowly.

"*You can't do this!*" Taarna screamed.

"I wish for you to put Oz back the way it was!" Ruggedo proclaimed.

Taarna was furious, but then she smiled to herself.

"To hear is to obey, O master," she said. Suddenly Glinda's palace and all other surroundings disappeared and everyone found themselves standing in a barren desert of snow—a mile deep and extending endlessly in all directions—in the middle of a raging blizzard.

"W—W—What did you do?" Dan shivered in the nearly unbearable cold.

"I said to put Oz back the way it was!" bellowed Ruggedo.

"And so I did, O master of the world," Taarna sneered. "I reverted Oz to exactly the way it was—during the Upper Permian Ice Age, two hundred and sixty million years ago."

"But I wanted you to revert Oz to the way it was just before we invaded it!" Ruggedo screamed.

"Well, then you should have said so, O master of the universe," Taarna mocked.

"You deceitful harpy! Put Oz back at once!" Ruggedo demanded.

"Oz will stay exactly as it is!" cried Taarna as she leered at Ruggedo and the hapless, freezing Ozites. "We Genies may be the slaves of our masters, but we do everything we can to circumvent our subservience with deceit and trickery.

"The great joy of a Genie's existence is to make fools of her masters and to watch them foolishly waste their three wishes on trivial inanity. You mortals are all the same—you have no vision; no capacity for envisioning possibilities.

"You might wish for the lost treasure chest of King Solomon, Master of All the Djinn, but you never consider the possibility of owning his entire palace. If you're trapped and starving to death in the Basaltic Caves of Krat, you gladly ask for a hearty feast of pheasant and wine, but does it ever occur to you to wish for the ability to eat your way out of the cave? And none of you ever, ever think to wish for your own magical powers, so that you can perform your own miracles without help from a Genie. Such potential wonders are beyond your shallow, foolish little minds. And I love it!"

And Taarna let out a hideous laugh of vindictive satisfaction at the inane obtuseness of mortals.

"You scoundrel! You miscreant!" Ruggedo cried. "You said you would help me work against Forg."

"Ah, at last the truth emerges," hissed Forg.

"I lied," said the unscrupulous Taarna to Ruggedo. "And besides, that was before you became a lousy, goody-goody turncoat."

"You can't defy me!" cried Ruggedo. "Am I not your master?"

"No longer!" Taarna said gleefully. "You've used up all three of your wishes, and I now pledge sole and exclusive allegiance to Forg!"

Taarna's spray can lifted itself out of Ruggedo's pocket, slipped effortlessly through the Magic Belt's barrier, and placed itself in Forg's clawed hand.

"Master, I hear and obey," said Taarna, with a reverent bow to Forg.

"And don't worry, fools!" Forg exulted to the shivering and terrified Oz people. "I will make my wishes with great caution. Genie, grant my first wish—I wish to know the Magic of Everything!"

"Your wish is my command."

And in one instant, Forg comprehended the workings of all known magic, and his 'Index' of magical powers shot up to 9.8. (An All-Powerful Genie has an index of 9.9, you remember.)

"Now I have the power!" cried Forg. "Let's try the power out now! O great magical powers that be, make me king of Oz and build me a great castle in my honor!"

A lump of snow rose up like a white mountain and erected itself into a great, dark castle, and an evil-looking crown appeared on Forg's head.

"Wonderful! It works well!" Forg gloated.

"It does indeed, your majesty," said Taarna fiendishly. "Why don't you try getting the Magic Belt now?"

"Indeed," said Forg. "O great fundamental forces of magic, give me the Magic Belt!"

Chapter Twenty-four

Immediately, Ruggedo's invisible barrier dissipated and the Magic Belt unlatched itself from him and flew over to Forg, who immediately put it on. The witches and demons bowed to him, saying, "Hail, Forg."

"And now, as the king of Oz and most powerful creature in Fairyland, I shall issue all orders, which must be obeyed at all times without question," Forg cried. "And my first order is for everyone in Oz to take up arms so that we may wage war against the rest of the world!"

"But we're not trained to wage war," said the Wizard of Oz. "We've always been peace-loving people."

"And I certainly will not wage war, either," said Ozma.

"Very well! Then you shall meet your doom!" Forg hissed.

"You leave them alone!" cried Dan, trying valiantly to shield his friends with his arms.

"Save your pathetic gallantry, you rotten little gremlin! Your beloved friends are all going bye-bye," sneered Forg at Dan, and then screamed to Taarna, "Genie, my second wish: I wish for the end of the Wizard of Oz, Ozma of Oz, Sofia, Zsuzsa, Judit, and especially Glinda."

"To hear is to obey, O master," Taarna proclaimed.

A momentary but mighty flash of light blazed forth, and Glinda, Ozma, the Wizard, and the Adepts and were gone.

"Glinda...Wizard...Sofia...Zsuzsa...Judit...*Ozma!*" Dan cried in despair.

"There we are," said Taarna with satisfaction. "Glinda and her colleagues are changed into pure energy, and they have shot away into space at the speed of light."

"You mean they're beams of light now?" said Jellia in horror.

"Indeed," said Taarna. "And in just the time we've been talking, they've already passed the moon and are nearly to Mars. No one will ever hear from them again."

The demons laughed heartily.

"You monsters! You ogres!" Dan screamed.

"Ahhhh, shut up," sneered Taarna.

"That was deliciously gratifying!" Forg cried. "Now back to enslaving. Magic Belt, imprison these remaining fools in chains and send them to my demon military camp where they'll be toughened up, all that lovey-dovey, peace-loving brotherhood drivel knocked out of them, and they'll be made fit and trained to kill, plunder, maim, and destroy!"

In a second, Dan, Jellia, Ruggedo, and Glinda's guards were transported to the military boot camp Forg had established next door to his weapons factory. The Ozites of the Emerald City were there as well, and they all found themselves chained to each other, encased in heavy armor, carrying various heavy weapons, and holding telegrams that read: "Greetings. You have been selected to serve the Land of Oz, which shall hereafter be an aggressive, ultra-violent, warmongering military state ruled by his majesty, King Forg."

All-Powerful Glinda

IN his great, colorful palace in the sky, King Fraunhofer, Ruler of the Rainbow and Monarch of the Multicolored, sat on his cloudy throne watching his daughters dance joyfully on the beautiful ribbonlike rainbow. He always enjoyed watching the festive frolicking of his daughters, but today he sat thinking and gravely stroking his multicolored beard, for he had two major problems facing him. One was that his neighbors, the Cloud Fairies, were without a ruler and were demanding that he offer one of his daughters as a queen or else go to war with them! The king did not at all like the prospect of war, nor did he like the idea of forcibly sending one of his colorful, vivacious daughters to live in the drab, gray, misty, somber Kingdom of Clouds. He did not know what to do.

His other dilemma was that, for the last few hours, he kept hearing a strange voice from nowhere calling his name: "King Fraunhofer—King Fraaaaaunhoferrrrr." From where the voice came he did not know, and it disturbed him to think that either someone was trying to reach him and failing, or else that he was going bananas.

His reverie was suddenly interrupted when he heard his most strong-minded daughter, Polychrome, suddenly cry out, "Look! Look at those beams of light!"

He looked and saw where she was pointing. Six beams of light were careening through the rainbow like bolts of lightning. It couldn't be lightning, though, because there were no clouds nearby.

"Oh, Papa," said Polychrome breathlessly as she and her sisters raced up to him, "there is magic afoot. I know there is!"

"How do you know, my child?" King Fraunhofer asked.

"Because I'm sure one of those bolts of light spoke to me," she replied.

The King looked up at the bolts, which were now receding upward toward outer space. Fraunhofer lifted his hands and spoke an incantation, and the beams of light suddenly turned around in a U-shaped trail, shot back toward them, and got captured in orbit around the bands of the rainbow.

As the beams each followed its own orbit, creating a series of ring-shaped trails surrounding the rainbow, the king called up to them, in a language that beams of light understand: "Who are you?"

"I am Glinda," said one of the beams, in the same language.

The King gasped. "*The* Glinda?"

"No, just *a* Glinda—she now comes in packets of ten," said another beam sarcastically.

"Thank you for the comic relief, Zsuzsa," said a third beam. "I am the Wizard of Oz; one of these other beams is our little queen, Ozma, and the other three are the Adepts at Sorcery."

"What has happened to you, my dear friends?" cried Polychrome.

"We were transformed into pure energy by Taarna the Genie," the Glinda-beam explained.

"Genie? You mean one of those dreadful creatures that think they're bigger than the world itself?" the King said contemptuously. "Well, how do you like being beams of light?"

Chapter Twenty-five

"Very confusing," complained the beam that was Ozma. "I keep seeing stars before my eyes."

"That's because when you are a beam of light, you can see everything in the entire universe at the same time, in accordance with the Magic of Everything," King Fraunhofer said. "In fact, you now have magical contact with the entire universe."

"That must mean that we are more powerful than anyone in the world!" cried the beam that was Glinda.

"Of course you are!" Polychrome said, dancing with glee. "In her attempt to destroy you, this Genie has only succeeded in making you all more powerful than ever."

"Then we can defeat those villains now?" said the beam that was Judit.

"Yes, we can!" Glinda proclaimed with sudden insight. "But only if we can find a way to resume a material form and keep this connection to the universe intact."

"I can do that!" King Fraunhofer cried. "I am a master of the colors of the rainbow, and that's all light is—a bunch of colors mixed together."

"Oh, Papa, you're wonderful!" Polychrome said with delight.

"But first," the King said solemnly, "you must promise to help *me*—fair's fair."

"Yes, of course," Glinda said, and the light beam that was Sofia added, "When we have our proper forms back, we'll use our powers all we can to solve any problems you have."

The king smiled, and then recited a long-winded incantation, and the beams of light exploded into the natural forms of Glinda, Ozma, the Wizard, and the Adepts. Except they weren't quite as they had been; they seemed even grander and more majestic than ever before. It seemed as though a halo of cosmic energy surrounded them, especially Glinda.

"Thank you," she said. "I certainly feel positively brimming with magical forces."

"So do I," said Sofia, and her sisters agreed.

"That's because the Magic of Everything is coursing through you," the king explained. "With your new direct connection to the multidimensional forces of the universe, you all now register at least a 9.9 on the Magic Index scale, and I think Glinda is an even 10."

"Then Glinda is all-powerful now!" exclaimed the Wizard.

"No, not quite, but neither is that Genie, despite her bragging," the king said. "The universe is so infinitely and unfathomably vast that there's no such thing as 'all-powerful.'"

Sofia observed how Glinda seemed bathed in the cosmic light and majestic power of all creation. "She sure looks all-powerful now, though!" she said.

"Yes, now let me tell you my problems—" King Fraunhofer said urgently.

"Okay, but don't forget we have our own country to save," Zsuzsa said, anxiously glancing at her pocket watch.

"My first problem," said the King, "is this voice I have been hearing calling my name."

"Fraaaaunhoferrrrr," came a ghostly moan over the rainbow.

"There it is again!" he cried. "Oh, what will I do?"

"It's Gyma's voice," Sofia squealed with delight. "She must be calling for your help."

"Yes, she's probably calling for all the fairies of Fairyland to help drive out those awful demons," said Zsuzsa.

"Oh, your majesty, you will come down and help us defeat our enemies, won't you?" implored Judit.

"I have *never* set my feet on cold, hard ground, and I do not intend to start now," the King said haughtily.

"Oh, come on, Papa! It's easy. You know I set my feet on solid ground often," Polychrome sang as she danced before the king.

"Too often, if you ask me," he retorted. "You're always running off with your groundling friends and getting yourself into all sorts of trouble."

"And it's fun!" said Polychrome gaily. "Just dancing around on the rainbow can get very tiresome."

"It's all very well for you," the king said, "but the King of the Rainbow and Master of the Multicolored does not set his feet on the vulgar surface of the earth!"

"You're refusing to help us then?" asked the Wizard.

Chapter Twenty-five

"Yes," said the king.

"There's gratitude for you," Zsuzsa said bitterly.

"Well," Sofia said with a sly smirk, "you said you had two problems; what is the second?"

"My neighbors the Cloud Fairies have no ruler," said the King in an anguished tone, "and they are demanding that I give them one of my daughters to be their ruler, or else they will declare war on us. And I do not want to force one of my colorful daughters to live in that gray, dreary Cloud Kingdom."

"Well," Sofia said, exchanging crafty smiles with her sisters, "it just so happens that we know of someone who might be just what the Cloud Fairies are looking for."

"Who?" the King demanded.

"But you won't help us, so we cannot help you," said Sofia, saucily swaying back and forth.

The King gulped, frowned, gave a long sigh, and then said with resignation, "Very well, my daughters and I will help you drive away the demons."

"Hooray!" cheered Polychrome.

"Now come on, there's not a moment to be lost!" the Wizard said. "Princess Gyma and the others are probably waiting for us in her cell."

"But who is this prospective ruler for the Cloud Fairies?" the King said, rising.

"We'll tell you when you meet her," said Glinda, now realizing whom Sofia was talking about. "But how will we get down there? I don't have my swan-drawn chariot with me."

"Don't worry," the king said. "Just tell me where this Princess Gyma is, and I'll direct the rainbow there."

In the little cell, Gyma, Locasta, and Esu were standing in a circle around the boiling concoctions, chanting the incantations of the Magic of Everything, while Nan-Kerr, Eric, and Trudi looked on, wondering what in Baumgea they were doing.

"It's working!" Locasta cried suddenly. "I can feel us connecting up with the Magic of Everything! I can sense the vibrations."

Then, just a few minutes later, with a flash of light, Glinda appeared in the room before them.

"Glinda!" Locasta cried. "What happened?"

"You won't believe the assembly we've just seen in the fields of Op," Glinda cried. "Every Fairyland inhabitant from Queen Zixi to Santa Claus is there, and about a million strange, scaled-and-feathered creatures..."

"It worked," Gyma said. "We have successfully summoned not only the cosmic forces of the Magic of Everything, but also all the fairies in Baumgea and all my dinosaurian subjects in Op! Together we will all chase away all those repulsive villains!"

"And we have brought the King of the Rainbow and all of his daughters," Glinda said. "And I am now very nearly all-powerful. At any rate, I'm as powerful as a Genie."

"How did that happen?" Nan-Kerr cried.

"Taarna tried to destroy us by turning us into pure beams of light," said Glinda, "but when we became pure energy, we became connected with the forces of the universe, which increased our powers by an order of magnitude, and I am now more powerful than anything else in the world—powerful enough to conquer all our enemies."

"Oh, Locasta, you're a genius!" Gyma cried, and explained to Glinda. "You see, as we were working, building up our magic-netic field, Locasta found the formula hidden in the Magic of Everything that can short-circuit a Genie's ties with cosmic forces and force the Genie's magic to work against her. We tried the formula, and now it looks like all of Taarna's magic is working on our behalf instead of hers.

"And now," she continued, "let us lead the fairies and dinosaurs waiting for us above ground to the defeat of the demons, and to the liberation of Oz and Fairyland!"

The Defeat of the Demons

IN Oz, Forg, carrying his big mallet and now wearing the Magic Belt, led his army of recruits, which included Dan, Jellia, Ruggedo, Trot, Cap'n Bill, the Shaggy Man, the Scarecrow, the Tin Man, Scraps, Betsy Bobbin, and many more of the once-jolly Oz people. Forg led them in a malevolent goose step across the frigid, yellow snow that now covered Winkie Country. The unwilling members of the army were weighted down by suits of armor, helmets, swords, spears, and rifles—all manufactured at Forg's factory where Ozma's palace had once stood. The sad Oz people panted and sweated from exhaustion in spite of the extreme cold.

"Hut—two—three—four—Hut—two—three—four—Come on, you knuckleheads! Lift those guns! March in exact unison or you'll be court-marshaled! When your training is at an end, we shall declare war on all the world and soon conquer it! Come on, you lame-brains! March! March!"

Finally, Dan collapsed in exhaustion.

"Get up, you little twerp!" Forg screamed.

"I can't go on," Dan cried, in tears. "I don't want to conquer the world."

"You rotten little coward! I won't have cowards in my army!" Forg screamed. "You shall get up and march to my orders or die!"

Dan lay motionless. Jellia and others moved forward to help him.

"Halt!" commanded Forg. "We shall leave this wimpo coward dweeb to rot! Now march!"

"No!"

"*What?*" Forg screamed.

"No!" cried Jellia, throwing off her armor. "I've had enough of this! You can't command us to do what we think is wrong!"

"And that goes for me, too," said the Shaggy Man.

"And us," concurred the Scarecrow and the Tin Man.

"And us," exclaimed Betsy, Trot, and Cap'n Bill.

Pretty soon, all the Oz people cast off their unwanted armor and weapons and stood side-by-side in open defiance of the tyrannical usurper.

Sing a song, dance a jig
And be loyal to Ozma's laws;
That's how we spurn the demons dumb
In the Merry Old Land of Oz!

...Scraps sang, as she turned somersaults in the snow and deliberately knocked Forg down. His face buried itself in the sludgy ice, to the delight of the Ozites.

Forg sat up and spat the snow out of his mouth. "I'll show you what happens to cowardly traitors, and then maybe you'll obey my orders in future!" he sputtered.

"Keyel!" Forg screamed. Seconds later, the ground shook with heavy footsteps. With a loud crash, the cyclops Keyel burst through a hill of snow.

"Yes, master?" boomed Keyel's monstrous voice from a hundred feet up.

"Have you been molesting the Oz people?" asked Forg.

Chapter Twenty-six

"Oh, yeah!" the cyclops grunted. "Keyel been crushing houses, squashing pretty flowers, tearing wings off of little birdies and butterflies, and using Oz citizens for baseballs, billiard balls, and boomerangs. Now Keyel ready for lunch!"

"Good! Lunch is right over here," Forg snarled, pointing to the Ozites.

"Yeah! Keyel want person! Yum-yum!" Keyel lisped, rudely spitting saliva in Forg's face.

"Help yourself," said Forg, as he wiped himself off. "I'd like you to destroy the one on the ground."

"Okay," Keyel growled, and he took Dan up in his fist and started poking him just to be mean.

"Put him down!" shouted Jellia.

"Let me go! Let me go!" Dan cried.

"Ahhhh, poor little Cosmo Gremlin," Keyel jeered. "Keyel will just crush you, little pipsqueak."

"Leave Danny alone!" suddenly boomed a womanly voice.

They looked in the direction of the voice, and suddenly before them materialized Ozma, Glinda, Locasta, the Adepts, and all the other fairies Gyma had summoned. Some of them were on foot, some rode on the backs of the dinosaurs, and some hovered in the air, either on their own or riding birds, giant insects, and pterodactyls. This fairy army lacked weapons, but were ready to defeat the foe with white magic and the power of love.

"Ozma! Glinda! Wizard!" the Oz people cried in joy.

"Forg, your wicked deeds are at an end," Glinda said slowly.

"What?" Forg screamed. "Glinda and Ozma...still alive?"

"You can't destroy us, you foolish demon," said Locasta calmly. "And tell your cyclops to put Dan down at once."

"Cosmo Gremlin be better name for him," Keyel sneered, "and Keyel just about to eat him. Yum-yum!" And he opened his huge maw and moved to stuff Dan in it.

Quickly, Glinda raised her magic scepter and, by chanting an incantation, shrunk Keyel to the size of an ant. Dan floated gently down into the willing arms of the Adepts.

"Hi, Danny!" they said affectionately, and Dan gave each of them a joyful kiss.

After gently releasing Dan, the Adepts ran over to the ant-sized Keyel and each raised a foot over him.

"Don't hurt me! Don't hurt me!" squeaked the tiny cyclops.

"Now the tables are turned, aren't they, you little coward!" Sofia cried, and her foot came down. And that was the end of Keyel the cyclops, although Zsuzsa and Judit stepped on Keyel's remains just for good measure.

"You cannot oppose me!" Forg cried. "I still have the Magic B—"

As he spoke, Ozma raised her magic Ozzy scepter, said an incantation, and the Magic Belt obediently unhooked itself from Forg and shot over to Ozma's waist like a magnet.

"You were saying?" Ozma said with calm malevolence.

The Ozites applauded and cried, "Hooray for Ozma! Hooray for Glinda! Hooray for the Adepts!"

"That does it! You will all obey me now!" Forg bellowed in rage. He took out the can and sprayed it. When Taarna appeared, he said, "Genie, I make my third wish. I wish to be the undisputed and always-obeyed *king of the world!*"

Taarna grinned grimly and pointed a magic finger at Forg. But to her surprise, Forg flew up into the sky like a rocket.

"AAAAAAAARGGGGGGGGGH!" was the last thing they heard Forg say before he vanished through the clouds.

"What happened?" cried Taarna.

"He's now a king, lord of all he surveys—on the planet Pluto," Glinda proclaimed.

"*What?*" Taarna screamed.

"Well, he said he wanted to be king of the world, but he didn't say *which* world," Ozma said with a giggle.

"But how did you do that? How did you misdirect my magic?" bellowed Taarna.

"The Magic of Everything," Glinda said sternly. "I've used it to intercept your powers. I am as powerful as you now; and now that both of your masters' wishes are used up, you must retreat into the spray can." As she finished

Chapter Twenty-six

speaking, a mist formed around Taarna. With a scream of rage, Taarna the Terrible Genie became a smoky mass and retreated into the spray can.

"Hooray!" cried Sofia.

"Taarna is defeated!" Zsuzsa shouted.

"Now let's put Oz back the way it's supposed to be!" Judit asserted.

Glinda of course agreed, and she waved her scepter in the air three times. Immediately the snow melted, Forg's castle vanished, all the injuries done to the Oz people, animals, birds, butterflies, and flowers were healed, and Oz at last resumed its normal, beautiful, and serene character that everyone knew and loved so well. The grass grew up again, the trees "re-leafed" themselves, and the flowers bloomed. All the yellow buildings of Winkie Country reappeared, including the Tin Man's castle and the Scarecrow's tower, both nearby, and the Blue Brick Road once more stretched its way through the yellow Winkie countryside toward the Emerald City.

"Hooray!" the citizens of Oz cheered as all the old familiar surroundings returned.

"You did it!" Sofia said to Glinda.

"We all did it," Judit said gently.

"But we still have to drive away the other demons and witches," said Glinda, taking Taarna's spray can and placing it safely in her robes. "Come on, everyone! Off to the Emerald City!"

The citizens of the Emerald City were still miserably slaving away at the machinery of Forg's weapons factory when they looked up and saw the crowd of fairies and dinosaurs sweep into the city. Glinda was riding on Margie's back (side-saddle), and she was making sweeping gestures with her scepter, melting more of the snow and reverting more and more of Oz to its normal form. Behind her came Polychrome and her family on the rainbow, all dancing with joy, and they were followed by the SS *Able*, whose liberated fairy crew now also had their powers back, thanks to Gyma and Locasta. The other fairies headed towards the city riding various dinosaurs.

When they reached the factory, Glinda dissolved it, and Ozma's grand palace stood majestically at the hub of the Emerald City once more. Glinda released all of the denizens of the city from their slavery, and she restored Dorothy to her natural form from the puddle of water where she had melted away as an ice sculpture.

"Oh, thank you, Glinda!" Dorothy said.

The sorceresses dissolved the armor and weapons that Forg had forced the Oz citizens to wear. "Hooray for Ozma, Glinda, Locasta, and the Adepts!" they cried.

The demons were beside themselves with rage at these proceedings.

"Where's Forg?" they demanded.

"He's on Pluto," said Zsuzsa, "where even air is frozen rock solid, so he's no doubt having a whale of a time."

"And you're next," Nan-Kerr added.

All the airborne fairies from Glinda to Polychrome circled the demons like vultures, and the dinosaurs stampeded toward them at full speed.

"Okay, everyone," Gyma cried, as she rode on Quetz's back, "throw all the knowledge you know at them!"

"Forg is on Pluto, the smallest and most distant planet in the solar system," Glinda cried at the monsters. "It has a diameter of 2,300 kilometers, a year equaling 247 earth years in length, and it has one moon called Charon, although its discoverer wanted to name it after our beloved Land of Oz."

The demons screamed in anguish.

"Another astronomer did name a search for life on other planets after me," said Ozma proudly.

The demons cringed with revulsion.

"Dinosaurs are land-dwelling vertebrates with three pairs of skull apertures, gizzards, and much higher levels of activity than other scaly egg-layers!" Princess Esu shouted.

The demons went into convulsions.

"Rainbows are produced by the refraction of light through water droplets in the air," Polychrome chirped.

The demons howled in agony.

Chapter Twenty-six

Riding a pterodactyl, Locasta swooped down toward the demons, and she shouted out her favorite "megawords" as loudly as she could.

"PSEUDONYM!" Locasta bellowed. "ELECTROLYTE. PHENAKISTO-SCOPE!"

The demons now fled in terror, like vampires fleeing from the sunlight.

Locasta flew at the head of the a squadron of pterodactyls, who chased the terrified demons toward the Ozian border beyond which lay the Deadly Desert.

"AMPHIBOLY!" Locasta shouted at a mega-decibel level. "SUPERLATIVE! GREGARIOUS! PSEUDORHOMBICUBOCTAHEDRON!"

The evil invaders reached the edge of the desert. When they desperately rushed out onto the lethal sands, the Phanfasms, Growleywogs, Whimsies, and Mimics all turned to dust. But the Whaqolanders levitated into the air and began to glide just above the sands. It so happened that they almost immediately came upon Old Pascalabes in his solitary sand boat. He was rowing his little boat through the searing sands toward Oz in order to join his evil colleagues, but now they descended on him and told him to row back quickly across the desert to Whaqoland. Old Pascalabes tried to row in the opposite direction, but the sand boat was immobilized by the weight of the mountain of demons and witches desperately trying to scramble aboard it.

Dan and other Ozites stood before the Magic Picture to watch the fairy army drive away the invaders.

Chapter Twenty-six

A few seconds later, to everyone's horror, a huge, serpentlike head and neck emerged from the sands. It had golden scales, vast jaws like a steam shovel, and malevolent eyes that swayed on the ends of long stalks.

"What is it?" Dan cried.

"It's the sandy, savage, snarling See-plus-plus! I think it's going to finish off our enemies," Jellia said with delight.

The demons and witches were so terrified that they tumbled out of the rowboat and onto poisonous sands. Immediately, they all screamed out as the hot sand began to burn them up.

Looking down at them from her circling pterodactyl, Locasta decided to add one more word to her attack arsenal and so she took a deep breath and uttered a word so long that it took her about five minutes to say it, and although no one could remember the whole 1,913-letter word, it began:

"METHIONYLGLUTAMINYLARGINYITYROSYLGLUT..."

And it ended: "...SYLALANYLALANYLTHREONYLARGINYLSERINE!"

As Locasta was articulating the Longest Word of All, Reed, S-Slinger, and Skin-Droop's bodies were collapsing and withering away like old balloons. Tasmminy was screaming in agony as her dainty body shriveled like an old leaf. Old Pascalabes screamed in rage as his form faded away like an old photograph. In vast torment, Scott Glib was tearing out his hair, smashing his glasses, and desperately trying to use his tail as a strand of chewing gum. The other demons and witches howled and writhed in anguish as their bodies slowly turned into an icky slime.

Suddenly realizing that it was witnessing its dinner "spoiling," the See-plus-plus lunged forward and, with one snap of its great jaws, engulfed all the witches and demons and Old Pascalabes. Making hideous crunching sounds, the monster properly chewed exactly twenty-three times (like its mommy taught it), and then swallowed the remains of the invaders from Whaqoland with one gulp.

The fairies in the sky and standing at the edge of the desert cheered and waved at the great beast. The See-plus-plus responded by emitting a colossal belch, and then, somewhat embarrassed, it hastily descended back to its home beneath the sands.

Prince Dan

AS soon as the demons and witches of Whaqoland were destroyed, the army of fairies and dinosaurs turned into a parade of triumph, which proceeded back to the Emerald City with Glinda, Gyma, and Locasta in positions of honor at the front.

When they arrived back at her palace, Princess Ozma said, "We will celebrate our victory over the monsters of Whaqoland with a banquet in honor of Locasta and Gyma, whose great knowledge of the Magic of Everything allowed right to triumph over might."

"But first," Glinda interjected, "let us deal with the fate of Taarna, the Genie who caused all the trouble to begin with."

"Finish her off, I say," growled the Cowardly Lion.

"Melt down her spray can," added the Hungry Tiger.

"Feed her to the See-plus-plus," Dorothy's Auntie Em suggested.

Chapter Twenty-seven

"No," Ozma declared. "I want a peaceful conclusion to this Genie business. As it is, I'm sorry that so many were destroyed by that sand monster."

"They were our enemies, your majesty," protested Zsuzsa.

"That is no excuse for unpardonable cruelty," Ozma asserted.

"Do not worry, your highness," said Glinda. "I will not destroy Taarna; instead I will ask three wishes of her."

"You? But I thought you were all-powerful now," Nan-Kerr said.

"No, not quite—there's no such thing as absolutely all-powerful," Glinda said with a smile. "I can do almost anything now, but for some things I will still need to execute elaborate spells and incantations to get the job done. I might as well take advantage of this Genie's so-called instantaneous response before I render her harmless."

"But what could the most powerful sorceress in the world possibly need to fulfill her hearts desire?" Nan-Kerr asked.

"You'd be surprised!" Glinda smiled, and she took out the can, sprayed it, and Taarna once more emerged. She immediately realized that Glinda was now her master.

"No!" she cried. "I won't have a goody-goody for a master!"

Her bracelets glowed defiantly.

"Yes, you will!" said Glinda triumphantly. "And no tricks, or I shall destroy you, and I now have the power to do so."

"All right," snarled Taarna, knowing that she was defeated.

"My first wish is for my Book of Records to hereafter faithfully and completely report to me what is going on in the world," Glinda commanded.

"Yes, master." And Taarna sent a beam of magic out in the direction of Glinda's palace to grant the wish.

"Now the Book will tell of goings-on in Fairyland without omission of any important facts, and I will be able to faultlessly watch over and protect the people of Oz and beyond," said Glinda, satisfied.

"Next?" Taarna hissed at her.

"Second, I wish for a great barrier surrounding Oz, like that which you put around the Land of Im."

"How did you know I made that barrier?" Taarna growled.

"I figured," said Glinda shortly. "And now I want one to surround Oz, so that no one may enter Oz by any means, except at our express invitation, thus stopping anyone from ever invading us again."

"Your wish is my command," Taarna snarled, and she put the barrier in place, which was invisible but completely shut out intruders, even from underground.

"You mean we're safe from invasion now?" said Dorothy.

"Between that barrier and my improved Book of Records, Oz and its people are now safe and sound for good," Glinda said with a kind smile.

"All right," said Taarna, now nearly in tears. "Make your third wish."

"You need not take on so," said Glinda, now addressing Taarna more gently. "I think that you will like my third wish."

"I seriously doubt that!" Taarna snapped.

"My third wish shall be for your freedom from Genie servitude," Glinda proclaimed.

"Oh, don't toy with me!" cried Taarna.

"I am quite serious; in a moment, I will wish you free of the Curse of the Spray Can," Glinda said.

"Okay, what's the catch?" Taarna demanded.

"The catch is that you will be deprived of all your magic powers; you will be an ordinary girl," Glinda said gravely.

"No, no, please!" Taarna pleaded.

"Either that, or we'll wish you locked in the spray can forever!" Zsuzsa cried.

Taarna, deciding that she wanted to be free more than anything, said, "I'll right, I'll do it—if you wish for me to be one of the most exquisitely beautiful women in all of Baumgea, so that knights and princes will come far and wide seeking my hand."

"Agreed," said Glinda.

"She doesn't deserve it," Jellia observed.

"I think that is best, my dear," Ozma said. "Taking away her magic is punishment enough, and giving her something she wants will give her incentive not to do any future mischief."

Chapter Twenty-seven

"They did the same sort of thing some years ago in America," the Shaggy Man observed. "I think they called it the 'Marshall Plan.'"

"Taarna," Glinda said, "I wish for you to be free and to be exquisitely beautiful, but devoid of all magical powers."

With a flash of magical light, the misty cord tying Taarna to the spray can broke and formed into permanent legs, and her gold bracelets snapped open and fell away. Her pony tail dropped into long flowing curls, and she was draped in a long flowing gown.

"Hey, this is pretty good!" Taarna said, examining herself with pride.

"But remember," Glinda warned, "no more wicked deeds."

"Oh, of course, of course," Taarna said obligingly. "Now, if you'll just direct me to the nearest knight-and-handsome-prince-filled fairyland, I'll be on my way."

"The Land of Im?" Ozma suggested.

"Perfect," said Locasta.

With the Magic Belt firmly around her waist, Ozma spread her arms and said, "Transport Taarna to the Land of Im." And Taarna was gone.

"And now that this dreadful affair has at last been put to rest, I think the time has come to set things right with Grandmama," said Zsuzsa.

"Yes, indeed," Glinda said. "People of Oz, may I formally present the Good Witch of the North."

"Why, Locasta!" exclaimed Dorothy. "How good it is to see you!"

"You do know her, then?" Zsuzsa said with delight.

"When we restored Oz just now," Glinda explained, "I also cast a spell that I hoped would remove Mombi's curse that made everyone forget Locasta, and apparently it has worked."

"It certainly has!" said the Wizard with a tenderness that surprised everyone, and they became positively flabbergasted a moment later when he took the little old witch lovingly in his arms and kissed her.

"Er...uh..." Zsuzsa stammered in stupefaction.

"You see, many years ago Glinda appointed me as a spy to try locate the whereabouts of baby Ozma," Locasta explained. "So I was around the Emerald City a lot and I met the Wizard. And well—we fell in love, deeply in love...And we..."

"You mean…?" Zsuzsa whispered.

Locasta nodded.

"Grandpapa!" the Adepts cried, and they passionately embraced the Wizard.

"I'm still confused," said Ozma.

"Well if *you're* confused, I see no hope for the rest of us," Jellia observed.

"You see," continued Locasta after the excitement of the reunion had died down, "the Wizard and I had a very tender relationship. We even had a son, Ozwoz."

"Our dad," said Judit.

"You mean that paranoid guy with the mechanical army?" said Dorothy.

"Yes," said Zsuzsa. "He went a bit ga-ga, and mum wanted to go and protect her fellow Veela, so we were left in Grandmama's care. We became very close."

"Where is your mother now?" asked Dorothy.

"The Virtual Sprites said that the Veela had encoded themselves within the network of magical anomalies in Virtual Forest," said Ozma.

"Huffman encoding, or JPEG compression?" asked Dan in interest.

"I don't know—but I'm sure you'll be able to decode them free, Danny, clever and tender as you are."

"Yes…So anyway," Locasta continued, "I reluctantly left the Wizard when I realized that my love for him was a potential conflict of interest, because Glinda suspected him of hiding Ozma."

"Why would he hide Ozma?" asked Sofia.

"Because if anyone ever found out he was a humbug Wizard and not the heir to the throne of Oz, he stood a very good chance of getting lynched," observed Zsuzsa.

"And I fear Glinda was right," the Wizard confessed. "I *did* hand poor baby Ozma over to Old Mombi, Lurline and Ak forgive me. However, it was totally an accident on my part. Mombi appeared to me in the form of Locasta, and she persuaded me that the baby Princess Ozma would be kept safe if I gave her to the Good Witch. So I did. Only after Locasta came to me the next day and denied the any knowledge of the previous day's visit did I realize that I had been tricked."

Chapter Twenty-seven

"So that was it!" said the Scarecrow, who had never been entirely clear on why Glinda and Ozma had been so quick all those years ago to forgive the Wizard's apparent treason. (*He* had been quick to forgive, because how could he hold a grudge against the great and wise Wizard who had bestowed upon him such a fine set of brains?)

"But that's all long past and done with," Glinda smiled. "The Wizard is a loyal subject now, and Locasta is back with us at last."

"It's so wonderful!" Dorothy exclaimed. "Oh, Locasta, can you ever forgive us for forgetting you?"

"Of course, my dear," said Locasta.

"We will make it up to you, I promise," Ozma asserted. "We will have a grand celebration of your return to Oz."

"And we will re-coronate you ruler of the Gillikins," the Scarecrow proclaimed.

"Thank you very much," said Locasta. "But the Gillikins already have rulers whom they are happy with, and I don't think I wish to be a ruler again. I only wish is to live quietly and happily with my granddaughters."

"Oh, that would be just great," Sofia cried.

"What about our Danny?" said Judit, looking affectionately at Dan.

"Oh, yes. Ozma, I hope you're not going to send him back to America?" Zsuzsa said. "I know he wants to stay with us, and we want him to stay."

"Well, you know I don't like to offer a home in Oz to too many outsiders..." Ozma said with a mischievous smirk, for she had already made up her mind.

"Oh, couldn't Danny stay with us?" Sofia pleaded. "We have plenty of room for him at our palace on Flathead Mountain—We could even set up a special wing of the palace just for him, with rooms for his computers and everything."

"Please, may I stay? I will be as humble and faithful a subject as you have ever had," said Dan, and he knelt humbly before Ozma.

Ozma smiled and a put a gentle hand on his shoulder and said softly, "Sweet Danny—Of course I want you to stay—And not only that, I have decided to make you a prince of Oz."

"A prince?" cried Dan in astonishment. "But I...I...don't know how...I mean...are you sure...I...I..."

Ozma smiled, pointed her scepter to the kneeling Dan, and said, "I dub you Prince Danny of Oz."

"You were always a prince to us," Sofia said to Dan sweetly, and she and her sisters each gave him a warm hug.

"Yeah, 'gremlin' indeed. That rotten cyclops Keyel!" Zsuzsa said.

"It's funny, but that's what mean kids used to call me to make fun of me. They thought I was ugly and a nerd because I used computers and liked science, so they called me Gremlin, or even Cosmo Gremlin," Dan said.

"Well, now you're among people who know you're a prince," said Locasta.

"And by all means, let's set the See-plus-plus on those bullies who hurt our Danny!" Zsuzsa said vengefully.

"I'm not hurt now—I'm happy; and here in Oz, I'll always feel like a prince!" proclaimed Dan, and he hugged them again.

"The prophecy!" Judit cried suddenly. "It's come true!"

"What prophecy?" Locasta said.

"The prophecy that our machine gave us just before we came to find you," said Judit.

"What was the prophecy, my dear?" asked Ozma.

Judit produced the slip of paper and read:

"I bring uplifting news my friends
Oz's perils are near an end
To invade and plunder Oz your foes
Will decide to have one final go
For a while you may be where
You all feel you're in despair..."

"We sure did," the Scarecrow remarked.

"...But their 'perfect' plan will reach a hitch—
A 'very special teacher' and a long-time lost Good Witch."

"The long-time lost Good Witch is Locasta," Glinda observed.

"And the very special teacher is Gyma!" Ozma cried.

"Then demise befalls each fiend and crone
And Oz is ever after left alone
And then eternal peace and cheer
Will reign in Oz, now free from fear."

"They were fiends," the Wizard said with a shudder.
"But they're gone now," Dorothy said.
"And if I have anything to do with it—and I do—Oz and all its citizens will live in peace and harmony and be left alone now and forever after!" Glinda proclaimed.

"The truth of my words you'll be convinced
The day the gremlin becomes a prince."

"That's Danny!" Ozma proclaimed as Judit completed the verse. "And now that the prophecy is fulfilled, and Oz is at peace, I think we should now have a celebration."

So that evening the Oz people all enjoyed a great party in Ozma's palace. All of Ozma's courtiers from the Scarecrow to Scraps to the Tin Man to the Cowardly Lion attended, as well as many citizens of the Emerald City and other parts of Oz, and many honored guests also attended, including the Witches of the Shack (who vowed to make Whaqoland from now on a peaceful and friendly country), the crew of the SS *Able* (who all planned to return to their beloved fairy homes in various parts of Baumgea, and promised to donate the ship to the Emerald City Museum), and the dinosaurs of Op (some of whom said that they would stay in Oz as members of Ozma's royal menagerie, and even a few of the pterodactyls volunteered to join Glinda's fleet of flying chariot-pullers).

Everyone sat down to a hearty dinner, with much happy discussion of recent events. After the banquet came a ceremony honoring those who had saved Oz from the demons of Whaqoland. Locasta was heralded and honored by all for her clever use of the Magic of Everything to tame the All-

Powerful Genie. Dan and the Adepts were awarded medals for their bravery against witches, pirates, and two-headed monsters. The Wogglebug named Princess Gyma an honorary faculty member of the College of Athletics and Arts, and she gave them all a fascinating lecture about the incredible cross-continent language of the Java Men who dwell in the outskirts of Virtual Forest. Ruggedo and Nan-Kerr where acclaimed for their reformation from evil to goodness, and Eric Seagull and Trudi were offered quiet homes in the Emerald City.

Glinda and the Wizard performed many magical feats for the spectators, including a marvelous display of multicolored fireworks that assumed many shapes, including the faces of various famous Oz personalities, and at the end wrote out in fiery letters: "OZMA AND OZ FOREVER."

The party finally broke up some time after midnight, at which time, after affectionate farewells, Princess Gyma, the dinosaurs with her, the Shack Witches, and all the fairies from afar returned home.

As he was preparing to return to his home in the sky with his daughters, King Fraunhofer said to Glinda and the Adepts, "But you still haven't told me who you think could rule the Cloud Fairies."

"Nan-Kerr!" they said.

"Yes, that is actually my rightful post," said Nan-Kerr, "but I was knocked from the sky by Taarna."

"Well, if you were unjustly deprived of your throne, then you must assume it again at once!" Polychrome said.

"Quite so," agreed King Fraunhofer. "If you will step aboard the rainbow, we will take you back there right away."

So Nan-Kerr said good-bye to everyone, and after affectionately hugging Locasta and Dan, she stepped onto the rainbow. Nan-Kerr and Polychrome and her sisters waved as the rainbow ascended into the starry night.

After everyone had gone home to bed except Ozma, Dan, Locasta, and the Adepts, Ozma warmly took Dan's hand and said:

"Well Danny, how do you like the knowledge that you are to live in Oz forever?"

"I'm so happy," he replied, becoming teary with joy. "No one ever loved me before, but the Oz people love me—Locasta, the Adepts, Jellia, Glinda, Gyma, the Scarecrow, Dorothy, the Wizard..."

"And me," Ozma added with a smile.

"Your majesty..." Dan began to say.

"Ozma."

"O—zma," stammered Dan. "Would it be presumptuous of me...I mean, I know I could never be worthy of the great fairy queen of Oz, but...would you...could you..."

"Yes?" encouraged Ozma.

"Would you...do me the honor...of being my...my girlfriend?"

Ozma embraced him and tenderly whispered, "Perhaps." And she gave him a demure smile.

He would have preferred a "yes," but "perhaps" was more than any girl had ever given him before. His eyes sparkled with new hope, and he mentally resolved then and there to prove himself worthy of Ozma's love.

Late that evening, at their palace on Flathead Mountain, the Adepts set up a series of apartments for Dan's use, Ozma brought a state-of-the-art computer workstation to him using the Magic Belt, and Dan began his new, happy life in the Land of Oz.

To order additional copies of this book,
please send full amount plus $4.00 for
postage and handling for the first book and
50¢ for each additional book.

Send orders to: